D0906136

"I can't say enough good things about this story! I was transported to the 1949 Louisiana bayou, where I fell in love with the characters and setting. Teacher Ellie Fields seeks to find herself while helping the people she's quickly coming to care about—especially one special little boy and his handsome uncle. Valerie spins a tale full of depth, detail, and humor, in which you can smell the bayou, feel the juice from the po'boy drip down your chin, and so much more. Come spend a few hours in Bernadette, Louisiana. You might find you don't want to leave! I know I didn't."

Lynette Eason, bestselling, award-winning author of the Danger Never Sleeps series

"There's just something about a novel by Valerie Fraser Luesse that feels like coming home. Reading *Under the Bayou Moon* felt like an invitation to sit with Valerie in her story shack so she could spin a yarn that made me fall in love with a place I've never been and care deeply for characters I've never met. This is the magic of good fiction, isn't it? And Valerie performs her enchantments with a lyrical Southern style that took my breath away. This is a book to be savored."

Susie Finkbeiner, author of *The Nature of Small Birds* and *Stories That Bind Us*

"With atmosphere dripping from every page like Spanish moss on a cypress tree, Valerie Fraser Luesse brings the Louisiana bayou to vivid life in this story of one woman stepping out in faith to pursue her purpose. This memorable tale of love—love for self, love for others, and love for the land—will expand in your heart just as the ripples from a boat's passage touch every secret corner of the bayou."

Erin Bartels, award-winning author of
We Hope for Better Things

"Steeped in the rich culture of the Louisiana bayou, Valerie Fraser Luesse's tale takes us to a place where love and community matter and an almost magical alligator enchants!"

Nancy Dorman-Hickson, coauthor of the award-winning
Diplomacy and Diamonds and a former editor for
Progressive Farmer and *Southern Living* magazines

"This compelling novel has a bit of everything: self-exploration, a sense of adventure, and fascinating characters. Valerie Fraser Luesse brings the beauty and mystery of the bayou to life as Ellie finds her home in more ways than one."

Krissy Tiglias, executive editor
of *Southern Living* magazine

UNDER THE BAYOU MOON

Books by Valerie Fraser Luesse

Missing Isaac

Almost Home

The Key to Everything

Under the Bayou Moon

UNDER THE BAYOU MOON

A NOVEL

VALERIE FRASER LUESSE

Revell

a division of Baker Publishing Group
Grand Rapids, Michigan

Published by Revell
a division of Baker Publishing Group
PO Box 6287, Grand Rapids, MI 49516-6287
www.revellbooks.com

Library of Congress Cataloging-in-Publication Data
Names: Luesse, Valerie Fraser, author.
Title: Under the bayou moon : a novel / Valerie Fraser Luesse.
Description: Grand Rapids, Michigan : Revell, a division of Baker Publishing
   Group, [2021] | Includes bibliographical references.
Identifiers: LCCN 2021002491 | ISBN 9780800737511 (paperback) | ISBN
   9780800740023 (casebound) | ISBN 9781493430420 (ebook)
Subjects: GSAFD: Christian fiction.
Classification: LCC PS3612.U375 U53 2021 | DDC 813/.6—dc23
LC record available at https://lccn.loc.gov/2021002491

Scripture used in this book, whether quoted or paraphrased by the characters, is taken from the King James Version of the Bible.

This book is a work of fiction. Names, characters, places, and incidents are the product of the author's imagination or are used fictitiously. Any resemblance to actual events, locales, or persons, living or dead, is coincidental.

The author is represented by the literary agency of Stoker Literary.

21 22 23 24 25 26 27   7 6 5 4 3 2 1

For all the teachers,
with loving memories
of a truly gifted one,
Patricia Donahoo McCranie,
"Aunt Patsy"

Prologue

1947

RAPHE BROUSSARD WAS JUST A BOY when he first saw it—glimpsed it, at least. Mostly hidden in the saw grass and canes, it had temporarily left the tip of its long alabaster tail exposed in the sunlight—a rare mistake. The streak of white offered only a hint of what lay hidden, the promise of what might be revealed. Raphe had watched silently, reverently almost, as the tail thrashed back and forth just once before disappearing into the green, leaving him to wonder if he had truly seen it at all. He told no one.

Over the years, Raphe would return to that secluded spot whenever his mind was troubled, as it was now. He had a choice to make, and it was weighing on him that day as he paddled deep into the bayou, gliding across remote but familiar waters where the pines and cypress trees towered above. They cast this solitary pool in perpetual shade as if a veil had been tossed over the sun, not blocking its hot rays entirely but reducing them to a warm softness. The water was glassy, carpeted around the edges with water hyacinth and duckweed. Floating here on still waters, in a pirogue carved out of a cypress tree by his grandfather, Raphe could quiet his mind and think. He could come to a decision about a thing.

Should he give up his freedom and become a father to his orphaned nephew, or listen to that preacher? Most of the evangelicals who had come into the Atchafalaya Basin seemed well-meaning enough, but there was a particularly strident one, Brother Lester, who had somehow gotten wind of Raphe's plight and urged him to give Remy, his blood kin, to a "good Christian family"—strangers. The child needed a mother and father, the preacher said. A single young man like Raphe—Cajun, Catholic, and therefore prone to drink— would surely be a bad influence.

Raphe imagined himself as a young father with no wife, limiting his own possibilities while praying he didn't make some horrible mistake that ruined his nephew's life. And then he pictured a choice he found completely unbearable— trying to live with the expression on Remy's face, the one that would haunt Raphe forever if he let strangers take the boy away.

That heartbreaking image—of a child realizing he had been abandoned by the one person he trusted most—was burning Raphe's brain when the alligator appeared. It came out of the cattails at the water's edge and silently glided in. What a sight! The alligator had to be twelve feet long and pure white except for a single swirl of pigment trailing down its back like curled ribbon. It passed so fearlessly close to Raphe that he could see the piercing sparkle of its blue eyes. On the far bank, it climbed onto a fallen tree in dappled light, taking in as much sun as its pale skin could tolerate.

Raphe had never put much stock in the swamp legends that the old-timers recounted again and again around campfires. He loved the tales about the white alligator, but they were just entertainment, nothing more. Still, he was comforted by the notion that this enigmatic denizen of the bayou was keeping watch while he wrestled with Remy's fate and his own conscience.

As he sat silently in his pirogue, the massive white head slowly turned, almost in his direction but not quite. In the filtered light, Raphe could see one side of the alligator's face, one of those sapphire eyes. Only a few seconds passed before it turned back, gliding slowly across the tree and silently disappearing into the canes.

Fishermen and hunters along the river called the alligator *L'esprit Blanc*, French for what the Indians had named it— "The White Spirit." It was strange—all of them knew about L'esprit Blanc, repeating stories they had heard for years, but all those who claimed to have actually seen it were taken by the storm. All except Raphe. While his neighbors speculated about the high price such a rare hide would fetch—if it truly existed—Raphe found it impossible to believe that anyone who laid eyes on something so extraordinary could bring himself to kill it. Still, he kept his sightings to himself.

Raphe looked up at a darkening sky. Rain was coming. He sat in his boat, listening to the wind stir the trees overhead and watching ripples begin to roll across the mirrored surface of the water. His choice was clear.

He would never tell a soul where to hunt the white alligator. And he would never send Remy away. Some things belonged right where they were.

ONE

ELLIE FIELDS SAT IN A BUSTLING MARINA CAFE in Bay St. Louis, Mississippi, watching a train make its crossing and wondering what it would be like to ride two rails suspended in air, the water below, the sky above.

"That be all for you, hon?"

Ellie smiled up at the waitress standing next to her table, holding a pot of coffee. She was wearing a pink uniform with a white apron and a name tag shaped like a dolphin. Her hair was strawberry blonde, teased and pinned into a French twist in the back. She looked about forty.

"That's all, thanks," Ellie said. "Hey, I like your name. I don't think I've ever met a woman named Geri before."

The waitress rolled her eyes. "It's short for Gertrude! Can you believe my mama hung that on me? It was her grandmother's name."

"You're definitely more of a Geri. I'm Ellie—short for Juliet. My little brother couldn't pronounce the *j* or the *l*, so he renamed me. I was 'Eh-we' till he got the hang of the *l*."

Geri put her hand on her hip. "It's not fair that your family gets to label you for life, is it?"

"No, it's not."

"I'll be right back with your ticket, hon," Geri said, pointing another customer to a booth on her way back to the counter.

Ellie looked out the window next to her table. The engine of the train had long since passed the trestle over the bay, while the caboose was still some distance away—one had yet to see what was already a memory for the other, yet they were part of the same machine.

She reached into her purse and pulled out a letter she had folded and unfolded, read and reread countless times since it arrived in her parents' mailbox in March. She spread it out on the table in front of her. Something about the letter gave her courage, which she needed right now. One more read couldn't hurt.

March 1, 1949

Dear Miss Fields,

We have never met, but I am the town physician in Bernadette, Louisiana, where it is my understanding that you have been offered a teaching position. While I have little influence with the school board, I do have one friend remaining among its members. He was struck by your application and thought I might be as well, so he forwarded a copy to my office. I was especially drawn to the way you answered, "Why do you want this position?" I believe I heard great sincerity in your answer: "I want to serve where I am most needed and to use whatever gifts God has given me to make the world a better place, especially for children."

Miss Fields, you will find no children in greater need of a gifted teacher than those in Bernadette, nor will you ever find another place where your efforts will be more appreciated. Should you decide to accept the position and join our little community, my wife and I will offer you our wholehearted support and will be happy to provide housing, free of charge. It might not be luxurious, but it will be safe and comfortable.

Sincerely,
Arthur Talbert, MD

"Here ya go, hon," Geri said as she laid a ticket on the table, drawing Ellie's attention away from the letter and back to the journey at hand.

"Could you tell me how far I am from New Orleans, Geri?"

"Gonna do a little partyin'?" Geri gave her a smile and a wink.

Ellie pictured herself embracing with abandon the revelry on Bourbon Street and shook her head. "I'm afraid a Birmingham ballroom on New Year's Eve is about as wild as I get. I just took a teaching job in a little town called Bernadette, Louisiana. It's supposed to be about eighty miles or so from New Orleans. Thought I'd stop over and see the city on my way."

"Well, congrats on the new job, hon! You're not too far. Just keep followin' 90 and you'll be there in about an hour. Some people call Bay St. Louis 'Little New Orleans' on accounta we get so many summer people from over there. You from here in Mississippi?"

"No, I'm from a tiny little town you never heard of—Maribelle, Alabama."

"And here I thought you was headed to the backwoods, but Bernadette might be a step up for you." Geri laughed and winked at her again.

Ellie remembered how a couple of Atlanta girls who lived down the hall at her college dorm always gave her grief about coming from a town that "didn't even get a dot" on the state map. "If Bernadette has more than one traffic light," she told Geri, "it'll be a step up, alright."

"Ain't nothin' wrong with that," the waitress assured her. "No shame in bein' a small-town girl. But now, you watch yourself on the road—'specially in New Orleans. All them one-ways in the Quarter's just murder to figure out your first time around. And you're gonna wind your way through some bayou country before you get there. I know we're supposed to be all modern and everything now that the war's over and done with, but there's some deserted drivin' between here and there. Make sure you fill up before you leave, okay?"

"I will—thanks, Geri."

The waitress stared down at Ellie and shook her head. "You got a face like an angel, you know that? You any kin to that woman in *Casablanca*?"

"No." Ellie smiled. "But thank you."

"You need to get you one of them hats that dips down over your eye like she wore. I bet that'd look real good on you."

"Maybe I'll find one in the French Quarter."

"You be *careful* in the Quarter, you hear?"

"I will," Ellie said, holding up her right hand. "Word of honor. Thanks for looking out for me."

Geri gave her another wink and a wave before hurrying to grab a water pitcher from the counter and greet a new customer. Ellie left a tip and then paid her check at the register.

She filled up at a local Pan-Am and got back on the highway, relieved to know she would make it to New Orleans in plenty of time to find her hotel before dark. Even though she had only a week to get settled before school started, Ellie had decided to allow herself one night in the fabled city, which she had never seen.

She had spent her first night on the road with her mother's sister in Ocean Springs, a pretty little town with cottagey storefronts and shady streets sheltered from the coastal sun by the craggy, arched branches of live oak trees. Her parents had insisted that she make a stop there and let her uncle give the old Ford a good going-over before she went on to Louisiana. She had bought the used 1939 Deluxe, which she named Mabel, with the salary from her first year of teaching. The old girl had been rolling for ten years now and was showing her age, but she still had some miles left in her. Ellie's aunt insisted on introducing her to just about everybody in town before she left, so she and Mabel had gotten a late start.

Her whole family thought she was crazy for accepting a teaching job in rural Louisiana when there were, as her mother put it, "perfectly good schools from Mobile to Muscle Shoals and enough bachelor vets in Alabama to marry every girl in ten states." But Ellie could no longer bear the burden of invisibility. That's how she felt—as if her truest self were invisible to everyone around her and had been for so long that it was now banging on her chest from the inside out, demanding to be seen and heard. If she could just go through the motions, everything would be so much easier, but that would be a lie of a life. And what Ellie yearned for— what she had come to demand for herself—was authenticity.

She had shown, more to herself than anyone else, that she was willing to walk away from anything, including marriage, if it demanded that she be satisfied with anything less than what she was meant for—whatever that might be. And now she felt it would be unkind to continue dating war vets who had been so homesick overseas that they never wanted to leave Alabama again. When they looked at her on a dance floor or took her hand in a movie theater, she couldn't shake the feeling that they were picturing her hanging diapers on the line or sliding a pan of biscuits into the oven before she poured their morning coffee and kissed them off to work. Even the one she had believed to be different turned out not to be.

All those soldiers had seen horrible things, Ellie knew, and she was ashamed to admit, even to herself, that she was jealous of them. They had left as boys and come home as men. They had *done* something. Ellie had gone from high school to college and back home again. Was that it—her circle complete, her story told?

Her mother insisted that Ellie just needed a little change of scenery and would "come home lickety-split" as soon as she got the wanderlust out of her system. But Ellie knew that wasn't true. What she longed for was not change but transformation. Just like the tall stands of pine trees and oaks that dissolved into water and sky as she crossed the Pearl River into Louisiana, Ellie hoped her old self would dissipate, releasing something new and interesting, something with purpose.

The highway sounded different as she drove onto the bridge that would carry her across Lake Pontchartrain and into New Orleans. Though Highway 90 spanned a narrow channel between marshlands, she could look to the northwest and see the vast, unknowable waters that stretched far beyond the tenuous safety of the bridge. Mabel's tires bumped along as they made it across, only to thread more water, with Pontchartrain on one side of the highway and Lake Saint Catherine on the other.

Ellie found herself surrounded by simple wooden houses on stilts—most with some kind of boat on a trailer parked in the yard—separated by the occasional bait-and-tackle shop or small grocery store. The landscape was flat and stark, the sky a brilliant sunny blue. Now and again, Ellie would glimpse a woman watering her flower beds or a man loading fishing rods into his boat.

As Mabel carried them through a string of small towns, they passed lakes and crossed bayous, sometimes on bridges so rickety that Ellie held her breath from one side to the other. She imagined Mabel doing the same. Though she had seen the bayous around Mobile and Biloxi, Louisiana was a different kettle of fish. Bayous here were boundless and dense, lit with shades of green—from deep ivy to bright chartreuse—as algae, lily pads, and water hyacinth spread over them. They were dotted with ancient cypress trees, their Spanish moss hanging like the lace-gloved fingers of a Louisiana debutante, reaching down to stir ripples on the water.

Ellie began to encounter more traffic and bigger houses as she drew nearer to New Orleans, guiding the old Ford along a now busy Highway 90 until she made it into the city and caught her first glimpse of the road sign she had been waiting for: Vieux Carré—the French Quarter. She followed Esplanade to Royal Street and almost wrecked Mabel as she marveled at the plaster walls in shades of yellow, burnt orange, red, and forest green, with weathered old shutters hanging just enough askew to show they'd lived a life. Scrolled black wrought iron framed upper balconies where hanging baskets bursting with ferns, begonias, and periwinkle spilled sweet potato vine all the way down to the sidewalk. Mysterious garden gates, tucked into alleyways, conjured notions of romantic assignations in the hidden courtyards that lay beyond. Ellie wondered what the gas streetlamps would look like once they began to flicker in the darkness. New Orleans was everything she had imagined and then some.

Careful to dodge bicycles, taxicabs, and street vendors, she slowly made her way to a hotel she had heard about from a fellow schoolteacher who moved to rural Alabama from Birmingham. Adele had grown up in New Orleans and gave Ellie a well-marked street map, circling all the things she "absolutely *must* see." Ellie had memorized every street name, landmark, and critical turn as best she could but still kept the map spread out on the seat next to her, stealing a glance whenever she came to a stop sign or traffic light.

At last she spotted it—the Hotel Monteleone—and sighed with relief. After parking Mabel, she made her way to the main entrance, a blue overnight case in hand, and tried not to look like a hayseed as she took in the palatial lobby with its grand pillars and gorgeous chandeliers. The Monteleone looked like something out of a movie, and Ellie imagined herself not in the cotton dress she wore but decked out in a sequined evening gown, an air of mystery about her. The thought of it made her giggle out loud—Ellie Fields gussied up like Ingrid Bergman.

"Now that's what we like to see at the Monteleone—a happy guest," said a voice behind her. She turned to see a smiling bellman in a crisp gray jacket and black pants. He tipped his hat to her.

"Between you and me, I'm not a guest yet," Ellie confessed. "I'm hoping they'll rent a room to an Alabama girl who has no idea what she's doing."

The bellman raised his eyebrows. "First time in New Orleans?"

"First time ever," Ellie said.

"Aw, you're in for a *treat!*" the bellman said. "My name's Theodore. I've lived here all my life. You have any trouble, you send for me." He gestured toward a long, ornate front desk. "It would be my pleasure to escort you to reception."

"Thank you so much." Ellie fell into step with him. "I'm Ellie—Ellie Fields."

"I'm honored to meet you, Miss Fields." Theodore led Ellie to the front desk and introduced her to a hotel clerk, who looked to be about her father's age. Then he took the overnight case from her. "This'll be waitin' for you in your room."

"Thank you again." Ellie was about to turn back to the clerk when she remembered Adele's instructions: *Don't forget to tip in New Orleans!* "Oh, wait, Theodore!" She caught up with him, slipped a quarter into his palm, and whispered, "Did I do that right?"

Theodore gave her a slight bow. "Perfect. And I thank you, Miss Fields."

Ellie hurried back to the front desk and checked in, then

caught the elevator to her floor and wandered several long corridors until she found her room. There, on a luggage stand just inside the door, was her overnight case as Theodore promised. She kicked off her shoes, removed her hat and gloves, and carried her friend's map over to the tall windows, where she set about getting her bearings.

The Monteleone faced Royal Street. With an upper-level room on the front of the hotel, Ellie could look across the block and see what had to be Bourbon Street, already lit up like a carnival even in the afternoon sun. She had heard tales of its debauchery but also of its music, which she intended to hear. With any luck, the serious sin wouldn't start until later in the evening. She could hear some jazz and retreat to the safety of the Monteleone before then.

The hotel bathroom was the fanciest Ellie had ever seen, all white tile and marble, with a gilded mirror, plush towels, and hand soaps that smelled like gardenias. She stared at her reflection in the mirror. Geri said she had a face like an angel, but Ellie couldn't see it. Her maternal grandmother, Mama Jean, would often say to her with great pride, "Your name might be Fields, but *you* are a Galloway!" Then she would trace Ellie's cheekbones with her fingertip. "You did not get those doe eyes and these fine Scottish features from *their* side!" she would proclaim.

Ellie splashed a little cool water on her face and patted it dry with a fluffy hand towel. She ran a brush through her hair, which she had always considered an indecisive brown. It looked like it couldn't make up its mind whether to be dark or light, so it had settled on deep brown streaked with a lighter shade here and there. Once, she had driven to the salon at Loveman's in Birmingham to get it colored, but the stylist flatly refused, saying, "Do you have any idea how much women in this city would pay to get what you're asking me to cover up?" Ellie had reluctantly agreed to a shoulder-length cut, which the stylist promised would still be long enough for her comfort yet short enough to ensure that she didn't look juvenile. It had a natural wave to it, so at least it was easy to curl. That was something, she guessed.

Her overnight case had room for only one outfit, and she would need that tomorrow. New Orleans would have to take her as she came—wearing a deep-rose cotton dress with a full skirt, cap sleeves, and a sweetheart neckline. She would wear her wide-brimmed hat to keep the sun off her face but forgo the formality of gloves. On this, her first trip to New Orleans, Ellie would embrace the storied city bare-handed.

TWO

AT THE CORNER OF IBERVILLE AND BOURBON STREETS, Ellie tried not to gawk. Nothing could've prepared her for this—the lights and the crowds, the noise and the music, and the sheer grit of this famous thoroughfare. Up and down Bourbon Street, jazz music seemed to seep through the iron-wrapped walls of Spanish-tinged buildings that looked hundreds of years old.

Ellie started walking, slowly making her way to St. Peter Street. She stopped whenever the music called, listening to street musicians and jazz bands before following her map to Jackson Square and St. Louis Cathedral. By the time she headed back to Bourbon, the sun was going down, making all the neon signs glow ever brighter, a beacon to the night-time crowd Adele had told her about, those ready to answer the city's call to *laissez les bon temps rouler*—"let the good times roll."

Somewhere between St. Peter and Toulouse Streets, she spotted him—a tall young man who looked to be in his twenties, taking pictures with a box camera. He was lean and tan, wearing khakis, a white cotton shirt with the sleeves rolled up, and a white straw fedora with a black band. Standing on the sidewalk across the street, he was aiming his camera at something beyond the open door of a bar called Tipsy's. Ellie watched as he peered inside, adjusted his stance a time or two, and took the picture, then ambled on. She had to wonder: In a place like this, swirling with people and music, what would've caught the photographer's eye?

Her curiosity drew her across the street to the doorway of the bar. Ellie immediately spotted the photographer's target. The room was narrow and tight, with space for only one line of bistro tables against the left wall and a long bar with an elevated stage behind it to the right. A girl in a red-sequined dress was onstage, singing "Love Me or Leave Me."

Seated on a stool at the corner of the bar, close to the door, was a blonde wearing a strapless blue cocktail dress that was a little too tight and a little too short for a woman her age. She was alone, smoking a cigarette as she stared at nothing in particular, absently running her finger around the rim of a half-empty highball glass. She wasn't so much beautiful as arresting, with a hardened glamour that made you wonder what she might've looked like ten or fifteen years ago. Was she waiting for someone, or had he already come and gone, abandoning her to this bar for the night? Perhaps many men had come and gone, dropping in and out of her life and leaving her alone in places like this.

Ellie was startled when the woman turned, met her gaze, and smirked at her wide-brimmed hat. "What's your problem, Bo Peep?" She practically spat the words. Ellie was stammering an apology when the woman raised her glass as if she were about to offer a toast, then threw the rest of her cocktail toward the doorway.

Mortified, Ellie fled, running as fast as she could until she was several blocks from the bar, where she stopped to catch her breath beneath a corner lamppost. She leaned against it as she took off her hat, using its wide brim to fan the steamy New Orleans heat off her face. She saw a couple of men on the street do a double take and checked to see if any of the hurled drink had landed on her skirt and stained it, but her dress looked fine. Who knew what made people in New Orleans stare? As Ellie had just proven, she was guilty of it herself.

She kept fanning with her hat, thinking of the day she bought it at Marlene's dress shop in Sylacauga. The saleslady had said it made her look elegant, and that's how Ellie always felt when she wore it—until a blonde woman on a bar stool suggested otherwise. Now she just felt stupid. She had presumed to judge and instead received judgment, revealing herself for what she was—a hayseed who didn't know how to handle herself in New Orleans.

Ellie eyed a metal garbage can next to the lamppost. She briefly clung to the hat and a memory of the girl who bought it, then slowly extended her arm above the trash can and dropped it in.

"I can't believe you just did that."

Ellie looked up to see the photographer watching her with a sad expression on his face, his camera pointed in her direction. She didn't know what to say. "It's just a hat," she finally said with a shrug as he approached her at the lamppost.

"I don't think so," he said, slowly shaking his head.

"It's kinda your fault, now that I think about it."

He raised his eyebrows and pointed to himself.

"That's right. If I hadn't been trying to figure out what you were taking a picture of back at Tipsy's, I wouldn't have made a bumpkin out of myself, staring at that blonde lady at the bar who, in case you're interested, called me Bo Peep and threw her drink at me."

The photographer winced. "Ouch! That was mean, even for Bourbon Street. Woulda made a great shot, though."

"Not for me, it wouldn't!"

The photographer laughed. "No, I guess not. Well, it seems I owe you an apology, which I sincerely offer." He took off his hat and bowed dramatically. "I am your humble and contrite servant, Heywood Thornberry of the Du Quoin, Illinois, Thornberrys. You may call me Heywood."

Ellie responded with a deep curtsy. "I am Miss Ellie Fields of the Maribelle, Alabama, Fields. You may call me Miss Ellie Fields."

They laughed together before Heywood looked around as if he were making sure no one could hear and leaned toward her. "I should advise you, Miss Ellie Fields, that the only women in New Orleans who park themselves against corner lampposts on Bourbon Street are, shall we say . . . open for business."

"What!" Ellie shrieked and leaped off the curb, which made Heywood laugh again. "Are you kidding me, Heywood?" she demanded, standing in the street with her hands on her hips.

He held up his right hand. "So help me, I speak the truth. I just thought you should know—before a line begins to form."

Ellie covered her face with her hands. "I'm an idiot!" she shouted, her voice muffled by her hands and dampened by the din that engulfed them.

Heywood pulled her hands away from her face and smiled

down at her. "Not true. You, Miss Ellie Fields, are merely out of your element. Temporarily. I predict you will own this fair city before it's over with. Now let us put your brief career as a lady of the evening behind us and grab some supper."

"You promise you're not a violent criminal?"

"Ma'am, I am far too poor to be a criminal and far too lazy to be violent. Also, I am betrothed to another and, therefore, completely safe."

Ellie's eyes narrowed as she frowned at Heywood. "Your intended doesn't mind if you pick up strange women on Bourbon Street?"

"She does not," Heywood assured her. "She says I have far more to say than one woman has the capacity to hear and therefore encourages me to engage the company of others."

Ellie had to laugh. "Well, in that case, I'm in."

Heywood offered her his arm. "Let us repair to a po'boy emporium."

He escorted her to a small café called Ollie B's a couple of blocks off Bourbon and found them a table.

"Heywood Thornberry, you better get up from there an' gimme some sugar!" cried an ample woman. She wore a long orange caftan—striking against skin the color of rich espresso—along with large gold hoop earrings and a bright orange-and-yellow turban.

"Miss Ollie!" Heywood shouted. He jumped up, hugged the woman, and kissed her on both cheeks.

"When you get back to New Orleans?" she said, holding him at arm's length and looking him over.

"Just a few days ago. You know I ain't stayin' here long before I got to have one o' your po'boys."

She slapped her leg. "I know that's right! Have mercy,

Heywood, I thought you's gon' turn into a big ol' shrimp last time you's here, what with all them po'boys you put away."

"Well, you oughtn' to make 'em so good! How's Mr. Welton?"

Miss Ollie shook her head. "Welton done got the cancer."

"Oh no." Heywood clasped her hand between his. "I am sorry to hear that. What's the doctor say?"

"Nothin' I wanna hear. But what you gon' do? You gotta just keep it goin', don't you, Heywood?"

"Yes, ma'am, you sure do. You let me know if I can help at all."

"'Course I will." She smiled and patted his cheek. "Now who dis?"

Heywood turned to Ellie, who was watching them from the table. "This is Miss Ellie Fields, fresh from Alabama. I accidentally got her into a mite o' hot water on Bourbon Street and thought I'd make amends with your fine cookin'."

"Pleased to meet you, Ellie," Miss Ollie said. "You in dang'rous comp'ny."

"I guessed as much," Ellie said with a smile. "It's nice to meet you, Miss Ollie."

"I best get back to my kitchen," she said. Then she turned to the bartender and called out, "Pinkie, cool 'em off with a storm—on the house."

The bartender nodded to Miss Ollie and soon arrived at their table with a tray that held two glasses of ice water and two tall cranberry-orange-colored cocktails.

"What's that?" Ellie pointed to the tall glass.

"That, Miss Ellie Fields, is called a hurricane," Heywood said. "Drink one and you'll forget all your troubles. Drink two and you might end up in the Mississippi River."

29

She took a tentative sip. "It's good." She took a long drink.

"Give it a second," Heywood advised.

She soon felt the effects of the drink and shook her head. "Maybe I'd better stick to Coke."

He motioned for the bartender to bring her one.

"Do you live close to New Orleans?" Ellie asked him.

"Not too terribly far," he said, taking a sip of his drink. "I work on an oil rig around Morgan City, but I slip up here now and again to take pictures."

"Is that what you want to do—become a photographer?"

He frowned and thought it over. "That was never my intent, but I seem to be drifting in that direction. There's just so much to look at down here. We don't have Spanish moss in Illinois. No alligators, either. Everywhere I look in Louisiana, there's something I want to remember, so I take pictures all the time."

Ellie nodded. "I can understand that. I've never seen anything like New Orleans. I'll bet there are lots of rich people in town with plenty o' money to hire a photographer for portraits and weddings and fancy parties. You could make money off that and photograph cypress trees and alligators in your free time."

Heywood smiled at her. "Yes, I suppose I could—if it turns out I'm any good. We'll just have to wait and see."

"Well, if you'd ever like someone to review your work, I happen to be the former senior photographer of the Maribelle High School yearbook."

"Truly?" Heywood said with a grin. "I had no idea I was in the company of a professional."

"I was perhaps best known for my blurry action shots," Ellie said, "but I am most proud of my beauty queen portraiture. I feel I captured their true essence, all the while keeping their tiaras in focus."

"I am in the presence of greatness."

A teenage boy brought their food out of the kitchen. "Extry sauce?" he asked.

"Not for me. Ellie?" Heywood asked.

"I'm fine," she said.

The two of them dug into po'boys—eight inches or so of crusty French bread, split down the middle and filled with the crispiest golden-fried shrimp Ellie had ever tasted. It was dressed with lettuce, tomato, and a sauce she couldn't exactly name—not quite mayonnaise and not quite tartar sauce but kin to both.

"Man!" she said, reaching for an extra napkin.

"It's the best, right?"

Ellie dabbed at the corners of her mouth. "What does Miss Ollie do to those shrimp?"

"I have no idea, but nobody else does it." Heywood took a long drink of his hurricane and leaned back in his chair. "The bread is key—comes from a local place called Beulah Ledner's. Well, it used to be—it's Gambino's now—and you can't find it anywhere else." He took another drink and looked at Ellie. "But enough about our mutual gluttony. Tell me your story. What brings you here from Alabama?"

"A job," she said. "I got a teaching position in a little town called Bernadette. Ever heard of it?"

"I know it pretty well." He picked up a stray shrimp and popped it into his mouth.

"What's it like?" Ellie wanted to know.

"Small. Rural. Whole lot o' water. It's got the biggest general store you've ever seen—Chalmette's—and you'll love the people. Most of 'em are Cajuns, but there's some Creole families down there too."

"I read up on Creole food for my trip to New Orleans, but what's Cajun mean?"

"Short for Acadian—French Canadians. The older ones don't speak English, so if you don't speak French, you might want to pick up a dictionary before you leave town."

"They don't speak English at all?"

"Just the old folks—most everybody else down there can *parle* some *anglaise*. Take 'em as they come, and they'll do the same for you. They're good people. Biggest hearts of anybody I ever met, but they've got a low tolerance for bull— that is, baloney—so always be straight with 'em. But you still haven't answered my question. What brings you *here*? There's gotta be plenty o' teachin' jobs in Alabama."

"True. But there are too many people there tryin' to tell me what'll make me happy. How can they know that when I don't even know myself?" Ellie took a small sip of her hurricane. "Whew, that's enough o' that," she said, pushing the drink in Heywood's direction.

A smile broke across his face as Ellie shook her head, trying to shed the effects of the drink, and reached for her Coke. "Don't let 'em put you in a bandbox, Ellie. Break that ribbon and climb on out o' there."

"I mean to try. I have no idea what'll come of it, but I do mean to try."

"And when did you call off your engagement?"

Ellie looked up at Heywood, who was draining the last of her hurricane. "How'd you know?"

He pointed to her left hand. "Now and again, you twirl a ring that isn't there."

"How do you know he didn't break it off?" she said, looking down at her hand.

"Because he'd have to be an idiot, and I doubt you'd ever date one."

"That's kind of you, Heywood." Ellie sighed. "His name was Gunter. We'd only dated for a few weeks when he tried to give me a ring. About a year later, I accepted. Or at least, I thought I did."

"Those naggin' doubts are a pill, aren't they?"

"Yes, they are." Ellie ran her thumb over the bottom of her ring finger. "He took me out to dinner in Birmingham a few weeks after he gave me the ring—we were about to start making wedding plans—and over pecan pie and coffee he said, 'I guess it's time for you to let the school know you won't be coming back.' Just like that, as if it were a given—a minor detail no more important than the reception punch or the rice bags. When I told him I didn't want to quit teaching, that I loved it and had worked hard to get my degree, he said, 'Now, Ellie, I can't have the whole community thinking I can't support my wife. Surely you can see how that would make me look.'"

"What a fathead."

"It wasn't just what he said, it was the way he said it—so sure I'd do whatever he wanted—and that he kept it from me, what he really thought. He said what I wanted to hear until we were headed for the altar, and then he pulled back the curtain when he figured it was too late for me to do anything about it. He figured wrong. I gave him his ring back right there and caught the bus home."

"Ellie, you're my new hero," Heywood said.

She absently toyed with the straw in her Coke, slowly

plunging it up and down in the ice. "Some hero. I let myself be totally fooled for a whole year—at least, that's what I tell myself. Maybe I was the one doing the fooling. And now here I am, going to a place I've never seen to live with people I don't know. I'm a hero, alright. Break out the ticker tape and throw me a parade."

"I predict enormous success for you in Louisiana," Heywood said. "I believe its untamed character will suit you to a T. Now quit worryin' about tomorrow and eat your po'boy before it gets cold."

They finished their supper, then went into the kitchen to say goodbye to Miss Ollie. Ellie saw Heywood slip her some cash money before paying their ticket and leading the way back to Bourbon Street. They spent a couple of hours ducking in and out of dimly lit, tightly packed clubs, listening to jazz and blues singers pour out their hard times and lost loves. Then Heywood escorted Ellie back to the Monteleone, stopping outside to buy her a rose from a woman selling them on the street. He ceremoniously kissed her hand in the grand lobby and promised to look her up in Bernadette. As she stepped onto the hotel elevator, Ellie wondered if Heywood really would come to see her. She hoped so. Right now, he was the closest thing she had to a friend this side of the Mississippi River.

THREE

THE FRENCH QUARTER WAS STILL SLEEPING when Ellie awoke and looked out her window the next morning. She had slept soundly, a better rest than she had enjoyed since she made the decision to leave home. She wasn't afraid of any challenges that lay ahead. She was afraid of coming up empty-handed, of going through all this upheaval only to discover that Louisiana held no more direction for her than Alabama.

Picking up the rose Heywood had given her, she breathed in its fragrance as she gazed down at the empty streets. A solitary woman was weaving her way toward the Monteleone from the general direction of Bourbon Street. She wore a vibrant purple dress with a yellow feather boa hanging off one shoulder and dragging on the sidewalk behind her. She carried her shoes in her hands. Ellie wondered what had happened to her last night. Where had she been and what had she done? Why was she walking the streets of New Orleans in clothes made for night, as daylight penetrated even the darkest corners of the French Quarter?

Something about her reminded Ellie of the blonde woman Heywood had photographed at Tipsy's. Did he spend a lot of time with women like that? Or did he just capture their image and walk away? Last night he had been a perfect gentleman, but Ellie suspected he was what her mother called "a hard dog to keep under the porch." She seriously doubted that he called it a night after dropping her off. And she wasn't sure she believed he was engaged. Even so, she was glad they had met. Heywood had a way of putting whatever she was trying to say into sharper focus, like the pictures he took with his camera. Sometimes she needed that.

The woman in the purple dress staggered, dropping one of her shoes as she struggled to steady herself, then turned down an alley and vanished, like a nocturnal vapor absorbed into the morning light.

What would that be like—to drop out of your life and disappear into a place like New Orleans, perhaps indefinitely, maybe even forever? The woman in purple seemed to have lost herself in the French Quarter, but could it be possible to find yourself here?

Ellie imagined never going home and never showing up in Bernadette but instead opening a corner bookstore—maybe on Royal Street—and living above it in a building with plaster walls painted bright yellow. It would have tall wooden shutters and a balcony wrapped in wrought iron. Each morning, she would water her hanging baskets as she called out a greeting to the shop owners across the street.

All of her friends would be musicians and artists—or waiters and carriage drivers hoping to become musicians and artists. She would dress for her own comfort and wear her hair in a long ponytail all the way down her back. Then again, maybe she'd cut it short. Her store would be a gathering place where interesting people shared interesting ideas over beignets and chicory coffee. She would sketch in Jackson Square on Sunday afternoons.

Ellie could see her bohemian existence plain as day. But then her own responsible nature reminded her that she had made a promise to Bernadette, and it would cost a lot of money to open a bookstore. Reluctantly, she pulled herself away from the window, bathed, dressed, and packed her overnight bag. She snapped the stem off Heywood's rose and pinned the bloom to her blouse. Then she took the elevator downstairs and went to the reception desk to check out.

"Leaving us so soon, Miss Fields?"

She turned to see Theodore the bellman smiling at her. "I'm afraid so," she answered. "If I'd known I was going to fall head over heels for New Orleans, I'd have gotten here a long time ago."

"Well, now, you'll just have to come back real soon. Can I help you to your car or call you a cab?"

"No thank you," Ellie said. "I sure do appreciate your kindness, Theodore."

He gave a slight bow and tipped his hat to her. "My pleasure. I wish you a safe and blessed journey."

ELLIE WAS ON THE LAST LEG OF HER TRIP, crossing a landscape that grew more watery by the minute. She had finally parted company with Highway 90, which faithfully carried her all the way across the coast, and was now following much rougher state highways over an endless series of bridges, some more questionable than others. In places, the roadway seemed little more than a roughly paved mound of dirt and gravel snaking through the water. The corner of

Louisiana she had crossed yesterday was flat and open, but as she drew closer to Bernadette, traveling deeper into bayou country, cypress trees soared out of the water, their moss-draped branches snow-tipped with white herons and egrets.

For the first time in her life, Ellie wished she were a real photographer like Heywood. He was right. There was just so much to see here. Louisiana looked like something out of a movie—dreamy and exotic, cloaked in green, with water everywhere you turned.

She drove back and forth over creeks, rivers, and swamp-land before she could finally see what must be Bernadette up ahead. The pavement had played out, and now Ellie was guiding Mabel over a gravel road that led into town. Drawing closer and closer, Ellie at last saw it—the general store Heywood had told her about. Chalmette's was a white clap-board building with a deep porch across the front and two gas pumps right by the street. It would've occupied a whole block if Bernadette had blocks.

What a pretty town it was—tiny, with one main street, and you could just about throw a rock from one end to the other. The wide gravel main street led to a beautiful old church fac-ing the town and watching over it like a sentinel. Its soaring steeple had a cross on top, silhouetted against a bright blue morning sky. Dotting both sides of the roadway between the store and the church was a scattering of storefronts: a post office, a sawmill that looked shuttered, a beauty parlor that appeared to be closed, and a cannery like the one back home, where all the women came together to put up peaches and tomatoes and green beans for winter.

Ellie couldn't help comparing Bernadette to her own home-town, which was small but not *this* small. Maribelle had a filling station, a town garage, a dress shop, a little café and a burger joint, a high school, and an elementary school.

Driving slowly down the street, Ellie came to a T in front of the church—St. Bernadette's. Now she knew where the town got its name. Maybe twenty yards or so to the right of the church was a tin-roofed structure even bigger than the general store, with picnic tables scattered around it. Just left of the church was a two-story schoolhouse, unpainted but neat and well-kept with a bell tower out front. Beside it was a white wooden building that looked like a small store, but "Doctor's Office" was painted on a sign out front.

So this was the place. The job offer Ellie had received by mail instructed her to report, upon arrival, to "the doctor's office." No address was provided, nor was the doctor's name, though Ellie knew it—Arthur Talbert, author of the letter that had spurred her on whenever she doubted her decision to move to Louisiana.

There were no signs of life at the schoolhouse or the church, so Ellie steered Mabel onto the graveled area in front of the white building and parked next to a black Ford. She climbed four wooden steps to the front porch, took a deep breath, and opened the screen door. A string of bells attached to it on the inside jingled as she stepped into the waiting room. Lined with ladder-back chairs, the room had a bench down the center and a big wooden desk with a telephone in the corner to the right of the front door. No one was sitting there.

Ellie heard voices coming from a closed door opposite the front entrance, but there was no one in sight. She took a seat in one of the chairs against the wall, holding her purse in her lap and hoping the doctor—whoever he was—didn't notice the wrinkles in her navy-blue skirt and polka-dot blouse. She wanted to make a good impression. Lightly running a finger over Heywood's rose, she tried to steady her nerves.

A glance down and she could see that her navy pumps were covered with dust. Bending over to brush them off, she heard a noise and looked up to see two hens underneath the desk. Each had an ear of dried corn, calmly pecking at it and occasionally looking in Ellie's direction. She was trying to figure out what chickens were doing in a doctor's office when the bells jingled on the screen door and a guy who looked a little older than Ellie came into the waiting room, carrying an ear of dried corn and another chicken. He did a double take when he spotted her.

"*Bonjour*," he said with a slight nod before placing the chicken under the desk with the others, pulling back the shucks on the corn, and laying it on the floor.

"*B-bon-jour*," Ellie attempted.

He immediately turned to her and frowned. "English?" he said.

Ellie nodded. "Sorry my French is so bad."

He shrugged and smiled down at her. "Not so bad." His deep voice was rich and smooth like chocolate. He was handsome in a working-man sort of way that Ellie had always found honest and appealing—tall and strong with slightly wavy black hair and tanned skin, no doubt from many hours on a fishing boat. His eyes were the color of cornflowers, with long dark lashes. He was wearing overalls tucked into rubber boots, his blue shirtsleeves rolled up to his elbows.

For a moment, he stared straight into her eyes. Then he said, "*Au revoir*" and left before Ellie had time to answer. Through the screen door, she saw him turn and walk up the street toward the general store just before one of the interior doors of the doctor's office opened. A kindly man of about sixty stepped out, followed by a young woman carrying a baby, with two more children holding on to her skirt.

"*Merci*, Doc," the woman said. She looked under the desk and nodded. "*Ça c'est bon*, he remembered to bring another hen."

"Well, that wasn't necessary, Kitty, but I appreciate it," the doctor said. "You remember to give the baby those drops three times a day and let me know if Sylvie and Luc have any kind of reaction to their vaccines."

The young woman was making her way to the door when she and the doctor finally noticed Ellie.

"May I help you, miss?" the doctor asked.

Ellie stood and offered a smile. "Hello. I'm Ellie Fields— the new schoolteacher."

The young woman recoiled, giving her a look that seemed equal parts fear and resentment. She wrapped an arm protectively around the child closest to her and hurried out the door.

"Welcome, Miss Fields!" The doctor clasped her hand between his. "I'm Arthur Talbert, but everybody around here calls me Doc, for obvious reasons."

"Want to tell me what that was all about?" Ellie nodded toward the door, still ajar, where the young mother had fled with her children.

"I'll do my best," he said with a sigh. "Let's have a seat and I'll give you the lay o' the land."

Doc was tall and broad-shouldered with neatly trimmed silver hair, blue eyes that twinkled when he smiled, and wire-rimmed glasses. His kind voice had the timbre of reassurance.

No doubt it had convinced many a frightened patient that everything would be alright. Ellie immediately liked him.

He offered her a seat beside the big desk before settling into the leather swivel chair behind it. The chickens, their dining hall disturbed, strutted out and began wandering around the waiting room.

"What would you like to know first, Miss Fields?" Doc leaned back in his chair, and Ellie noticed how very much at home he appeared in his office. He probably spent as much time here as he spent at his own house.

"Could we start with the chickens? And please, call me Ellie." She watched as the birds leisurely roamed about, softly clucking.

"They're payment for services rendered," Doc explained. "Feathered currency, if you will."

"Your patients pay you with chickens?"

"Now and again." Doc smiled and ran his hand slowly back and forth over the blotter on his desk as he explained his unique billing system. "This is a wonderful community, Ellie, but it's not a rich one. There was a time when all the families around here lived completely off the land—still do to some extent. They grow their own fruits and vegetables in a community garden right down the road." He pulled back the curtain covering a window behind his desk and pointed toward town. "And then the women get together at the cannery and put everything up.

"The men hunt, fish, and trap—there's a big market down in Morgan City," Doc went on. "That's where they sell what they don't need. Some o' the younger ones have found paying work on the oil rigs or big shrimpers in the Gulf. And some of them pick up extra work from the timber companies that operate around the Atchafalaya River. Anything they can't make, catch, or shoot, they buy at the general store. And when they don't have money to pay me, why, they pay me however they can, sometimes with chickens, sometimes a pig—whatever they have. Sick young'uns can't wait for payday."

"My uncle's mercantile back in Alabama works the same way," Ellie said. "Thursday is chicken-plucking day. I just never saw it happen in a doctor's office. Speaking of which, why am I here—in your office instead of the school board's, I mean?"

"I know it seems strange, but my office doubles as the town hall. If something comes up that involves the whole community, we use the dance hall, but when only the men need to get together, we just do that here or at Chalmette's."

"Did you say dance hall?"

He chuckled and nodded. "You'll soon see that Bernadette has a fine sense of rhythm."

"Are you from here, Doc?"

"Born and bred," he said. "I worked my way through medical school and spent a few years on the staff at a hospital in New Orleans. But I was never happy there. I guess I always felt the pull of the bayou—must've been God's way of telling me I was needed here. What about you, Ellie? What convinced you to come all the way from Alabama—and all by yourself?"

She pulled an envelope out of her purse and held it up. "Your letter had a lot to do with it. To tell the truth, I'm not sure what I'm doing here. I just knew I wasn't where I was supposed to be. Guess I'm trying to figure out where that is."

Doc nodded. "I remember that feeling. You'll have to decide for yourself if Bernadette is the place of your calling, but

I can tell you this much: You'll never find another community that needs you more. That's part of the reason I stay. I have to spend a couple of days a week working at the hospital in Lafayette to pay the bills, but I'm here the rest of the time and can't imagine being anyplace else."

Ellie felt something soft brush against her leg. She reached down and picked up a red hen that had wandered away from the others and let it settle onto her lap.

When she looked up, Doc was smiling at her. "Farm girl?"

"Oh yeah," Ellie said. "Daddy raises cotton and Mama's in charge of the henhouse—which means I was in charge of the henhouse till I left for college."

"I understand you graduated from Alabama Polytech?"

Ellie raised her right arm and shook an imaginary football pom-pom. "War Eagle."

Doc smacked himself on the forehead. "I'll never be allowed back into LSU stadium if word gets out I've recruited a rival Tiger to teach in Bernadette."

"What grade will I be teaching, Doc? I don't think I saw that in my letter from the school board."

"No, I expect they left that out on purpose for fear you wouldn't come. You'll be teaching the lower grades."

"*Grades?*" Ellie leaned forward in her chair, her eyes wide.

"All the children under age eleven will take their lessons with you on the ground floor, then they'll go upstairs to Miss Etta Harrison—most of them stay with her till they're fourteen or fifteen. After that, the boys go to work, and the girls help out at home till they get married."

"But I've never taught more than one grade at a time. How many kids are we talking about?"

"People around here tend to have large families. Best guess, I'd say no more than forty or fifty."

"*Fifty?*"

The hen stood up, flapped its wings, and clucked a few times before settling back down in Ellie's lap. She ran her hand over its feathers to settle it down.

"Now, don't worry. We can recruit one of the older girls in the community to help you keep order. There's usually one or two mamas willing to give up some of their help to bring a little extra money in. We don't pay much, but a little's a lot when you don't have anything."

Ellie was speechless. To come all this way—uproot herself when everybody back home warned her not to—only to learn she had landed herself in a school with precious few resources. She'd do well just to keep the children in the building, let alone make a difference in their lives.

"I expect I know what you're thinking," Doc said.

Ellie stroked the hen as much to calm her own nerves as to relax the bird.

"You're wondering how quickly you can make it back to Alabama. But just hear me out first. Till we built our school, the children on the bayou had to paddle downriver to the bus stop and then take a ride every morning and every evening. It's too much to ask of them, Ellie. Children shouldn't have to paddle a boat *and* ride a bus back and forth just to get an education. It's not fair, especially for the little ones. For the longest time, all the school board did about it was complain that the Cajun children were a hindrance to the others because they couldn't stay awake in class."

Ellie let out an exasperated sigh. "Well, I guess not! They were exhausted."

"We finally convinced the board that if they'd let us have our own school, we'd build it ourselves—which we did, down to the last nail. The town pays Miss Harrison, and the powers-that-be provide one teacher for the lower grades—usually a bad one."

Ellie had stopped petting the chicken, which rubbed its head against her arm, reminding her of her duties. She ran her hand over its feathers, thinking how strange it would be anyplace else to discuss a new job with a chicken in her lap, but somehow it made sense in Bernadette, Louisiana.

"There's something I don't understand, Doc," she said. "If school is so important to the people here, why don't they like teachers?"

Doc removed his glasses and wiped them with a white handkerchief he took from his shirt pocket. Ellie thought his eyes looked sad without the protection of the lenses. He put his glasses back on, folded the handkerchief, and returned it to his pocket, then reached into a desk drawer and pulled out a sealed envelope, which he handed to Ellie. She saw the school board's insignia in the upper left corner.

"Those are your instructions from the board," Doc said. "You can read them after you get settled in, but I'll go on and tell you the part that'll answer your question. About twenty years ago, the federal government decided that any-body moving to the United States from another country had to assimilate and 'become American,' which, to a bunch of politicians, meant everybody had to sound the same."

"How so?"

"Cajun people who'd been speaking French since they moved here a couple of centuries ago were told their language was un-American, unacceptable, and strictly prohibited in public schools." Doc grew more emotional and animated as he spoke, his voice rising, his hands waving in the air. "That, of course, was in addition to the prejudices against them already present in Louisiana. Being called backward and having their native tongue openly mocked—years and years of that have made many Cajun parents ashamed of their own language. And their children—by official mandate now—can be punished if they speak it in school."

"Punished? How?"

He slapped the top of one hand with the other. "A ruler whack on the hand, writing 'I will speak English only' over and over on the chalkboard after school, public humiliation like standing with their nose in the corner of the classroom . . ."

Ellie crossed her arms. "I'm flat-out not doing that."

"They'll say you have to," the doctor countered.

"They can say whatever they want."

The doctor leaned back in his chair and smiled. "A rebellious nature will make you feel right at home in Louisiana. I apologize for getting so worked up, but we're talking about the education—the future—of our children."

The chicken stood up in Ellie's lap, ruffled its feathers, and then sat back down. She scratched its soft neck. "Why does the state of Louisiana even care what the people do in a town this small and remote? I think the children need to learn English, but what harm could possibly come of letting them speak French too, especially if that's how they communicate with their grandparents?"

"Absolutely none," Doc answered. "And I'm not sure the state would be so adamant about stamping out French if it weren't for pure old-fashioned Louisiana politics. There's a powerful state senator named Roy Strahan—'Big Roy' to his cronies. He's gotten filthy rich off shady dealings to buy up oil rights all over the state, and he recently got his son, Boone, made the superintendent of education. Never mind that young Boone's college degree is in forestry. He knows absolutely nothing about educating children. Big Roy let him work for the park service for a few years before he decided it was time for Boone to enter the family business, which is crooked politics. The senator always has Junior right there when he takes to the stump to preach on progress, promising to stamp out 'the scourge of French' so Louisiana can join the rest of America in the great march forward, now that the war's over."

"Do they honestly believe that?"

"The Strahans believe in the Strahans, or at least Big Roy does," Doc said. "Apparently, he means to pave the way for Boone to follow in his footsteps whether he wants to or not, and the state department of education's as good a place as any to start. It's got plenty of visibility—not much of a budget but a valuable pulpit."

"And you don't think Boone's up to the job?"

"I'm telling you, Ellie, Louisiana has schoolchildren without food to eat, children who don't get proper medical care and don't have warm clothes in the wintertime—all worthy pursuits for the superintendent. But no, the senator would rather have his boy devote himself to making sure innocent bayou kids aren't bilingual. If you ask me, it's just an excuse to snoop around down here, looking for oil. And they've been helped along by an evangelist named Brother Lester Dobbs who believes French is the language of Catholics and Catholicism is idol worship. He travels all over Louisiana preaching to packed tents filled with people all too ready to believe that anything they don't understand must be evil."

"How often does the superintendent come down here?" Ellie asked.

"The last one came the first Monday of every month—and let me tell you, he was a true believer. He really thought French speakers were holding back the whole state. It's an unfortunate quality of human beings that we're prone to condemn the unfamiliar. I don't have any reason to expect better from a Strahan, but I'll reserve judgment till Boone makes his first appearance. In any case, the end result of all this nonsense is that we have a community full of Cajun children who either hate school or are scared to death of it."

"Children can't learn when they're afraid."

"No, they can't. I agree that all of these children need to learn English—they've got to be able to speak it, read it, and write it if they want to get on in the world. But to punish one—especially a little one—because he slips into French now and then? That's not right."

"How on earth will I ever convince the people here to let me teach their kids?" Ellie asked.

"They'll send their children to school because they want them to learn, in spite of all the obstacles and hardships the state has thrown at them. These folks have a sad history, Ellie. The British banished their ancestors from Canada because they wouldn't take sides with them against the French. Acadian people were put on ships to who knows where—with no regard for keeping families together, and no notion of where they were being sent. You had parents who never saw their children again, husbands and wives separated forever. And now here they are, nearly two hundred years later, persecuted just because they sound different from the rest of us and want to raise their families their own way."

Doc reached into a desk drawer and pulled out two books, which he handed to Ellie. One was a French-English dictionary. The other was a thick volume called *Acadiana*. "Cajun French is a little different from what you'll find in this dictionary, but it will at least help you start learning the language," he explained. "And this history will tell you what you need to know about them."

"You say 'them'—you aren't Cajun yourself?" Ellie asked.

"No, my father came here from a little town in southern France, and my mother's family is German, but they settled in the bayou. I've always felt the most at home here. I guess that's what makes me so mad about the way my community is being treated. These are some of the warmest, most open-hearted, truly *interesting* people you'll ever meet—probably got finer musicians and storytellers in Bernadette alone than you'd find in ten states put together. But all this interference with their language and their children has made them suspicious of people from the outside, and I don't blame them one bit."

"You think they'll give me a chance?"

"I do. But I won't lie to you, Ellie. None of our other elementary teachers has stayed more than a year, and the one you're replacing was the worst we've ever had. She didn't care a thing about the kids and seemed to enjoy punishing those who broke the English-only rule. She wouldn't even live here—commuted from Morgan City and decided after a couple of months that it was too much of a hardship for her to teach five days a week, so she only came for three. That said, I believe the families here will bring their children to school, and once they do, I have every confidence that you can win them over."

"Sure hope you're right."

"I generally am," Doc said with a grin.

"I want to thank you for your letter, Doc," Ellie said. "Every time I thought about backing out, I'd read it again and find my courage."

"Well, I'll never regret anything I did to persuade you to come."

"You mentioned housing?"

"I did indeed," Doc said. "My wife, Florence, says the bayou makes her claustrophobic, so I had to build her a house on the river, but we still have the cabin I grew up in. It would put you close to some of the local families and help them get to know you. And it's yours, free of charge, if you want it."

"That's awfully kind of you, but I'd have to pay you something."

"For a cabin standing empty? No, you won't owe us a thing. And if you find you aren't at ease in the bayou, why, you're welcome to come and stay with us on the river, or we'll help you find a place in Morgan City."

"I'm sure the cabin will be fine," Ellie said. "I wouldn't want to spend all my time traveling back and forth. I want to be part of the community, especially being so far from home."

"What if you decide you miss home too much to stay?"

Ellie looked down at the hen and ran her hand over its feathers. "I can't go back, Doc," she finally said, looking up at him. "Whatever I'm meant to do with my life, it's not in Alabama. I don't know if I'll find it in Louisiana either, but I do know that I keep my promises, and I've promised to teach these children this year."

The doctor looked out the screen door—at what, Ellie couldn't see. Then he turned back to her. "They've never had a teacher like you, Ellie. Most young women from the outside don't want to live in the bayou or become part of our community. We've had to make do with teachers who didn't even have college degrees, or recent graduates who finished at the bottom of their class and couldn't get a job anywhere else. The only one who's stayed is Miss Harrison, and she's seventy-five years old, retired from the public school system, with no family and no place to go. Can't hear it thunder and forgets herself from time to time, but what can we do? She at least reviews the basics, mostly because she doesn't remember teaching them the week before. Everybody pitches in to pay her a little bit to supplement her retirement, which isn't much, and we all look after her. You're the only one who's come because you wanted to be here. You're the only one I've felt was truly led to Bernadette."

"I'll do my best," Ellie said.

"That's all anybody can ask. Why don't you use my phone to call your family and let them know you're safe? Then I'll introduce you to the bayou."

FOUR

DOC HELPED ELLIE UNLOAD her teaching supplies at the school and park her car at the town landing on Bayou Teche. He carried her two suitcases to a bass boat tied to a tree on the bank and put them in. Then he took the overnight case Ellie was carrying and helped her into the boat before untying it and climbing in himself. He pushed off with an oar and then moved to the rear seat to crank the motor.

"Most of the locals paddle, but I've got a touch of bursitis that's acting up again," he said as they took off. "Also, I'm lazy."

A warm wind blew Ellie's hair away from her face as the boat glided across water that began as a clear, narrow channel but soon opened into a maze of towering, bald cypress trees, clusters of water lilies popping up here and there. Back home, the land, river, and sky were all distinct from each other. Not in this place, where ancient trees rose out of water and into the blue. It was beautiful and mysterious, and Ellie was smitten right away. She reached over the edge of the boat to trail her hand in the water.

"I wouldn't do that," Doc said with a wink. "Alligators!"

Ellie quickly drew her hand back. "Duly noted!" she

shouted over the motor noise. Alligators notwithstanding, she couldn't stop smiling as they traveled a watery wonderland of moss-draped trees filled with exotic birds you didn't see on the Coosa River back in Alabama. Fallen logs became sunporches for sleepy turtles. Now and then a bullfrog or two would leap off a lily pad and splash into the water. Ellie kept her eyes peeled for snakes and alligators but saw none, though she knew a place like this was likely crawling with them.

Doc steered them off the main channel of Bayou Teche and into a narrow tributary. It was peaceful and serene, completely shaded with tall trees. Houses on stilts began to appear, clinging to the banks, where they perched as if they had grown right out of the bayou. People on their porches waved and called out to Doc with what sounded like a friendly greeting, but it was all in French. He answered back in kind with a smile and a wave.

Soon they came to a small cove with just two cabins on stilts—one at the mouth of it, facing the channel, and another tucked deep inside it. Doc steered them to the more distant cabin, which had a long, wide dock with a built-in wooden bench near the end. It looked a lot newer than anything else on the property. Another bass boat with a motor was tied to one side of it. Up on the bank near the water was a long, narrow wooden boat, sharply pointed at the bow and stern, with low sides and a flat bottom.

Doc helped Ellie out, then set her luggage on the dock and climbed up to join her. "Right this way," he said, picking up her suitcases. Ellie grabbed her overnight case and followed him to the cabin with a screened porch all the way across the front and a gingerbread-framed screen door. On the porch, Doc opened the heavy wooden front door, which was decorated with a carving of an alligator painted white, and held it open for Ellie.

The floors and walls were made of wide cypress boards, well chinked to keep out the elements. All the kerosene lamps scattered about told Ellie there was no electricity.

A small rectangular wooden table with four chairs anchored the room near the center. Against the back wall were a woodstove, a sink with a hand pump, an icebox, and open shelves filled with dishes, canned goods, sacks of flour and sugar, boxes of salt and pepper, a bread box, and a couple of tins that likely contained coffee or tea. Onions and garlic hung in bundles from a beam overhead, along with an iron rack that held a few pots and pans and a cast-iron skillet or two. A small worktable was tucked into the back corner.

Against the right-hand wall, beneath one of the tall front windows, was a twin bed with no headboard or footboard. It was covered with a cheery red-and-white quilt and five or six throw pillows.

On the wall to the left was a huge stone fireplace with cast-iron kettles mounted on hinges that could swing them over the flames. Floor-to-ceiling bins on either side of it were filled with firewood. Facing the fireplace was a piece of furniture that looked wildly out of place in a bayou cabin—the longest, poufiest sofa Ellie had ever seen, covered in forest-green fabric, an attempt, perhaps, to accommodate its rustic surroundings.

"Florence says a living room needs a sofa," Doc said with a grin. "And who am I to argue? I'll put your things in here."

Ellie followed him through a doorway next to the woodstove and into the only other room, which was as long as the one in front but not as deep. One end held two iron beds with a nightstand between them. At the other end, Ellie saw a pine wardrobe with double doors next to a washstand, which had a mirror hanging above it. Against the back wall was a galvanized bathtub with a bucket and a brick next to it.

"Here's a convenience my father thought of," Doc said. He walked over to the tub and pulled out the drain plug. "There's a hole in the floor beneath the tub so it'll drain by itself. You'll only need the bucket to fill it, not to empty it. Just remember to replace the plug afterwards or a snake might decide to crawl through and join you. Florence puts that brick on top of it, just to be on the safe side."

Ellie shuddered at the thought of a water moccasin in her bed. "Believe me, I won't forget that plug. Or the brick."

Doc opened what looked like a closet door next to the washstand. "And this is something Florence insisted on if I ever wanted her to spend a weekend out here fishing with me. She said she was done with outhouses."

Ellie peeked inside and saw an actual functioning toilet. "That's the most beautiful thing I've ever seen," she said, which made Doc laugh.

"You have to fill the tank with the bucket, but it works. One day, Florence will have me plumb the whole cabin, but she's satisfied for now, no more time than she spends here," Doc said as the two of them returned to the front room. "You had written that you'd likely arrive today, so Florence put some fresh eggs and butter and a bottle of milk in the icebox, and I put a big ice block in there this morning, so everything should stay cool. There's a little smokehouse out back where you'll find plenty of bacon and boudin."

"What's that—boudin?" Ellie asked.

"Never had it before? It's a Cajun sausage. Best thing you ever tasted, 'specially when you dip it in a little cane syrup. We also took the liberty of leaving you a jug of Florence's homemade muscadine wine—strictly for medicinal purposes if you happen to be very Baptist."

"Good for what ails you?" Ellie said with a grin.

Doc winked at her. "Absolutely. That cabin we passed on the way in—it belongs to an older couple. Everybody calls them Tante Dodo and Mr. Hudie. Tante Dodo took it upon herself to learn English for the sake of her grandkids, so she can communicate with you. I've told them you might be staying here. If you ever needed anything or had any kind of trouble, you could just go straight to their cabin and they'd do anything in the world for you."

Ellie stepped onto the porch and peered across the water. From here, all she could see of the other cabin was its chimney, barely visible through an opening in the trees. "Doc, I'm not sure I feel right about this, taking your fishing cabin away from you and your wife," she said as he came out to join her.

"Ellie, you have no idea how happy we would be to host you, for as long as you're willing to stay. I can fish anywhere. This is Louisiana, for heaven's sake. And Florence only comes down here to humor me. You aren't taking a thing in the world away from us. Just the opposite, in fact. So what do you think? Could you be happy here for a while?"

Ellie looked out at three ducks swimming across the cove as a heron took flight from a cypress tree. "Yes, Doc," she said with a smile. "I think I could be very happy here."

FIVE

RAPHE STOOD ON THE SCREENED PORCH of his cabin, took a sip of coffee, and looked out at the downpour pelting the bayou. He had always loved the rain, even though it hindered fishing. He relished the stillness it brought. There was something so peaceful about that.

Peace would be hard to come by after this week. Another school year was beginning, and though Remy tried his best to hide it, Raphe knew he was terrified of going back and would likely be miserable every minute he was there. The boy would stop eating again. And he would cry into his pillow at night, which Raphe could hear when he sat on the porch underneath Remy's loft up above. He was always torn: Should he interrupt the tears to comfort Remy or allow him privacy to spill his sadness into a pillow without the embarrassment of being seen doing it? A real father would know the answer to that.

Remy was such a gentle soul, always trying hard to please, never asking for anything, determined to endure without complaint—as if abandonment lurked like an alligator in high grass, waiting to snatch him away from home if he made a wrong step.

Raphe had done all he could to alleviate his nephew's fears, but they were buried so deep he couldn't touch them. And now Remy had to go back to that school and face whatever poor excuse for a teacher the parish school board had persuaded to come way down here for a year, one who would no doubt work daily to *instill* fear of something as harmless—as beautiful—as the language his people had spoken for centuries. If he thought it wouldn't bring all kinds of trouble down on them, Raphe would keep Remy away from school and do his best to teach him to read and write at home. But it wasn't possible.

He heard the door open behind him.

"More coffee, Nonc?" Remy had the pot in his hand.

Raphe smiled as he held out his cup and let Remy top it off. The boy returned the pot to the stove and then came back out.

"*C'est une grosse pluie, non?*" Remy immediately slapped his hand over his mouth.

"Yes, it's a big rain." Raphe put an arm around his nephew. "Come over here. We can sit in the swing and watch it."

They took a seat in the porch swing they had built together, Raphe rocking it back and forth as they listened to raindrops splashing outside. Remy was only seven and small for his age. His feet didn't reach the floor.

"Listen to me, Remy. I've been tryin' to make sure we speak English at home so you get in the habit because I know you gonna get into trouble if you speak French at the school. But there's nothing wrong with French. That's just other people telling us what to do. The law lets 'em get away with it for now, but I bet you it won't always be that way. You got to do what they say while you're in that school, but at home—

we're not gonna let anybody make us feel ashamed o' who we are. You understand?"

Remy smiled up at him and nodded.

"And I'll tell you this," Raphe went on. "If that teacher thinks she's gonna hurt you or make you feel scared, you let me know. You and me, we can stop that right away. You tell me anything, and we gonna handle it together. *D'accord?*"

"*D'accord.*" Remy smiled again and rested his head on Raphe's shoulder. "Will you tell me the story of L'esprit Blanc, Nonc?"

"*Oui,*" Raphe said, looking out at the darkened bayou and listening to the rain. "Long time ago, there was a boy named Jacque Babineaux who spent so much time deep in the swamp, watchin' the alligators and listenin' to the sounds they made, that he learned how to talk to 'em . . ."

SIX

ELLIE HAD MADE HERSELF BREAKFAST FOR SUPPER, with scrambled eggs, some boudin from the smokehouse, and a small pan of biscuits with cane syrup she found on one of the kitchen shelves. Doc was right about the boudin. Ellie had never tasted anything like it.

Tomorrow she would try to catch some fish for supper, but tonight she just wanted to relax and let herself sink into the bayou. Kerosene lamps were burning in the front room, filling the cabin with warm light. She finished eating, washed her dishes, and put them away, then put on her nightgown and poured some of Florence's muscadine wine into a coffee cup. Wrapping herself in a shawl Mama Jean had brought back from a trip to Scotland, Ellie went onto the porch. She sat down in a rocking chair and pulled the shawl a little tighter. It was made of lightweight wool, plaid, in peacock shades of blue, wide enough and long enough to swathe her whole upper body.

She put her bare feet up in the rocker and took a sip of the wine, which reminded her of all the times she and her brother had trekked through the Alabama woods, picking up muscadines that fell from wild vines and eating them on the

61

spot. She would write Lanny a letter as soon as she settled into school. Hard to believe he had already graduated and was helping work the farm.

Relaxing in the rocker, Ellie closed her eyes, listening to the rain and the night sounds of frogs and crickets. A cool wind was blowing through the screens wrapping the porch. She heard something, distant but clear as a bell, drifting across the water from somewhere upstream. It was a plaintive fiddle playing a tune Ellie couldn't describe—like a sad song trying to be happy, or maybe a happy song that couldn't mask a touch of sadness. It was beautiful. A man's voice, aged but strong, began to sing. "*Parlez-moi d'amour . . .*"

She thought about Gunter. Nagging doubt, Heywood helped her to see, had kept her from accepting his ring for many months, but when she finally said yes, she had felt happy, hadn't she? The minute he made it plain, though, that he intended to be the decision maker in their lives, that what was important to him would always come first, some sort of switch flipped inside her. She hadn't cried about their parting—not once—because she didn't feel sad. Mostly she just felt foolish.

If she really dug down deep and thought about it, there had been signs, things she dismissed as overprotectiveness on Gunter's part. In fact, he had been slowly, over time, exerting little bits of control, imperceptible when taken one moment at a time but painfully obvious when she looked back on the accumulation. Maybe she, too, was guilty of deception, only she had deceived herself, not her intended. She wasn't sure which was worse.

Ellie took another sip of wine, set the cup on the porch, and closed her eyes again. Tomorrow she would go to the school and do her best to transform those two dreary class-rooms into a proper space for children. She would plan every minute of her first day—how to make it fun and interesting so her students would look forward to school instead of dreading it. She would find a way to make every child feel safe and special. But for now, she would simply breathe in the night, listening to the crickets and the night owls. She would follow Heywood's advice: Let tomorrow take care of tomorrow and enjoy the here and now.

SEVEN

RAPHE GRABBED A COKE FROM THE RED COOLER on the porch at the general store and went inside to pay Emmett Chalmette at the register. It would be good to get out of the midday heat. Just inside, he found Emmett on his hands and knees, gathering up white alligator carvings. They had been displayed on a small table near the front of the store. Now the table was lying on its side, the wooden alligators scattered everywhere.

"What happened?" Raphe asked as he set the Coke and his money on the counter and started helping Emmett.

"Scoot the table back a little closer to the register where I can watch it better if you don't mind, *mon ami*," Emmett said.

Raphe moved the table back and began gathering up the larger carvings.

"That preacher Lester done come in here," Emmett said, shaking his head. "I won't let him on my property no more, but he stands 'cross the street preachin' about what he calls graven images and sayin' we all goin' to hell on accounta we worshipin' the white alligator."

"What made him think that?" Raphe asked, setting a stack of carvings on the display table and then spreading them out.

"Somebody musta just put the notion in his head, 'cause he done seen these carvin's o' Freeman's alligators on doors an' porches 'round the bayou for over a year now, an' he ain't said a word," Emmett said. "But here in the past few months he's gone on a tear about the white alligator. Says it's bad enough us Catholics worship statues—that same ol' crazy business—but now we done bowin' down to a reptile. Come in here shoutin' about it just now and turned my table over 'fore I could stop him."

"He still putting up a reward for anybody that kills it?" Raphe asked.

"Oui," Emmett said, replacing the smaller carvings while Raphe grabbed a broom from behind the counter and swept around the table. "I don't know where a preacher woulda got $5,000 to spend on an alligator reward. But they say he draws big crowds to his tent revivals. That collection plate must be fuller'n my crab traps on a mighty good day."

"You still seeing a lot o' hunters from the outside?" Raphe asked as he returned the broom.

"Naw," Emmett said. "They made a big noise 'bout gettin' the white gator and collectin' all that money, but folks like that got no idea what they doin' when they come down here. Most of 'em just rode up and down the main channel—like you'd ever find a white alligator out in broad daylight. They've all 'bout give up."

Raphe took a sip of his Coke. "Why people got to meddle with things they don't know about?"

"You go on and figure that one out, Raphe, so you can explain it to the rest of us."

"Freeman's carvings still selling good?"

"Oui," Emmett said. "Most people buy the smaller ones

for the kids, but some o' the ladies get the bigger ones to put on their front door. Leta's got one nailed to ever' post on her porch. Looks real nice."

"That's good," Raphe said. "Helps Freeman bring in a little extra money. Even harder for a colored family than the rest of us. Knowing his daddy, Freeman's been raised to work hard."

"How long you an' Lawyer been playin' music together?"

Raphe took another sip of his Coke as he tried to remember. "Don't know. Since way before Freeman was born. I haven't seen him in a long time."

Emmett smiled at him. "That's 'cause you ain't picked up your fiddle in a long time, Raphe. What's it gonna take to get you back on that stage at the dance hall?"

"Time," Raphe said with a long sigh. "Ain't got any."

"I hear you, *mon ami*."

"I see *le conseil* is meeting today." Raphe pointed at the five men gathered around a long piece of plywood resting on sawhorses at the back of the store. They were peeling boiled crawfish and sipping from cold bottles of beer that Emmett iced down in a galvanized trough.

"Aw, they really got it goin' today," Emmett said with a grin. "Didn't hardly look up when ol' Brother Lester tipped my gators."

"What's got 'em so stirred up?" Raphe asked.

"The new schoolteacher. She come in here to buy supplies, and when I rung her up, she said '*merci*'! Even bought a white gator. I thought Leo and Andre was gonna hit the ground! They near 'bout *ran* to the Teche to fly the flag so they could tell the others. Goin' on two hours now, they been back there hashin' it out, talkin' over each other 'cause they so excited. I'm gon' make me a killin' off all the beer they drinkin' while they eat them crawfish and work on this new development."

Raphe smiled and shook his head. "Reckon I better get back there and see what they decided. I left my Coke money on the counter."

"Merci, Raphe."

He had known the group of men around the table since he was a boy. They were good friends to Raphe's father before the storm took him away. Leo and Andre Castile were brothers, both in their seventies and both fishermen. Clayton Menard, Binkie Melancon, and Clifton Chavis were their cousins—all about ten years younger than Leo and Andre, and all three alligator hunters. Because the five always seemed to know everything about everybody in the whole parish, the community affectionately called them *le conseil*—the council. To make it easy for one to summon the others for discussions like these, Leo had erected a flagpole at the town landing and had his wife fashion a white flag with a big purple fleur-de-lis. When the flag was flying, news was breaking, and they all knew to gather at Chalmette's.

"Raphe!" Leo called out. "Put down that sorry Co-Cola and come have a beer with us! It's on me."

Before Raphe could answer, Leo put a cold beer in his hand. Raphe thanked him and set his Coke on the table.

"Well, don't just stand there!" Leo said. "Pull you up a stool and help us eat this crawfish! I hauled in a mess of 'em."

Leo was a character—tousled gray hair with a few remaining dark streaks and usually capped with a straw hat, a twinkle of mischief in eyes black as coal, and a thick mustache framing a jolly smile. His skin was dark, his face lined with age, but he had the muscular body of a thirty-year-old and still worked like one.

Raphe pulled up a stool and joined the men eating from a mound of crawfish piled onto newspaper in the center of their makeshift table. "Tell me 'bout that teacher," he said.

"Well, I can tell you this much fo' sure: You might want to pack you a lunch pail and tell her you done forgot yo' ABC's," Leo said with a grin. "She's a pretty one, that teacher."

"*Mighty* pretty," Clayton agreed.

"And she said 'merci'!" Andre added before sucking the meat from a crawfish shell.

"Bought one o' Freeman's alligators too," Binkie added. "What you make o' that, Raphe?"

"Don't know." Raphe took a sip of his beer and pinched the head off a boiled crawfish. "Maybe she don't hate us like the last one. Or maybe she wants to know how we answer when we don't think twice. Testing us a little bit for the school board?"

"Never heard a teacher say a word o' French," Leo said. "I think it's a good sign. Maybe Remy'll have a better time this year."

"Maybe so," Raphe said. "Can't get any worse, that's fo' sure."

"Hey, what you hear from ol' Heywood lately?" Leo asked him.

"Not much. Passed through on his way to New Orleans. I look for him to stay up there a while—bet you he's got that camera goin' ninety to nothin'."

"That's the truth." Leo smiled, nodding in agreement. "That boy loves to take his pictures. Heywood's a good friend, Raphe. You got to hang on to your *bon amis*—'less you want to get stuck with a bunch like this!" Leo gestured to his relatives around the table and laughed. "You a sorry sight when don't nobody love you but your own kin!"

"And we just here fo' the beer and the crawfish," Binkie said. "He run outta food, we gon' leave him fo' good!"

Raphe laughed with his father's friends. Sometimes he wondered what they had all been like when they were young, waltzing and two-stepping with the girls on Saturday nights and spending their days on the water. Raphe had enjoyed such a carefree life—hardworking but carefree—before the storm changed everything. Heywood had a way of bringing back those days. Raphe had almost forgotten how to laugh and pass a good time till the lanky photographer turned up on the bayou, asking for help getting his bearings on the Teche and the Atchafalaya. Right away they hit it off and had been friends ever since.

Heywood probably had that effect on everybody. He wasn't from Louisiana but had moved there from Illinois, following work in the oil fields. He always said he could ride a billy goat around the world backward and never see anything more exotic and beautiful than Louisiana. To Raphe, the bayou wasn't exotic—it was home—but it was beautiful, alright. There were no ills a paddle down the river couldn't cure, no problem he couldn't sort out with a fishing rod in his hand. Raphe wasn't restless like Heywood. He just knew he had a missing piece, with no idea where to find it.

EIGHT

THE METAL DOOR ON THE MAILBOX clanked shut as Raphe dropped an envelope in. Though the post office was open, he hated getting tangled up with Miss Ernie, who ran it, and opted for the mailbox out on the porch instead. Miss Ernie was a nosy old woman who brazenly pried, sharing her information with the whole community. She even kept a notebook where she wrote down the more interesting addresses on local mail so she could ask you all kinds of questions about them: "Who you know in Mobile, Alabama? Why you gettin' mail from a hospital in Baton Rouge? Somebody in your family been sick? Y'all havin' trouble payin' the bill?" Everybody felt sorry for her husband, Mr. Jimmy, who was as sweet and kind as she was vexing.

Raphe stared at the poster nailed to the post office wall.

He pulled the sign off the wall and threw it into a trash barrel. Cajuns didn't worship alligators any more than Catholics worshiped statues. The very idea that such a misguided notion might destroy something so purely beautiful as the white alligator was more than he could stand. He was about to walk back to the landing and head home when he paused and thought about the new teacher. Maybe she wouldn't terrorize Remy the way the other one had. Even so, it wouldn't be a bad idea to let her know here and now that he wouldn't stand for it. He took a chance that she might still be at the school and made his way there.

The double front doors were propped open, and the ground-floor windows were raised. Raphe climbed the steps and went inside. He could see that all the desks and chairs had been pushed into the dogtrot that ran from the front to the back of the building, creating a wide, breezy corridor that separated the two large classrooms on the ground floor of the school. The walls of the dogtrot had wooden shutters that could be opened, creating cross breezes with the exterior windows. All of them were open now.

Through the open shutters, he heard a radio playing and a woman singing "Lovesick Blues." She must've thought there wasn't another living soul in sight, because she was really belting it out. Raphe liked her voice. It would sound mighty good with a fiddle. But that didn't mean she wasn't a terror like all the others.

He followed the music into the open doorway of the classroom to his left. The teacher was wearing overalls rolled up to her knees. She was barefoot with her hair in a ponytail. Raphe watched as she poured herself a cup of coffee from a thermos on the desk, sprinkled in some sugar from a paper sack, and splashed it with milk from a mason jar. She took a few sips and then climbed onto a step stool by one of the windows, standing on tiptoe to try to hook a curtain rod onto a nail she had no hope of reaching.

"Can I give you some help?" he asked.

She gasped and dropped the curtain rod.

"Sorry—didn't mean to scare you," he said, hurrying to retrieve the rod and help her down off the stool.

Breathing hard, she put her hand to her forehead. "I think you just took a few years off my life. Guess I had it coming, though—probably deafened you with my singing."

"What?" Raphe cupped his hand over his ear.

That made her laugh. And what a fine laugh it was, light and clear.

"Hey, I know you," she said. "Or at least, I've seen you, right? In Doc's office?"

Raphe looked closely. It *was* her. The brown-eyed girl with the gold-streaked hair was the new teacher? He couldn't decide whether she was prettier in her teacher clothes or barefoot in overalls. "That was me." He rested the curtain rod in the windowsill.

She extended her hand. "This one's fairly clean," she said. "I'm Ellie Fields, the new teacher—though, from what I hear, that won't exactly put me on your Christmas list."

He shook her hand, which felt soft but strong. "Raphe Broussard."

"Pleased to meet you. I guess I'll be teaching your kids?"

"Nieces and nephews. I don't have any kids."

She gave him a puzzled frown. "I thought I counted three."

"Three?"

"Children—at the doctor's office?"

He nodded as he remembered. "My sister's. She needed help. Her husband was out on a shrimper."

Raphe surveyed the classroom. Usually musty and dark, it looked and smelled as if it had been scrubbed clean. He caught the faint scent of lemon. There was a box of colorful paints and brushes against the back wall and a big stack of quilts in a rocking chair next to the desk up front. More boxes were stacked in a corner of the room.

"So if you don't have any kids, what brings you to the school?" Ellie had a way of looking straight at him that Raphe liked—no hedging or hiding.

"My nephew Remy—he lives with me. He's seven. Remy . . . he had a rough time last year. I thought . . . I guess I thought I'd stop by and . . . and . . ."

He was searching for the right words when she gave him a big smile. "You thought you'd stop by and tell me if I'm mean to Remy, I'll be sleeping with the alligators?"

"Something like that," he said, smiling at her in spite of himself.

"Listen, Raphe," she said, "I don't believe in punishing children for speaking the language they grew up with. Don't get me wrong, they need to learn English. It's the only way for them to live and work outside the bayou if they should ever have to—or want to. But to humiliate a child just because he can speak two languages instead of one is cruel and stupid. And I'll say that to Big Roy and Little Roy, or whatever his name is, and the rest of the department of education if they ever ask for my opinion, which is highly unlikely."

A brief silence fell between them before she picked up one of the quilts from the chair. "Are you in a hurry or can you help me with something?"

"No." He closed his eyes and shook his head as he corrected himself. "No hurry, I mean."

"I'm trying to hang curtains and figure out how to rig up some quilt racks on the wall so I can brighten up this awful room. But I have to be able to get the quilts down at nap time so the children can lie on them."

"Nap time?"

"That's right."

"You gonna let the boys and girls sleep—in school?" Raphe had never heard of such a thing. School was about memorizing and ciphering and trying to stay awake.

"Just the little ones," Ellie said. "The older children can make it through the day fine, but the first and second graders need to rest for a while after they've had their lunch or they'll be too tired to concentrate in the afternoon. Will you help me?"

"Sure."

She led him to a box of supplies from Chalmette's. "I bought some dowels that might work—just need to figure out how to mount them on the walls. I thought I'd hang three quilts between the outside windows and then three more between the shutters open to the dogtrot."

Raphe knelt down and rummaged around in the box of supplies to see what he had to work with. Then he went to the rocker and picked up one of the quilts, which was well made and heavy. "You gonna need something stronger than those dowels," he said. "I'll be right back."

He went to his truck and sorted through scrap lumber till he found some pieces that would work. "Show me how you want to hang them," he said to Ellie. He watched as she took a blue-and-yellow quilt from the rocker, folded it lengthwise a couple of times, and then draped it over her arm.

"Something like that, maybe, so it hangs long and covers up a lot of that heinous drab wall?"

Raphe nodded, took note of the quilt's length when it was halved, and set to work on the first rack. "Try this one," he said when he was finished.

She draped the quilt over the rack just as she had held it on her arm, looked up at Raphe, and smiled. "Amazing what a little color'll do. Now get busy."

He gathered more lumber and finished the racks so Ellie could hang her quilts, which brought a dramatic change to the brown walls, splashing them with rings and squares and triangles of cotton cloth in every color of the rainbow.

"You make these?" he asked her.

That brought an exasperated sigh from her. "You think all women should stay home to quilt and cook?"

He had touched a nerve without meaning to. "I think all women should do as they please," he answered calmly, as if he hadn't noticed the rancor in her voice. "I just wondered who made quilts this fine." Raphe ran his hand slowly over the blue-and-yellow one with its intricate circular patterns and felt the fine stitching with his fingertips. He turned to see Ellie watching him.

"I'm sorry," she said.

For a split second, she looked like she was about to cry, which affected Raphe more than he would've expected. Gazing at her delicate face with the fine bones and full mouth, he asked, "Is Ellie your real name?"

"No."

"I didn't think so."

She was smiling again, thank goodness. "Well, now you have to guess what it's short for: Melanie, Adele, or Mary Nell."

He shook his head. "None of those."

She looked startled, like a deer jerking its head up from a stream at the sound of a snapping twig. "How did you know?"

"Because you are none of those," he said.

For a moment, she stared at him, wide-eyed and silent. "It's . . . Juliet. My name's Juliet. But nobody's called me that since I was about four."

"Ah," he said. "Juliet. I can see it. But which name do you feel?"

Again she stared at him straight on, without hiding behind flirtatious laughter or a clever remark like so many women did. "Nobody's ever asked me that before. I guess I'd have to try on Juliet and see how she suits me. What about you? Are you really Raphe?"

"Christened Raphael," he said, "but only Mamou—my grandmother—called me that."

"And what do you choose—Raphe or Raphael?"

He thought it over. "Raphe, I think. I believe Raphael is too much name for me."

"Well then, Raphe," Ellie said, "would you allow me to tell you the story of my quilts even though I've behaved badly?"

"Oui."

"Merci," she said, giving a small curtsy in her overalls. She pointed to the quilt in blue and yellow. "This one's called Cathedral Window. It's really hard to sew, which is probably why it's the only one my Mama Jean makes. She's my grandmother on my mother's side, and she doesn't mind telling you that her Scottish ancestors were smarter, stronger, braver, and generally better than everybody else. But she's always in my corner. We're really close. She made this one, and Mama made the purple one just like it in the center over there. Hey, they look really good the way you hung them opposite each other."

"Merci," he said.

"The two on either side of this one are called Rail Fence, and they're really old. My great-grandmother on Daddy's side—he called her Mamie—she made those out of flower sacks. The little flowers on the fabric are all faded, but I still think they're beautiful. Mamie had nine children—*nine*—but three of them didn't live to grow up. That happened a lot back then."

"It happens still if you're too poor to care for your children," he said.

There it was again—that startled, wounded expression on her face.

"You are not to blame, Juliet," he said, regretting that his own words had brought her unexpected pain. "Tell me about the others?"

She nodded, still looking at Raphe, not the quilts. Finally, she turned to the breezeway wall with the open shutters. "The ones on either side of the Cathedral Window over there are called Arkansas Traveler. My Aunt Joyce made one, and Aunt Vivian made the other. In our family, we call the four of them—my mother, the aunts, and Mama Jean—'the sisters.' Daddy started it, and the rest of us picked it up somewhere along the way. "

"So you brought them with you to Louisiana—*tes soeurs.* Your sisters."

He watched as she looked around the room and then smiled, nodding in agreement. "Oui," she said, "I guess I did. My *soeurs.*"

Raphe wondered why such a woman was alone—and what had made her so sad way down deep below her smile. "I should hang your curtains and get out of your way."

"You're not in my way—but I'd sure appreciate it if you hang my curtains."

One by one, he lifted the four rods with white cotton curtains over the outer windows, where they fluttered in the afternoon breeze. Then he surveyed the room with approval. "Now it looks like a cabin instead of a jail."

"Let's hope I can convince the kids that I'm their teacher, not their warden," she said. "Hey, can I ask your opinion about something?"

"Yes."

"When I bring the desks back in, I'm gonna put them two deep in a circle all around the room. So I thought I'd paint something on the floor in the center—something from a storybook like the yellow-brick road from *The Wizard of Oz* or maybe Humpty Dumpty sitting on his brick wall. It'll have to be simple because I'm not a very good painter, but do the children here know those stories?"

Raphe shook his head.

"Can you tell me a story they *would* know—something familiar I could paint on the floor? Maybe a folktale that has something to do with the bayou?"

"I might know a few," he said.

She offered him the rocking chair and took a seat on the desk, her legs and bare feet dangling above the floor. He sat down in the rocker and absently scratched his jaw, mentally riffling through the catalog of bayou tales he had heard all his life.

"Lotta the old stories, they're kinda scary," Raphe explained. "Prob'ly to help keep the children from going where they got no business at night—like *le feu follet*, lights floatin' around the bayou at night. You'll be so glad to see 'em in the dark swamps, but they don't mean to guide you—they mean to lead you in the wrong direction so you get lost and drown. And the Rougarou—in the daytime, he looks like everybody else—could be your neighbor, your cousin, your best friend—but at night he's got the body of a man and the head of a wolf, and he'll hunt you."

Ellie shook her head. "It's a thousand wonders Southern children can sleep at night. You grew up with the Rougarou, and I grew up with Rawhead."

"Rawhead?"

"Daddy told us he lived in the barn at night and would eat us if we went anywhere near him," she said. "Definitely kept us away from the poison he had to keep stored out there to keep the bugs off his cotton. Can we think of something a little less horrifying, maybe?"

Raphe rocked for a few seconds, thinking before he spoke. "Remy's favorite is a story about *le cocodrie blanc*—the white alligator."

"*Cocodrie* means 'alligator'?"

"It does."

"What does *Teche* mean?"

"It comes from an Indian word that means 'snake.'"

"I live on Snake Bayou?"

"You could say that."

"That oughta keep me from dangling my feet in the water. And I'm guessing the white alligator in your story is the one I keep seeing everywhere—the one I bought at Chalmette's?"

"That's the one. We call it L'esprit Blanc—the White

79

Spirit. Nobody knows where it came from or how long it's been in the swamp. Some people say it's not real at all—just an old Indian tale to scare white men away. Others swear they've caught a glimpse of it—the tip of its tail before it disappeared into the swamp grass or a peek at its snout right before it vanished into the Teche. They say L'esprit Blanc is snow white, with eyes the color o' sapphires."

"He must be mighty old if the Indians saw him."

"Either that or there's more than one."

"Is L'esprit Blanc good or bad?" Ellie asked.

Raphe raised his eyebrows. "That's always the question, *non*? I'll leave that to you. There's all kinds o' stories about him. Some say he'll cast a spell on you—*un gris-gris*. Others say he's pure goodness—that's why he's so hard to find. Remy's favorite goes like this: A long time ago, there was an orphan boy named Jacques Babineaux who lived all alone on the Atchafalaya. One day, Jacques gets so lonesome, livin' all by hisself, that he decides to leave the river—which he knows like the back of his hand—and paddle deep into the swamp, lookin' for some company. All the callin' birds and the singin' frogs, they make him feel a little less lonesome. But most of all, he loves the alligators. And he spends so much time listenin' to the sounds they makes that he learns how to talk to 'em. A lot o' people don't know this, but alligators are fine company."

Ellie grinned. "Is that a fact?"

"Pretty good card players too." Raphe slowly rocked in the chair as he continued the story. "Jacques, he loves bein' with 'em so much that he don't ever want to go home. He stays and he stays, and he talks and he talks till he starts gettin' on the alligators' nerves, but they don't want to hurt his feelin's, you know?"

"I've heard alligators are very sensitive," Ellie said with a straight face.

"Absolutely. So the gators, they wait till Jacques falls asleep, and then they hold *le conseil* to decide what they gonna do 'bout dis boy 'fore he runs 'em all crazy. Well, they bicker and they fuss, till finally the oldest one of 'em says they oughta send Jacques out to search for the white alligator. Now, L'esprit Blanc's got the powerful gris-gris—whenever you see him, he gonna make hisself look like the thing you want most. You spot him when you want a new shotgun, that gator's gonna look like the finest Remington at Chalmette's, only soon as you reach for it, he gonna show hisself—pull you in the water and drown you fo' sure. Dat's how come he never been found, never been caught, never been killed. You sure you wanna hear this whole thing?"

"If you stop now, I swear I'm gonna sing to you, and we both know you don't want that," Ellie said.

"Even the gators, they can't say for sure if L'esprit Blanc is real," Raphe went on. "They just wantin' to keep the boy occupied long enough to give their ears a rest."

"Do alligators have ears?" Ellie asked.

"They do. So the boy, he wakes up and the alligators tell him they got a big job for him. They need him to catch this white alligator and bring it back alive so it can give 'em the gris-gris. Well, Jacques, he can't wait to go—here's a big adventure on the bayou and a chance to prove hisself to the alligators."

Raphe stopped rocking and leaned forward, his elbows propped on his knees. "Right away, Jacques, he lights out in a pirogue. Minute he's gone, the alligators go to celebratin'— they throw a big boucherie, dancin' on the banks o' the Teche and playin' music and roastin' a pig. They can't imagine what it's gonna be like to sleep late without Jacques wakin' 'em up early to talk about the weather or keepin' 'em up late to talk about what they gonna do tomorrow. They fill up on barbecue and go to bed, thinkin' they ain't got a care in the world, and they gonna sleep till lunchtime the next day 'cause Jacques, he'll be out lookin' for that white alligator for a real long time."

"Something tells me things won't go as planned."

"Don't be jumpin' ahead now," Raphe said, leaning back in his chair. "The next morning, all the alligators are havin' the best rest they had since the boy turned up on the bayou. They all dreamin' and snorin' and sleepin' so fine. But then right at daybreak, they hear the awfullest commotion out on the water—something splashin' and Jacques singin' at the top o' his lungs and playin' his accordion. That sleepy bunch o' alligators, they come staggerin' down the bank to find Jacques standin' on the back o' L'esprit Blanc, ridin' him like a pirogue as he glides down the Teche, with Jacque's boat tied to his tail. Jacques unties the boat, hops off the white alligator, and leads it up the bank to where the others are all waitin', half-asleep and yawnin', ever' one of 'em. You ever see a whole bunch o' alligators yawnin' at the same time?"

"As a matter of fact, no, can't say that I have," Ellie said, laughing.

"The oldest gator, he says to Jacques, 'How you find that white alligator when nobody else in the bayou could?' Jacques, he just smiles and says, 'Guess I wanted it more than they did.' That's when the white alligator speaks up and says, 'I'm fixin' to give y'all the only gris-gris you need: You gonna find what you want most 'cause you gonna see it like nobody else.' And before they could stop him, he backed into the bayou and swam away. Nobody's seen him since. But one o' these days, somebody's gonna want that white alligator more than anything else. And when they do, they gonna find him."

Ellie applauded from her perch on the desk. "That's a *fine* swamp tale, Mr. Broussard," she said with a big smile. "And I'm especially excited because I don't think an alligator will be all that hard to draw. I'd be in a real pickle if you'd told me a story about a panther or a bear or something. By the way, do you realize your accent changes when you tell a story?"

He smiled and nodded. "My sister says I speak in my own voice, but I tell stories in our papa's. I don't do it on purpose. It just happens."

He could hear the soft thud of her heels against the desk as she sat there, slowly swinging her legs back and forth. He sat silently for a while before he said, "What you having for supper tonight?"

"Me? Well . . . I guess it's too late to catch a fish, so I'll probably have the same thing I ate last night—scrambled eggs, boudin, and biscuits. And before you ask—yes, I can cook."

"Will you let me and Remy cook for you? We can drop your boat off at Doc's cabin, and I can get you home after so you don't have to travel the bayou at night."

She looked down at her overalls and bare feet. "Can I clean up a little at the cabin?"

"Sure."

"Then I'd love to."

NINE

ELLIE STOOD BEFORE A MIRROR HANGING over the wash-basin at Doc's cabin. She had hurriedly splashed a little soap and water on "the critical regions," as Mama Jean called them, and changed into a lavender cotton dress. There was no time for her hair, so she just brushed it and pinned it into a twist on the back of her head. Slipping on a pair of gray leather flats, she went out to join Raphe. He stood up when the door opened onto the porch.

"Well, at least I'm clean—sort of," she said. "Is there anything I can bring?"

"Just your company," he said. "You got a porch lamp?"

"A what?"

"It'll be dark when we get back," he said. "Good idea to leave a lamp on your porch so you don't have to try and find your way in a dark house."

Ellie stepped inside and grabbed a lamp and matches from the table. She set them on the porch next to the screen door. "All set."

Raphe held the screen door open for her, and they walked down to the dock, where he helped her into his boat. Once he cranked the motor, they were off, skimming across the slough and back into the main channel of Bayou Teche, traveling farther south over water Ellie hadn't seen before. The sun was low in the sky, casting the whole bayou in dusky twilight and cooling its bright daytime greens to the softer shades of early evening.

"I think it would be hard to live someplace else if you grew up here," Ellie said to Raphe, speaking up so he could hear her over the motor.

"Why is that?"

"Because it's not like anyplace else, not even close. I think I'd miss it if I left, and I haven't even been here a heartbeat."

Raphe smiled at her. "Mamou would've said the bayou water's done got in your blood."

They hadn't traveled very far—maybe five or ten minutes—when Raphe steered the boat into a canal off the Teche and slowed the motor to an idle. As they glided under a cypress tree with a low-hanging curtain of Spanish moss, he took an oar from the boat and used it to hold the moss off of Ellie.

The banks of the bayou were dotted with cabins on pilings about six feet off the ground. Outside one of them, Ellie saw the woman from Doc's office, the one who had paid with chickens Raphe brought. "Is that your sister's house?"

"Yes, my sister Kitty," he said.

The channel made a bend to the left and emptied into a small slough. It held only one cabin, long and narrow, with a steep roof, shutter-framed windows, and a screened porch across the front. It sat on heavy posts about six feet off the ground, close to the water. Raphe steered the boat to a small dock and tied it up. He offered Ellie his hand and helped her to the ladder on the dock, then followed her.

As they climbed the steps to the cabin and stepped inside

the screened porch, a boy came out to greet them. "Hey, Nonc!" He stopped and stared when he saw Ellie. He was a pretty child, with dark, short-cropped hair and big brown eyes. He was wearing dungarees, a light blue T-shirt, and sneakers. What looked like a St. Christopher medal hung around his neck.

"Remy, we've made a new friend," Raphe said. "This is Miss Ellie. She's the—she's our new neighbor stayin' over at Doc's cabin."

"Pleased to meet you, Remy." Ellie held out her hand and smiled.

Remy timidly shook it. "Hello."

"We're gonna cook supper for Miss Ellie—make her feel welcome," Raphe said.

"Okay," Remy said. "I got the oysters and the shrimp shucked. Put the rice on too."

"Well, you already did the hard work. All I got to do is stir it up." Raphe gave Remy's hair a gentle tousle. "Why don't you show Miss Ellie to the table and I'll get things going?"

Ellie followed Remy inside. The cabin was laid out much like Doc's, with a main room that held a kitchen, fireplace, and table, and a door on the back wall, likely leading to a bedroom. Ellie had noticed stairs on the front porch. There must be a loft.

Remy pulled a chair out for her.

"Why, thank you," Ellie said, smiling at him as he sat down next to her.

Raphe got busy at a small butcher block next to the sink, chopping vegetables that released the savory aroma of celery, onion, and bell pepper.

"How old are you, Remy?" Ellie asked her table companion.

He was studying her face as if he were trying to make up his mind about her. "I'm seven."

"So you'll be in second grade this year?"

"Yes, ma'am." Remy stared down at the table, tracing the wood grain with his finger.

"If you don't mind my saying, you don't sound too happy about it."

"No, ma'am."

Ellie glanced up to see Raphe looking at Remy before he resumed chopping a rib of celery. "I'm sorry to hear that," she said. "Is there anything at all you like about school?"

Remy looked up at her and scratched his jaw, just as Raphe had done when he was trying to think of a story to tell her. "I like story time, but we don't get to have it if the teacher thinks we've been bad, and she pretty much always thinks we've been bad."

"But you won't have the same teacher this year, right?" Ellie asked.

"No, ma'am, but she prob'ly won't like us any better than the other one did. That's what all the older kids say. Just thinkin' about school makes my stomach hurt."

Ellie reached over and laid her hand on his. "That makes me sad, Remy. I think school should be fun."

"*Fun?*" Remy said, his eyes wide in disbelief.

Ellie had to laugh at the stunned expression on his face. She could hear Raphe stirring something in a cast-iron pot as a nutty fragrance drifted from the stove.

"It's true," Ellie said. "What could be more fun than learning how to read? And how to count things and tell what color they are? You get to hear stories about the settlers who came here to farm and fish—people from faraway places like Germany and France."

"France?" Remy said. Ellie knew she had his attention now. "You can't talk about *nothin'* French in school, Miss Ellie."

"You mean 'anything'—you can't talk about *anything* French in school—but I'm not sure that's true."

"Oh, yes, ma'am, it's true!" Remy said, as if he needed to warn her away from the Rougarou. "If the teacher hears you say anything *en français*, she'll yell at you and maybe hit your hand with a ruler and tell the whole class you're acting un-American."

The nutty fragrance from the stove was growing stronger. Whatever was in the pot sizzled and hissed as Raphe poured the chopped vegetables into it.

"Well, I think that's wrong," Ellie said. "And I know your new teacher fairly well. She'll think it's wrong too."

"She will?"

"Mm-hmm. So I don't think you should worry too much about getting hit with that ruler."

"Sure hope you're right," Remy said.

"What else? Besides the ruler, I mean. Is there anything else that makes you dread going to school?"

"I still can't read. Not good anyway. Everything I learned to read, Nonc taught me. He likes books a lot." Remy pointed to a bookshelf on the wall opposite the fireplace. It was probably six feet tall and four feet wide, filled to overflowing with books. "In school, the teacher said we oughta be able to pick it up from hearin' her read to us and followin' along in our books, but three of us had to share one, and it was hard to see. I just can't get the hang of it."

Ellie saw Raphe retrieve what looked like a large glass jar of stock from the icebox and add it to the pot. Whatever was in there smelled divine. She hadn't realized how hungry she was till just now.

Leaning over to the boy and lowering her voice, she said, "I'll let you in on something, Remy: There's a secret code to the alphabet, and once you learn it, you can read *anything.*"

"*Vrai?*" Remy asked, his eyes wide as saucers.

"Now it's your turn to teach me," Ellie said. "I don't know what that means."

"It means 'really' or 'truly,'" Raphe said as he lifted a bowl from the sink and poured its contents—fresh shrimp and oysters—into the pot. "Is what you say really true?"

"It's definitely true," Ellie told Remy. "There are five magic letters that sound different depending on where they land in a word. Once you learn which spot makes which sound— boom—you're reading, because most of the other letters always sound the same. Want to say the magic letters with me? A-e-i-o-u."

Remy smiled and repeated the letters.

"A-e-i-o-u—back to you," Ellie said.

"A-e-i-o-u," Remy echoed with a grin.

Raphe set steaming bowls of rice and gumbo in front of Ellie and Remy, then brought one for himself and put three glasses and a pitcher of cold sweet tea on the table. "I never heard that before—about a-e-i-o-u. And I guess you know it's gonna be running through my head all night long."

"I had what you might call a radical language professor in college," Ellie said. "And I do apologize for disturbing your mind after you were kind enough to invite me to supper."

She poured the tea as Raphe placed a crusty loaf of bread on the table and sat down to offer thanks.

Remy looked at Ellie. "You don't sign the cross?"

"Remy, we don't pry," Raphe said.

"Sorry." He stared down at his bowl.

"It's okay, Remy," Ellie said. "I grew up in a different kind of Christian church, that's all. You might say they speak different languages—my church and yours—but they're saying the same thing. Oui? Yes?"

Remy smiled and nodded, then pulled a piece of bread from the loaf and dunked it into his gumbo.

Ellie dipped a spoon into her bowl and tasted fresh shrimp flavored by the oysters she hadn't managed to scoop up yet, and a broth so rich she couldn't begin to describe what was in it. She could taste the onion, celery, and bell pepper for sure, but there was so much more going on. "Holy cow!" she said.

"It's my favorite," Remy said, wiping his mouth with the back of his hand. Ellie saw Raphe motion toward Remy's napkin and wink at him. Remy took the napkin and wiped his mouth again. "Nonc makes it for me all the time."

"What's that mean—Nonc?" Ellie asked.

"Uncle," Raphe said.

"How about that, Remy? I've only been here a little while, and already you've taught me *vrai* and *nonc*."

Remy grinned at her and watched as she took another bite of gumbo. "Miss Ellie, are you my new teacher?"

She glanced at Raphe as she blotted her mouth with her napkin.

"Yes," he answered Remy, "Miss Ellie is your new teacher."

Remy put down his spoon, bowed his head, and said,

"*Merci, Bon Dieu*," making the sign of the cross before resuming his supper.

Ellie looked to Raphe, who explained, "He thanked God for you."

AFTER SUPPER, Remy begged to come along with Raphe and Ellie for the boat ride back to Doc's cabin.

"You need to go to bed, Remy," Raphe insisted.

"Please, Nonc?" the boy pleaded. "I never get to go on the bayou at night. *Please?*"

Raphe sighed and looked at Ellie.

"This'll cost you, Remy," Ellie said. "If we let you come along, you have to promise you'll tell all the other kids that I'm no relation to the Rougarou. And that I don't have fangs, at least none that you could see. Deal?"

"Deal," he said with a grin.

"Remy, go upstairs and get your pillow and the blue quilt Aunt Kitty made you," Raphe said.

"But why—"

"Remy, go."

"Yes, sir."

Raphe shook his head as his nephew scurried up the stairs. "This is not like him. Remy never argues."

"He's just excited," Ellie said.

Minutes later, they heard the thump of little feet on the stairs as the boy came running back with his blanket and pillow, which he handed to Raphe.

"We'll take the pirogue if that's alright?" Raphe asked Ellie. "It's slow, but a lot o' the old folks go to bed early and I don't want to wake 'em with the noise from a motor."

"I don't mind," Ellie said.

Remy ran ahead to the bank lit by a half-moon. Raphe laid the blanket and pillow in the stern of the boat, behind one of two seats a few feet apart in the center, and pushed the boat halfway into the water. As he climbed in, his nephew moved to follow him.

"Remy, ladies first—always," Raphe said.

Remy waited as Raphe held his hands out to Ellie and helped her into the boat and onto the back seat, then motioned for him. "I'll sit by you, Miss Ellie," Remy said.

Raphe stood in the center of the pirogue, his back to Ellie and Remy, and took up a long oar to push them away from the bank. He maneuvered the boat out of the slough, through the narrow canal that had brought them there, and back to the main channel of the Teche.

Remy's head was turning this way and that as he tried to take in all the sights of the bayou, from the tall cypress trees to curtains of Spanish moss grazing the water. But Ellie's eyes were riveted on the tall figure standing before her, his white shirt lit silver in the moonlight, his head slightly turning now and again as he scanned the bayou, effortlessly pulling them through the water. Raphe looked a part of it—of boat, bayou, water, and sky.

For a while, Remy pelted Ellie with a barrage of conversation, telling her where all the night sounds were coming from and pointing out who lived where in each of the cabins they passed. But the farther they traveled, Raphe paddling through tunnels of trees and watery fields of lily pads, the more Remy's chatter began to ebb, fading into yawns—occasional at first, but then coming in waves, one after another. Raphe turned to Ellie and smiled.

She took Remy's blanket and made a pallet behind their seat. "Here, honey," she said, tucking the pillow under his head. "Why don't you lie down on your blanket. We'll play 'way up high in the sky.'"

"I don't know that game," Remy said as he obediently lay down, looking up at the sky. Ellie removed his sneakers and folded the edges of the quilt over him.

"Here, I'll show you. Way up high in the sky, tell me what you see." Ellie raised her arm over her head and pointed up.

"The moon," Remy said.

"What does it look like?"

"Well," Remy said through a big yawn, "it looks like a big round window with a black curtain hanging over half of it."

"That's a great way to describe it, Remy. Let's go again. Way up high in the sky, tell me what you see." Again she pointed to the sky.

Remy yawned again and pulled the quilt tighter around him. "I see . . . some stars."

"Good!" Ellie said. "See if you can count ten of them."

Remy made it to five before his voice faded and he turned on his side, curling up in the quilt and falling fast asleep.

"He's a goner," Ellie said.

Raphe stopped rowing and looked at his nephew. "I knew he'd never make it to Doc's."

He started to row again, but she stopped him. "Would you mind if we just sat here for a minute?" she asked, looking up at a towering cypress they had drifted under. "I just . . . I can't quite take it all in."

Raphe dipped his oar in the water. "Not wise to be under a tree—snakes like the moss. Let me get us to a safer spot."

He rowed them away from the tree and into a watery clearing of sorts, with the moon gleaming down on the water, its lily pads and water hyacinth casting shadows on the surface. Raphe and Ellie were surrounded by colossal trees that had to be hundreds of years old. He sat down and laid the oar across the seats, near the edge of the boat.

"It's beautiful, *non*?" he said.

"So beautiful," she said. "I'm glad we came in the pirogue so we didn't spoil the night sounds. You do this a lot—come out on the bayou this late?"

"Used to," he said. "About every night—sometimes by myself but usually with my brothers. That was a long time ago."

"Your brothers don't go out on the bayou anymore?"

"They're gone. Storm took all of my family except for Kitty and my older sister—Remy's mother. She died later. So did her husband."

"Oh, Raphe—one storm killed your entire family?"

"Yes. My parents and grandparents, all of my brothers and their families."

"I—I just can't imagine. I don't know what to say. I'm so sorry. When did it happen?"

"When I was seventeen. Hurricane—a bad one. Took half the town. Lot o' people lost family."

"How did you and your sisters—I mean—"

"How did we live when everybody else died?"

Ellie felt sick, unconsciously wrapping her arms around her stomach.

Raphe repeated what he had said to her at the schoolhouse: "You are not to blame, Juliet. We lived because we weren't here. It's strange—you can save your life or lose it just

94

by choosing where to be when the sun rises." He looked up at the moon, and then his eyes rested on Ellie. "My sisters had a friend getting married in Ville Platte that day. Papa didn't want 'em to go up there alone—takes a couple of hours or more. He wanted me to drive them, so I did." Raphe shook his head at the memory of it. "I remember being so aggravated that I had to miss a day of fishing to go to a wedding, but you didn't say no to my father."

"Was there any kind of warning?" Ellie was still trying to wrap her mind around a storm killing an entire family. "Any sign that bad weather was coming?"

"There was talk of a hurricane. Some of the older fishermen said they felt a change in the air. The sky was overcast, and I remember a stiff, cool wind starting to build the day before we left. It had grown much stronger by the morning of the wedding. My sisters kept talking about how glad they were that they wouldn't be sweaty when we got to Ville Platte."

"But it wasn't stormy?"

"Not that we could see—the storm was still out in the Gulf—but the weather turned during the celebration after the wedding. By the time we were ready to leave, the wind was very strong, like a tornado was coming. We went to somebody's root cellar—can't remember their name—but that's where we rode it out. Took us a couple of days to get home because of all the trees over the roads. I had to cut our way through with the chainsaw Papa kept in his truck. Once we finally made it back here, well . . . wasn't much left. Water got so high when it came in—over twenty feet—you'd need a miracle to survive that kind o' water."

"What about Remy's parents? You said they made it through the hurricane?"

"They weren't married yet. She met him at the wedding that saved us from the storm. And then he put her right in the middle of another one, promising her the high life in New Orleans. But the high life ended both of 'em. He was shot to death in the street over gambling debts. She used the last of their money to get Remy back here to her family and died of pneumonia a few weeks later."

"I just can't imagine—everybody you love . . . just gone . . ."

"Do you always do that?" Raphe asked. "Take on the hurts of other people, I mean?"

"I feel for other people, if that's what you're talking about."

He shook his head. "No, it's more than that. You don't just feel *for* them. You feel *them*. It's a lot to carry, *non?*"

They were silently staring at each other in the moonlight when something slammed against the boat, hard.

Ellie gasped and instinctively moved to get up, but Raphe put his hands out to stop her. "*Non*—stay where you are," he said. "You'll tip the boat."

She did as he said, not at all sure why she was trusting a man she barely knew. Peering over the side of the pirogue, Ellie watched as a six-foot alligator swam right alongside them before disappearing into the moonlit bayou. When she turned to face Raphe, her eyes and mouth wide open, he was smiling at her.

"You should maybe breathe now," he said.

Ellie hadn't realized she was holding her breath. She took a few deep ones to calm herself.

"You never want to be in the water with an alligator," Raphe explained. "But most of the time, if you don't aggravate them or do something to make them see you as food, they'll be about their business."

"Most of the time?"

"Most of the time. You alright?"

"I think so." As she looked at him, she couldn't stop a smile from slowly spreading across her face. "I just saw an *alligator!*"

"You did," Raphe said, laughing with her.

"I guess that's one more good thing about the bayou. If there's a lull in the conversation, just wait a minute and a ferocious reptile will swim by."

"You mind lulls in the conversation?" Raphe asked. He stretched his legs out, resting his hands on his thighs.

Ellie had always thought you could tell a lot about a man by looking at his hands. Raphe's looked like a cross between a farmer's and a musician's—strong and weathered yet lithe and graceful. "I don't mind the lulls, but I've always been taught that I should put an end to them."

"Why is that?"

"Because Alabama women think making conversation is like making a decent biscuit."

"Or sewing a quilt?"

"Exactly. It's just something we're supposed to know how to do. Mama always said silence makes a man nervous, so a woman needs to know how to fill it up."

"And what do you say?"

Ellie turned her face to the moon and closed her eyes as she considered Raphe's question. When she turned back to him, he was staring straight at her the way he had the day before in Doc's office.

"I think I'd rather just find somebody I could be quiet with."

"That what you're looking for in Louisiana?"

"I seem to be looking for everything in Louisiana." Ellie took a deep breath and looked up into the trees silhouetted against the sky. "It's a lot to ask of one place, I guess."

"Maybe not too much," he said.

They stopped talking and listened to a night owl's call, deep and sonorous as it drifted over the bayou.

"Raphe," Ellie said when the owl was quiet, "was the school here in Bernadette when you were Remy's age?"

He shook his head. "No. Me and my brothers and sisters used to get up way before daylight to do our chores and then paddle to the school bus stop. We'd ride the bus to Morgan City, go to school all day, then make the trip back. When I think about school, I mostly think about being tired."

"How long did you go?"

His brow furrowed. "Till I was fourteen or so, I think. Then I started fishing and oystering. My papa was a fine mechanic and took up a lotta time with me, teaching me. A couple o' the bigger towns have marinas that call on me for engine work on the shrimpers between seasons. Helps me do for Remy. What about your family? Everybody go to college?"

"No, I was the first," Ellie said. "And if the war hadn't brought so many jobs to Alabama, I couldn't have gone either. I was able to work my way through, with a little help from my folks."

"Did you like it—going to college?"

"I was a fish out of water that first year, coming from a little bitty school in a small town. There were all these girls from places like Atlanta and Birmingham and Miami. Felt like I had 'country bumpkin' written across my forehead. It took a whole lot of conversations with Mama Jean to keep me from quitting that first year."

"Why didn't you?"

"Because I loved hearing those professors from all over the country talk about everything from history and literature to art and music. I just made up my mind that no matter how backwoods some of those girls tried to make me feel, I wasn't about to let them keep me from learning. And I couldn't imagine anything better to do with my life than pass that excitement along to small-town kids like me, you know?"

"I can see you thinking in that direction." Raphe shooed a mosquito away and ran his fingers through his hair. "Is this your first job—as a teacher, I mean?"

"No. I did my practice teaching in a little town called Opelika—it's right there near Alabama Polytech, where I got my degree—and then I taught for a while in Childersburg, Alabama, which isn't too far from where my family lives."

Ellie was startled by a splash in the water.

"Bullfrog, most likely," Raphe said. He was looking straight at her again. "What made you come here, Juliet? You have schooling. You have prospects. You have family back in Alabama."

Ellie thought carefully about her answer. She wanted to be truthful, with Raphe more than anybody, though she couldn't say why. "Because I was unhappy. Because I was tired of everybody telling me who I was and what I was supposed to be. Because I almost made a really stupid mistake and got myself engaged to somebody who thought I should give up my life's work just to make him look better at his. Because I couldn't breathe in Alabama anymore. What about you? Are you happy in Louisiana?"

He looked up at the silvery sky as he thought about it. "No," he finally said, looking back at Ellie, "but I'm home."

He picked up the oar and began rowing the pirogue through the cypress trees. Ellie took it as a sign that their moment of truth was over and sat quietly, watching the bayou drift by.

At last Raphe rowed them into Doc's slough. Once they were at the bank, he laid down the oar and jumped out, pulling the bow of the pirogue onto the bank. As Ellie stood up, he wrapped his arm around her waist and swung her out of the boat, then pulled the rest of the pirogue onto the bank. He picked up Remy, who barely stirred, sleeping soundly on Raphe's shoulder.

Holding his nephew with one arm, he took Ellie's hand with the other. "Might be a little risky to leave him in the boat," he said as he guided her to Doc's steps.

They climbed the steps and went onto the porch, where Ellie lit the lamp Raphe had advised her to leave outside.

"Want us to go in with you—make sure everything's okay?" he asked her.

Ellie nodded. He followed her into the cabin, where he waited by the fireplace, holding Remy, as she walked through to the back room, making sure there were no unwelcome visitors—human or reptile.

"All clear," she said as she returned to him and set the lamp on the table.

He was looking down at her in the lamplight, Remy's head on his shoulder, when she felt a sudden surge of emotion, as if the wave of anger and hurt and disappointment that had pushed her all the way from Alabama to Louisiana was about to break right on top of her and knock her off her feet. Her eyes were stinging and she couldn't speak.

Raphe reached down and laid his palm against her face.

Ellie slowly raised her hand to rest on top of his. Neither of them moved. Ellie could hear him breathing and feel the warmth of his hand against her face.

Remy suddenly stirred. "Nonc? Where are we, Nonc?"

Raphe and Ellie slowly let their hands fall. "We're on our way home," Raphe said quietly. "Go back to sleep, Remy." And then he was gone.

TEN

ON MONDAY MORNING, Ellie arrived at the schoolhouse an hour early. Her classrooms were already arranged, her lessons planned, her cookies baked for the children. Still, she wanted to get there early, to settle into her first day before the boys and girls began streaming in. Would the parents come with the little ones? Back home, the answer was yes, but she had no idea what to expect from Cajun families.

Doc had recruited one of the Toussaint sisters—there were twelve brothers and sisters in all—to help her keep order. Bonita Toussaint was engaged to be married in the summer, but for now, she was happy to help out and earn a little extra money to start her household. For the morning, Ellie planned to get the terrified first, second, and third graders acclimated while Bonita managed fourth, fifth, and sixth.

"Anybody home?" Doc came into the classroom, followed by Bonita and another young woman about the same age.

"Ready and waiting," Ellie said. "And mighty grateful for your help."

"Ellie," Doc said, "I'd like you to meet Bonita's sister Gabby. She'll be helping out at the school too."

"I can't thank you enough, Gabby," Ellie said.

"It'll be some fun, fo' sure," Gabby said.

"Doc, where's Miss Harrison? I don't think I've seen her this morning."

He clasped his hands together and took a deep breath. "Well, Ellie . . . she died."

"She *what?*"

Gabby shook her head sadly. "Poor ol' thing passed in her sleep, but at least she's with her maman and papa now, God love her."

Ellie was close to panic. "Doc, what are we gonna do? I can't teach the whole school by myself!"

"I know it's a lot, Ellie," he said in a voice she imagined he reserved for expectant mothers in labor. "But you can do it. I'm sure you can. Bonita and Gabby will be right here with you every step of the way. And my office is a stone's throw away if you need me."

"Doc, I've never taught high school." Ellie looked frantically about, as if she might find a rescuer somewhere in the classroom. "I don't even have lesson plans for them."

"Everything'll be alright, Ellie," Doc assured her. "Like I told you that first day, Miss Harrison, rest her soul, was way past teaching the older children anything more than the very basics, which they repeated year after year. And most of the bayou students leave school when they're fourteen or fifteen. So they're not *really* high school students. They're just a touch older than what you're used to. That's all."

"But there are so many children for one teacher!" Ellie insisted.

"One teacher and two *fine* assistants," Doc countered.

"You not gonna quit, are you, Miss Ellie?" Bonita asked

her. "We got kids at home needs to learn how to read and do their numbers. You not gonna leave us, are you?"

Ellie pulled up a chair and sat down to collect herself. She took some deep breaths to steady her nerves and then answered, "No, Bonita, I'm not a quitter. I just need to figure out how to manage all these children."

"You don't have to manage 'em all by yourself," Gabby said, putting a hand on Ellie's shoulder. "Me and Bonita's been wranglin' kids since *we* was kids—you give us mean boys, you give us gigglin' girls, we can handle 'em."

Ellie looked up at her. "Y'all really think we can do this?"

"'Course we can," Bonita said.

"Fo' sure," Gabby agreed.

"Well, then," Ellie said, standing up, "I reckon we'd better get after it. And y'all can drop the 'Miss Ellie.' Far as I'm concerned, the three of us are soldiers in the trenches, so I'm just plain ol' Ellie from now on."

"Ellie it is," Gabby said with a smile.

"Alright then," Ellie said. "Here's how we'll get through today. Since we've got to handle all the kids, I think it's best to keep them on one floor. Otherwise we'll run our legs off going up and down those stairs. The classrooms are huge, so we should be able to manage it. This morning, I'll take first through fifth. Gabby, you and Bonita take the older kids. There's a blank class roll on the desk. You just need to get every student's name on there. And then there's a record book where I like to keep the names of each child's parents and any other close relative I could call on in case of emergency. Y'all mind doing that?"

"We'll do it," Bonita said. "Where they gonna sit—the extra kids from upstairs?"

Gabby was quick with a solution. "We gonna make them big strappin' boys haul us down some desks. Ain't gonna hurt 'em to do a little work fo' their school."

"Thanks, Gabby," Ellie said. "Once they're all settled in, I want y'all to have each student write a letter—to me—and they don't have to sign it if they don't want to. But I want them to tell me everything they hate about school and how they wish it were different. I want them to write down all the things they want to learn about and anything they wish they could change."

Gabby and Bonita stared at her, openmouthed. "You serious, Miss—I mean Ellie?" Gabby asked her.

"Very serious," Ellie said. "I can't make them love school till I find out why they hate it. Is it just the nonsense about never speaking French, or is there more to it than that? I really want to know."

A clearly doubtful Bonita shook her head. "If you say so."

"The truth'll set you free, ladies," Ellie said with a grin. "It's about time for all the kids to get here, so why don't we meet them outside by the school bell and sort them into our two classes. And may the good Lord help us all."

"Amen," Doc said. "Ellie, I'm mighty proud of you."

"Why, Doc? I haven't done anything yet."

"Oh, yes you have. I'll be in my office if you need me."

Ellie and the Toussaints followed Doc outside just in time to see a drove of children, lunch pails in hand, walking toward them. Ellie shored up her courage and rang the school bell. Normally, schoolchildren would come running at the sound of a bell, but not these Cajun students. They walked glumly toward Ellie with a look of pure dread on their faces. Many of the little ones were wiping tears. Ellie was so shocked by the sight of such misery on the faces of innocent children that for a moment she couldn't speak.

Remy stepped from the back of the crowd and came to her rescue. "This is Miss Ellie, y'all. She's not mean and scary like all the others. Let's say good mornin'."

Oddly enough, even the older kids were so unhappy to be there that they took direction from a seven-year-old and offered a grim "Mornin', Miss Ellie."

Ellie managed to gather her wits and force a smile. "Good morning, everybody. And thank you, Remy. I want all of you students to do me a favor. Raise your hand if you hate school."

All the littlest hands shot up, but the older children looked at each other, unsure of what they should do.

"Come on," Ellie said, "tell the truth. Raise your hand if you hate school."

Every student haltingly put up a hand.

"Well, let's get busy changing that," Ellie said. "First, we need to split you into two classrooms. If you haven't had your eleventh birthday yet, I want you to line up right here in front of me. If you're eleven or older, please line up in front of Miss Gabby and Miss Bonita over there. Let's go, boys and girls!"

Apparently too bewildered to do anything but obey, Ellie's pupils fell into their lines, the older ones directing the littlest. Before they even made it into the schoolhouse, Ellie could see that Gabby and Bonita would have no trouble managing their group. A couple of older boys were sneaking up behind the girls and pulling their hair. Gabby and Bonita each took one of the mischief makers in hand, grabbing his ear and twisting it till he hollered and fell in line.

Ellie led her terrified youngsters into the room Raphe had helped her decorate. She watched their eyes widen and their mouths fly open when they spied the colorful quilts on the wall and the white alligator she had painted on the floor.

"L'esprit Blanc!" exclaimed a tiny little girl with long blonde braids, pointing at the alligator.

"No French!" an older girl loudly whispered, putting her arms around the younger, both of them clearly fearing Ellie's retribution.

All the other children stared at their teacher, waiting to see what punishment she would mete out.

"Tell you what, boys and girls," Ellie said, "let's take a little time to get to know each other. You two fellas over there—what are your names?"

"I'm Antoine Doucet, and this is my brother, J.D.," answered a boy with dark hair and eyes.

"And how old are you boys?"

"I'm ten," Antoine said.

"I'm nine," J.D. said.

"I'm very pleased to meet you, Antoine and J.D. Now I need your help. Would you please take three of the quilts off the wall and spread them here in the center with the alligator?"

Antoine and J.D. obeyed, laying Ellie's quilts all around the alligator.

"Thank you, boys," Ellie said. "Everybody, kick off your shoes and find a spot on the quilts."

The children hesitated at first, but then Antoine gave them a nod and they followed him to the quilts, where everybody took off their shoes and sat in a circle.

Ellie sat barefoot with them, spreading her full skirt to

cover her legs. The little girl with the blonde braids was silently crying.

"Sweetheart," Ellie said, "are you scared?"

The child nodded.

"You've got nothing to be afraid of, honey—come over here and sit with Miss Ellie."

The child came and sat down on her lap, pressing her face against the peacock-blue cotton of Ellie's dress.

"What's your name, sweetheart?" Ellie wrapped her arms around the little girl, who was shaking all over.

"Jean," the child whispered.

"Jean? Why, that's one of my favorite names in the whole world. Did you know that?"

Jean looked up at Ellie and shook her head. Ellie wiped her tears away.

"It's my grandmother's name. I call her Mama Jean. And her family came here to America from a country called Scotland, way over the ocean, just like your families came here from a place called Canada, way up north."

J.D. was frowning at her. "But I thought we was French."

"You mean *were*, J.D.—'we *were* French,' not 'we was,' okay?" Ellie corrected him.

"Yes, ma'am, I thought we *were* French."

"Oh, you are," Ellie assured him. "But your families didn't come here from France. They came from a country called Canada, where a big community of French people—much bigger than Bernadette—had settled. They were called Acadians. And over time, people shortened the last part of that word—'cadien'—to Cajun. See how that works? 'Cajun' is just a short way of saying Acadian, which is another way of saying French Canadian. Your ancestors were French Canadians."

"What's a—a—*ansister?*" Jean asked, looking up at Ellie.

"Your an*cestors* are the people you came from—people you're related to—who lived hundreds of years ago. Isn't that something, class? Just think, you and your families here in Louisiana are connected—kin, even—to people who lived hundreds of years ago in a place so far north that the snow gets as high as swamp grass in the wintertime."

There was a brief moment of silence while the children took in Ellie's story. And then the floodgates opened as they peppered her with questions.

"Why did we leave Canada? How did we get there in the first place?"

"When did we move to Louisiana?"

"Are there bayous in Canada?"

"Were there alligators up there?"

"How come our other teachers never told us about Canada? How come Maman and Papa don't talk about it?"

Ellie kept an arm around Jean and put up her free hand to quiet the children. "Hold on, everybody! Hold on!" she called out over them, laughing. "Listen, boys and girls. The story of your people is amazing. It's sad and it's brave. It's an adventure and it's a love story—"

"Yuck!" said one of the older boys in back, which made everybody giggle.

"I promise you we'll get to all of it," Ellie said. "But I'll be honest with you, class. I hadn't planned on being the only teacher here. I thought I'd be able to separate you older children from the little ones, but it looks like we need to find a way for all of us to learn in this one room together. I'll need you to be patient with me and with each other till we figure out the best way to go about that. Will you help me?"

A chorus of "Yes, Miss Ellie" followed.

"Thank you! Now there's something very important we need to talk about. Here at school we speak only English, *d'accord*?" Ellie gasped and put her hand over her mouth, pretending she had accidentally slipped into French, which brought laughter from her students. "Listen, boys and girls, there's nothing wrong with French. It's a beautiful language. It's the language of your parents and grandparents and great-grandparents. It's part of who you are. But when you grow up, you might need to leave the bayou for one reason or another. Maybe to find work. Maybe for marriage. I know, I know—*yuck! Marriage!*" Ellie made a face and had the students laughing again. "It's very important that we speak English in school, but no one's going to punish you if you slip into French now and then. We'll just try it again in English, alright?"

The children smiled and nodded.

"Good! Now let's go around the circle, and you all tell me your names. We can't be strangers if we're going to learn together."

AFTER LUNCH AND RECESS, Ellie swapped classes with Gabby and Bonita. Looking around the room, she saw not the open, trusting faces of young children but the suspicious, dismissive ones of adolescents and teenagers. Their eyes grew wide when she sat down on top of her desk instead of in the chair behind it.

"Class," she began, "I believe in being honest with young men and women. And the truth is that most schools would have three, maybe even four, teachers for the number of students we have here in Bernadette. Your school has one, plus two wonderful assistants that we're lucky to have. I expect you to treat Miss Gabby and Miss Bonita with the same respect you show me—and I expect you to show me plenty, because there are many of you and just one of me. I can't teach you what you need to know—what you *want* to know, based on the letters you wrote this morning—if I'm spending all my time making you behave. So I need you to just do that on your own. Just behave. Period. I can't force you, so it's up to you. Will you do that for me?"

The older students looked dumbfounded. They exchanged glances before a girl of about fourteen stood up in back and said, "We can do it, Miss Ellie."

"Thank you." Ellie smiled at her. "And what's your name?"

"Marceline," the girl said. "Marceline Ardoin."

"I appreciate your help, Marceline, and I'm pleased to meet you." Ellie picked up the stack of letters the students had written that morning. "I spent your lunch period reading these letters. And I want you to know that I take everything you said very seriously. This school doesn't have the resources to teach some of the things you want very much to learn, but don't worry—I have a few resources of my own, and I'll use them to teach you as much as I possibly can about the subjects you're excited about. Things will be different from now on. I promise you that. Now about this English-only rule . . ."

ELEVEN

"LEMME SEE 'IM."

Lura Poteet looked up from her desk in the outer office of Senator Roy Strahan's suite at the capitol building in Baton Rouge. She calmly adjusted her reading glasses, peering over them at the man standing before her. Cheap fedora, dirty boots, bowie knife in a holster strapped to his belt. Trash. Pure-D trash.

"Take a seat," she said. She met his stare, unblinking, as he narrowed his eyes and leaned on her desk.

"You think just 'cause you gotta press some button to unlock his office, that makes you the queen o' Sheba?" he said.

Lura slowly rose to her full height—all six feet eight inches of her—and opened her desk drawer.

"Now we're gettin' somewhere," the man said. "Go on and press your little button."

But Lura had no intention of pressing any buttons. Instead, she reached into her desk, pulled out a Smith & Wesson, and cocked it as she aimed it squarely at his head, her voice as steady as her gun. "Who do you think you're talking to?"

SENATOR ROY STRAHAN heard gunfire in the outer office. Somebody must've ticked off Lura. Likely Luetrell. Just showed what a poor judge of character he was. Lura grew up on the toughest cattle ranch in Texas. Sure, you had to repair the occasional bullet hole, replace the occasional lamp, pay the occasional hospital bill. And should he ever actually need statehouse security, they wouldn't show because they had grown accustomed to the sound of Lura's Smith & Wesson. But Big Roy never had to deal with anybody he didn't want to, and he always knew what trouble was brewing in the statehouse before anybody else. On any given day, he could tell you what the governor had for breakfast and any other details of his personal life that might come in handy. Lura saw to that.

Big Roy was sitting at his polished mahogany desk, studying a geological map of his state's southwestern parishes as he puffed on a Cuban cigar—the gift of a very grateful, filthy-rich constituent whose no-account son would've landed in the penitentiary without a word to the governor from Big Roy. He held a magnifying glass over three red X's marked on the waters of Bayou Teche. Gig Luetrell might be a cur dog that deserved to be put down, but he had a sixth sense when it came to crude oil. He could find it every time, especially under water—just didn't have the means to get it out. But Big Roy did, and he paid Luetrell handsomely for his services.

The Teche was covered up with French-speaking Cajuns who kept to themselves—made it dang near impossible to find out what they were doing or thinking when it came to oil rights. And bribes were useless down there because they didn't trust anybody who hadn't lived on the bayou longer than the alligators. On the upside, a convenient prejudice against Cajuns had flowered in Louisiana—a happy accident helped along by a crazy preacher. Big Roy threw gas on that fire—and money at it—every chance he got, especially now that Luetrell had marked three spots and was sure there were more.

Then there was Boone, the only son Big Roy loved but couldn't respect. He was so much like his late mother, rest her precious soul—not an ounce of fight in him. It was just a bonus that the need for discretion around Bernadette had at last created some use for him. Big Roy had already decided that once the boy served his purpose in the bayou, he'd cut him loose and let him ride off into the sunset to whatever state park he wanted to oversee. For now, however, Boone would play his part, which was giving Luetrell cover. That roughneck would stick out anywhere, but in a little bayou town like Bernadette? No. Best to tamp down local curiosity before it even flared up.

Big Roy was having another look at those enticing X's on the map when he heard a second gunshot in the outer office. He chomped his cigar and chuckled. Luetrell better mind his manners or he'd be leaving the statehouse in an ambulance. Lucky for him Lura didn't shoot to kill. Most of the time.

TWELVE

ON SATURDAY MORNING, Ellie had just dried the last of her breakfast dishes when she heard footsteps on the front porch, followed by a knock at the door. She opened it to find Doc standing beside a woman holding a casserole dish covered with tinfoil.

"Well, this is a nice surprise." Ellie welcomed them both inside.

"I've come to introduce you to my bride," Doc said with a grin.

Doc's wife was petite and fair, with chin-length, wavy auburn hair streaked with touches of gray, warm brown eyes, and a dimpled smile. "So nice to meet you, Ellie." Florence handed her a covered dish. "This is for you."

"Thank you," Ellie said as she took it. "Doc has told me so much about you. Won't y'all sit down? It's your house, after all." She set the dish on the kitchen work table. "Can I get y'all anything? Some coffee, maybe?"

"No, thank you," Florence said. "We've already had our morning cups."

"Florence limits my coffee," Doc said as Ellie joined them at the table. "She says too much of it makes me ornery."

"Well, we can't have that, now can we?" Ellie said.

"I wanted to surprise you tonight, but Florence said absolutely not," Doc explained. "She said you might already have plans, and even if you didn't, you'd want time to get ready."

"Ready for what?"

"The *fais-do-do*."

"The what?"

"He means the Saturday night dance," Florence said. "Sometimes I have to remind him that he is not of Cajun descent."

"Wouldn't you like being married to a handsome Frenchman?" He gave her a wink and a nudge with his elbow.

"I *am* married to a handsome Frenchman," she said.

"If only my people had come here from Nova Scotia instead of Europe," Doc went on, "I'd be Cajun—and a fine fiddle player, no doubt."

"Then who would I dance with?" Florence countered.

"Every fella in the dance hall." Doc turned to Ellie. "Florence is the best dancer in Bernadette."

His wife rolled her eyes and shook her head.

"It's true," Doc insisted. "Better than any twenty-year-old on that dance floor. But don't take my word for it, Ellie. Come and see for yourself tonight."

"And where might I do that?"

"At the dance hall—every Saturday night."

"I remember you told me about it, but I don't know where it is."

"Right next to the church—it's that big metal building that looks like a barn," Florence said.

"Everybody shows up around six o'clock," Doc explained, "and the ladies all bring covered dishes. In between dances, we eat the best food you ever put in your mouth. Florence fixed her jambalaya for you to take so you won't have to worry with cooking."

"It really is fun," Florence agreed. "And it's a good way to get to know the community."

"By all means, count me in," Ellie said.

"Wonderful!" Doc clapped his hands together. "Would you like for Florence and me to swing by and pick you up?"

"I'd appreciate that." Ellie laid the back of her hand against her forehead, feigning a swoon. "Bless my heart, I simply *cannot* go stag."

Florence laughed and patted Ellie on the arm. "I don't think you'll have to worry about that for long. Frenchmen appreciate women. I doubt you'll be lacking for company once they realize what a dear you are. Don't take it personally if the ladies are a little standoffish at first. They're just used to schoolteachers making their babies cry. They've never met one like you."

"Thank you, Florence. What should I wear?"

"Let's go pick something out together!" Florence suggested.

"Doc, hold the fort," Ellie said. "I'm about to turn your wife loose in my closet."

ALREADY ELLIE COULD HEAR THE MUSIC. Doc had tied up his boat at the town landing and helped Florence and Ellie ashore. Walking with this couple, together for years, made Ellie feel a sudden pang of loneliness. There was something in the way Doc kicked stray limbs and rocks out of his wife's path, her grip light on his elbow as he carried both covered dishes, that made Ellie long for something she couldn't name.

Not marriage, necessarily, but belonging—not the possessing kind but the accepting kind.

As they approached the dance hall, the music got louder and louder—fiddle, guitar, accordion, washboard, and triangle. The front and back doors were thrown open. Folding chairs and quilts covered the grounds, which were dotted with a few picnic tables. Inside, a Cajun band was playing from a small stage not quite a foot above the dance floor. All down one side of the hall was a line of wooden tables already laden with food. Horse troughs were icing down beer, Coca-Cola, and jugs of tea and lemonade. Down the other side of the hall was a row of what looked like pallets with quilts and pillows.

"Do y'all dance till you fall asleep?" Ellie asked Doc, pointing to the pillows.

"Wouldn't be a bad idea!" He was tapping his foot to the music. "Those are for the children who are too little to stay awake for the festivities. Their mothers just tuck them in, and everybody watches over them while we dance."

"I think I'm getting some looks," Ellie said, watching some of the women set their dishes down and whisper to each other as they cast glances in her direction.

"You'll be fine!" Doc assured her. "They're just sizing you up."

Two of the women waved to Florence, who took both dishes from Doc and walked over to the tables to greet them. The band began playing a Cajun waltz.

"Oh, that's a good one!" Doc said. "I'm afraid you'll have to dance with me, Ellie. Florence is busy."

"I'll do my best," she said.

Doc escorted her to the center of the floor, where about ten other couples were waltzing round and round in a circle.

"Ha!" Doc shouted over the music. "You're a fine dancer, Ellie! A fine one indeed."

"Thank you, Doc! But if it gets any more complicated than a waltz, Florence will have to coach me."

"She'll be glad to!"

"You sure you don't mind being seen with the schoolteacher?" Ellie caught the sidelong glances of some of the dancers.

"Far as I'm concerned, you're an answer to prayer, Ellie. And I'll tell anybody on this dance floor."

THIRTEEN

"HEY, BROUSSARD! Get down here, you lazy river rat!"

Raphe heard a familiar bell ringing and stepped outside to see Heywood Thornberry standing in his boat, the *Whirly-gig*, which was idling at the small dock down below. It was an old fishing trawler with a tiny cabin and bunk, a boat that afforded Heywood as much time docking for repairs as fishing on the river, but he didn't seem to mind. Raphe walked down to meet him.

"There's a dock fee for ugly boats," he said, catching the rope Heywood tossed up to him. Raphe secured the *Whirly-gig* while Heywood grabbed two large buckets and set them on the dock, then climbed up the ladder.

"Good to see you, my friend," Heywood said, shaking Raphe's hand. "Brought you food in one bucket and drink in the other."

Raphe peered into the buckets, one filled with fresh oysters, the other with bottles on ice.

"Let's go throw 'em on the fire," Raphe said, taking the oyster bucket from Heywood, who followed him into the house.

Heywood opened two bottles and handed one to Raphe,

who took a drink before dumping the oysters into the sink and making short work of cleaning them. Then he melted some butter from the icebox and sprinkled homemade hot sauce into it, giving it a stir to make sure the color was right. He put the cleaned oysters on a rack and handed Heywood a wooden breadboard loaded with the butter sauce, crusty bread, and a handful of kitchen tools, then picked up the rack and headed out. Heywood got their drinks and utensils settled on a wide stump between two low cypress chairs next to a fire pit by the water as Raphe gathered a few small logs from a woodpile by the porch and got a fire going. When the heat was just right, he set the rack of oysters on top and sat down with his friend.

"You been in New Orleans all this time?" Raphe asked, taking a drink and relaxing as he kept an eye on the fire.

"Not all of it—just a couple o' weeks. Before that, I had to go to a wedding in St. Francisville. Got some good pictures there too."

Raphe used a fire poker to adjust one of the logs in the pit. "Is there a wedding in your future, *mon ami?*"

Heywood shrugged. "Claudette wants a long engagement."

Raphe kept looking at the fire. "So you'll wait till you're maybe thirty, *non?*"

"Sounds about right," Heywood said, raising his bottle of beer and taking a long drink.

The oyster shells were popping open. Raphe grabbed a pair of tongs Heywood had brought from the kitchen and lifted the oysters off the fire and onto the breadboard. He slipped a glove over his left hand to protect it from the heat and deftly opened each one with a shucking knife before returning it to the breadboard.

"How in the Sam Hill do you do that so quick?" Heywood asked.

"Practice," Raphe said. "Been doin' it since I was Remy's age."

They each took an oyster shell, pried the meat out with small, two-pronged forks, and then dipped it in the butter sauce. "Merciful goodness—that's a taste o' heaven," Heywood said as he swallowed the oyster and pulled off a piece of bread to dip in the butter. "Where is Remy, anyway?"

"With Kitty," Raphe said. "He wanted to go to the dance hall with her family, so he's spending the night over there."

"And why are you not at the dance hall on a Saturday night?"

Raphe reached for the bread and tore off a piece. "Because I'm stuck here talking to you."

Heywood downed a couple of oysters, one right after the other. "I know better. If you were goin', you'd already be there. What you sittin' here for, Raphe? You've got the night free, and there's women and music and a ton o' food just up the way."

Raphe took a long sip of beer, leaned back to rest his head against the chair, and closed his eyes. "Because sometimes I just wanna be still."

They could hear music from the dance hall drifting on the early evening air.

"Hey, I met the new schoolteacher in New Orleans," Heywood said.

Raphe sat up and looked at him. "Ellie?"

"Ah, so you've met Miss Fields?"

Raphe shrugged him off. "Small town. Bound to happen." He couldn't stifle his curiosity. "What was she doing in New Orleans?"

"Stopped there on her way down here. Said she wanted to see the French Quarter. Remember what a time you and me had up there?"

Raphe smiled at the memory. "I do."

"You can still go to the French Quarter, Broussard. Remy'll be fine with Kitty every now and then."

"I know. But it makes him so sad for me to leave him. I hate to do it to him. Besides, you'd just get me into something again."

Heywood laughed. "That I would. I got Ellie into something."

"What kind of something?" Raphe was suddenly serious.

"Now, now—not what you think," Heywood assured him. He relayed the story about the woman at Tipsy's and the drink thrown at Ellie.

"That was mean," Raphe said.

"Embarrassed Ellie to death. I felt bad about it. I really did. And by the way, Miss Fields deserves your immediate attention."

"And not yours?"

"Sadly, no." Heywood grew uncharacteristically serious. "Ellie's special, my friend. But she's not as restless as she thinks she is. In the end, she wouldn't be happy with a vagabond like me. She needs an anchor—one that doesn't weigh her down too much. You would do nicely."

"Me? What could I give her but a child to raise and precious few comforts?"

"She's a teacher, remember? Children are her forte. And you, *mon ami*, could afford more comforts than you allow yourself. You just don't want to get attached to anything that might get swept away."

Raphe took a long sip from the bottle in his hand. "She'll be gone in a year, Heywood."

"Not if you get off your keister and do something about it. I swear, Raphe, you gotta learn to use your looks. I thought all you Cajun boys were ladies' men."

"Who told you that?"

"A Cajun girl, in a sadly memorable moment when she suggested I up my courtin' game."

They each had one last oyster before all the shells were empty. Heywood carried the shells to the bank and pitched them in the water, then filled the breadboard with all their utensils and empty bottles. "Raphe, ol' boy," he said, "get up from there—we're goin' to the dance hall."

"Heywood, I already told you—"

"Yeah, yeah, yeah, you wanna be still and all that nonsense. Well, you can do that when I'm not around. Go grab your fiddle and let's have some fun."

FOURTEEN

BY THE TIME RAPHE AND HEYWOOD made it to the dance hall, the whole town was there and the dance floor was packed. The accordion player, Lawyer Richard, immediately spotted Raphe and motioned for him to join the group onstage.

"What'd I tell you?" Heywood said. "You know you love to play—and as long as you're up there, you won't have to talk to anybody. Get after it, son!"

Raphe made his way along the edge of the dance hall to the small stage and joined the other players. Heywood spotted Ellie pulling a Coke out of a galvanized tub and made a beeline for her, standing behind her as she opened her drink.

"I see you're hittin' the sauce," he said.

Ellie whirled around. "Heywood!"

He picked her up and twirled her around. "I am delighted to see you again, Miss Ellie Fields!"

"You're gonna make me spill my Co-Cola all over you! When did you get here?"

"Just now."

"Is your fiancée here?"

"She is not."

Ellie put a hand on her hip and demanded, "Heywood Thornberry, are you really engaged, or do you just use that line to pick up women?"

He bowed his head and put his hand to his heart. "I am deeply, *deeply* wounded that you would think me capable of such deception."

"Answer my question."

Heywood held up his right hand. "I, Heywood Thornberry, do solemnly swear on the long and happy life ahead o' me that I am betrothed to Miss Claudette Sonnier of the New Iberia Sonniers. She thinks it best to put me on a long leash and let me exhaust myself before allowing me the honor of sleeping under her porch."

"Well, I want to meet Claudette because she must really be something."

"Oh, she is. She is indeed." Heywood offered Ellie his arm. "Would you take pity on a poor boy from Du Quoin, Illinois, and honor me with a dance?"

ELLIE HAD DANCED a couple of waltzes and a two-step with Heywood before some of the older men started cutting in. Back home, young people danced with young people, but not in Bernadette. Here, everybody danced with everybody. If all the men and boys were taken, the women and girls danced with each other. And as the individual couples danced together, the whole group moved in unison in a circle around the dance floor. From above, Ellie imagined, they must look like a giant spinning wheel with little wheels turning all over it.

Within an hour or so, she had danced with a man named

Leo and several others she remembered from Chalmette's, as well as a few giggling teenage boys, Doc, Remy, and a group of children who held hands in a circle with her as they revolved around the dance floor together.

When she thought she couldn't dance another step, Ellie took a seat in a folding chair near the front doors, the unofficial rest area, and looked around. For the first time since she started dancing, she took notice of the musicians onstage. Some were white, some colored; some were not the same as those who were playing when she first got there. One of the fiddle players, she was surprised to see, was Raphe. Not only was he playing, but the others appeared to be following his lead. His fingers danced gracefully up and down the neck of the fiddle as he stroked the strings with the bow. Just as he had melded with the bayou on the night he and Remy took her home, now he was one with the fiddle and one with the bow, conjuring music out of thin air.

Ellie turned her attention to Heywood. All the young girls—and some of the grandmas—wanted a spin with him, which he happily obliged. Heywood seemed blissfully unattached, as if he could twirl in and out of your life as easily as he could spin first one woman and then another around the dance floor. Whoever he held in his arms at the moment, always at just the slightest distance—perhaps in deference to Claudette—had his undivided attention and unabashed admiration, but his interest ended with the music as he shifted his attention from one partner to the next, never looking back. Ellie had watched him enough to see that. She wondered if the other women saw it too. Did Claudette Sonnier—or was she the exception?

Ellie didn't have much time to think about it before more

invitations to dance came her way. She made it through more waltzes and two-steps than she could count, finally seeing a chance to catch her breath when she and her partner—a sweet, soft-spoken old gentleman—found themselves near the front doors when the music stopped. Ellie smiled and said, "Merci" as he bowed to her and sat down to rest. Before anyone else could claim a dance, she ducked outside into the cool night air.

Walking all the way around the hall, she weaved through folding chairs and quilts spread on the ground until she made her way to the rear doors, also open to night breezes. The dance hall backed up to a wide creek that forked off the bayou. As the musicians took a break, Ellie could hear the water flowing over rocks and fallen logs.

Unlike all the cabins in the bayou, downtown Bernadette had electricity, and the strings of lights that zigzagged above the dance floor cast a glow outside the open doors. She stepped beyond it, into the darkness closer to the creek, and listened to the flowing water babble and sigh as the night breeze lifted her hair and cooled her face.

"*C'est belle, non?*" said a familiar deep voice. The sound of it made Ellie picture rich chocolate flowing over a silver spoon and into a cup of warm milk. She turned to see Raphe standing behind her.

"*Oui, c'est belle,*" she said, "if *belle* means 'beautiful'?"

"Yes, beautiful," he said.

"It's very beautiful. So is your music."

"Merci," he said with a smile that struck Ellie as a little bit sad. "I haven't played this much in a long time."

"Why not? I mean, if you don't mind my asking?"

"I don't mind." Raphe bent down, picked up a rock from the sandy bank, and tossed it lightly into the water. "I used to play all the time. My whole family did. If we weren't working, we were playing. But then after the storm . . ." He picked up another rock and gave it a toss.

"You miss your family more when you play?"

"Yes."

"And a prying woman only makes it worse?"

"A prying woman is a thorn in a man's side," he said, but he was smiling. "Did you know, prying woman, that there's a dance floor in the middle of the creek?"

"A dance floor—in the water?" Ellie thought he was teasing her.

"You don't believe me?" he said, looking down at her.

"You told me alligators can play cards. Your credibility is questionable."

"Then I will show you." Raphe offered Ellie his hand as he had done before, when he'd helped her in and out of the boat or guided her up the darkened path to Doc's cabin. But this was different somehow. With their fingers laced together, Ellie felt that he wasn't so much guiding her as sharing something with her. There was both excitement and comfort in that.

They walked together down the sandy, moonlit bank and followed it around a bend just beyond the dance hall, where Ellie could see a huge, flat limestone rock in the creek, maybe ten feet wide and almost as long. It filled the creek bed, leaving just enough room for water to flow around it.

"The dance floor," he said, gesturing toward the rock.

"It really does look like one." Ellie smiled up at Raphe, who was still holding her hand. Inside the dance hall, the musicians were playing again. She recognized the tune. "What's that song? I heard someone singing it on the bayou my very first night here."

"It's called 'Parlez-Moi d'Amour'—'Speak to Me of Love.'"

"It's pretty," Ellie said, absently swaying slightly to the music. "But I can't tell if it's happy or sad."

"Maybe both," Raphe said. "Would you dance with me to this sad, happy song?"

"I would," she said, "as long as you don't let me drown."

He kept her hand in his as they stepped off the bank and onto the rock. Then he slipped his free arm around her waist. Dancing with Raphe wasn't at all like dancing with Heywood—or anybody else. There was no distance between them. She could feel his strength and his warmth as they waltzed in the darkness over the water. Raphe made every turn with an easy grace. He rested his face against her hair, and she wrapped her arm tighter around his shoulder, letting her hand glide slowly up to touch his neck and his hair, which felt like silk under her fingers. She heard him whisper, "Juliet."

They stopped dancing. He let go of her hand but kept his arm around her waist, pulling her closer. Ellie slowly lifted her face to look at him in the moonlight. He stared down at her as he traced the lines of her face with his fingertips. The creek gurgled and splashed around the limestone as night birds called across the bayou and voices from the dance hall drifted on the cool breeze. Above it all, somehow, Ellie heard the sound of Raphe's breathing, feeling it on her face as he drew closer.

"Ellie! Ellie, are you out here?" It was Doc.

Without taking her eyes off Raphe, Ellie answered, "H-here, Doc. I'm—I'm right here."

Raphe smiled as he raised her hand to his mouth and kissed it, then guided her to the creek bank, beyond their secluded dance floor cloaked in darkness, and into the invasive light.

FIFTEEN

"THERE YOU ARE!" Doc came hurrying toward her as she and Raphe climbed the creek bank and returned to the dance hall grounds.

"What's the matter, Doc?" Ellie said.

"Florence twisted her ankle and needs to go home."

"Of course! Should I grab her dishes from the table?"

"No, that's alright. I already loaded them into the boat with her. I don't want to ruin your evening, so I asked Heywood if he and Raphe could get you home. He said they'd be glad to."

"Are you sure?" Ellie asked. "If you and Florence need my help, I don't mind coming with you at all."

"We're fine!" Doc assured her. "You go on and have a good time. I'll get her home and put some ice on it. She'll be good to go in a day or two. We've been dealing with this trick ankle for years."

Ellie still wasn't convinced she should let them leave alone. "Well . . . alright then—if you're sure."

"I'm absolutely sure."

"Please tell her to call on me if I can help."

"I'll do that," Doc said before hurrying out to the landing.

Ellie looked up at Raphe. "You know Heywood?"

IT WAS NEARLY TEN O'CLOCK when Raphe and the other musicians stopped playing, the dancers began to disperse, and the women started gathering their dishes.

"Mademoiselle, your transportation awaits." She turned to see Heywood giving a deep bow. "May I escort you to your well-appointed river craft, which some refer to—most indelicately, in my estimation—as a bass boat?"

"You may. Is the staff aware of my impending arrival?"

"They have been so advised."

Ellie took Heywood's arm. "So tell me," she said, "how long have you known Raphe?"

"Raphe?"

"Yes, Raphe."

"Let me see if I can remember," he said as they approached the landing. Ellie could see Raphe standing by the boat, laying his fiddle case on the floor of it. "Now that I think about it, me an' Broussard go way back," Heywood said with a grin. "I'm the one who dragged him to the dance tonight, wasn't I, *mon ami*?"

"He was," Raphe said, stepping into the front of the boat and holding his hands out to Ellie. He helped her climb in and make her way to the rear seat with him.

Heywood poled them away from the bank and then sat down facing them. "Perfect!" he said as Raphe started the motor and sent them cruising down the Teche. "Now I can see you both as we journey down this fine waterway."

Even in the dark, Raphe seemed to know every stump, every fallen tree, every possible snag in the bayou, skirting around them all with ease. For a time, they rode along in silence, all three enjoying their nighttime glide over water with no one else in sight.

Heywood stretched his legs out, leaned back, and looked up at the full moon. "Hey, you know what, Raphe? I think it's high time we showed Ellie the open water. If we stay in this bayou under a full moon, the Rougarou might get us. We're almost to the lower Atchafalaya. Let's pick up that little jaunt that connects it to the big daddy river."

Raphe hesitated and looked at Ellie. "Are you tired?"

She shook her head. "No, I'm okay."

Raphe looked up at the sky lit with silver. "Can't see wastin' a moon like that." He rounded a bend and turned into a narrow canal that was only a few yards wider than the boat on either side. The canal snaked through the dense trees and swamp grass until it abruptly straightened into a long corridor of water before opening into the Atchafalaya River.

"Need a minute to take it in?" Raphe said.

Ellie turned to see him smiling at her. He had remembered what she said about the bayou.

"I do." She smiled back at him. He shut off the motor and let the boat drift.

All around was water dotted with cypress trees, their twisted trunks anchoring them to the river as craggy branches bearing thick tufts of green cast primeval silhouettes against the night sky. Spanish moss cascaded off the trees, swaying like a silk gown in the night breeze. Moonlight spilled over the water, its glimmer interrupted here and there by the dark shadows of lily pads scattered about like stepping-stones.

Sitting silently with Raphe and Heywood, listening to the water lap against the boat, Ellie pictured herself hopping from one lily pad to the next, all the way down the river to the Gulf of Mexico. The eerie beauty of such a place in the moonlight made her shiver.

"You cold, Ellie?" Heywood asked her.

She shook her head.

"Ah, Raphe," Heywood said with a smile, "I do believe our Ellie is overcome by the wonders of the Atchafalaya."

"Anybody would be," Ellie said.

Heywood shook his head. "You'd be surprised." He pulled a flask from his hip pocket and took a long draw from it before offering it to Raphe and Ellie. "Barrel-aged elixir, anyone?"

Raphe shook his head. "Might steer us into a tree."

"I'd be asleep in two minutes," Ellie said. "To think that anybody could see this and not be amazed—that's just plain sad."

"Sad that they're so stupid," Heywood said, an edge to his voice. "Or so greedy."

Ellie frowned at him. "What do you mean?"

"Money and politics." Heywood took another drink. "Both can cloud your vision, Ellie, especially when the cash in question is oil money and the politicians in question are crooked."

"But you work on an oil rig, don't you?"

"True—which gives me a bird's-eye view." Heywood was scanning the river like somebody trying to memorize it. "Louisiana has good stewards and bad ones. The good ones want to drill for oil *and* protect the waterways. The bad ones—the greedy ones—just want to get in and take what they can as fast as they can. They don't care at all whether any of this is left when they're done." He dipped the river water with his hand and watched it slowly trickle out. "I wonder if any of it will still be here in twenty or thirty years. Glad I won't be around to see it disappear." Again he lifted the flask and took a long drink.

"You don't know that, *mon ami*." Raphe reached for the flask, which Heywood surrendered, and slid it under the seat.

"What are you talking about?" Ellie asked. "Heywood, are you sick?" She heard the tremor in her own voice.

Heywood's eyes met hers, and he smiled. "No, Miss Fields, I'm not sick. I'm just doomed. Longevity does not appear to have a place in my bloodline. Let's talk about something else."

"Are you out o' your mind, Heywood?" Ellie stood up, precariously rocking the boat.

Heywood grabbed onto his seat as Raphe reached up, put his hands around Ellie's waist, and slowly pulled her back down beside him.

"Sorry," she said. "But seriously—are you out o' your mind, Heywood, to think you can say something like that and then just move right along? I want to know what's wrong."

"It runs in my family," he said with a long, tired sigh. "As far back as anybody can remember, the oldest boy among the first cousins—every bloomin' generation of us, every single one—has died before he turned thirty. Sometimes it's sickness. Sometimes it's an accident. One cousin got tired o' wonderin' when it was gonna happen and shot himself. But he always dies. And I'm that cousin. I'm the oldest male. So I reckon I'll be the fifth—the fifth that we know of."

"Well, if some of them died in accidents, then it's not an inherited disease," Ellie insisted. "There's nothing in your body that will make you die young, Heywood. Your family's just had a string of coincidences—awful ones, I'll grant you that—but it's nothing more. And just because it happened to the others doesn't mean it has to happen to you. The one who shot himself doesn't really count, when you think about it. How old are you now?"

"Twenty-nine—and then some. When I got drafted, I thought for sure that was it. Question answered. Date set. I'd die overseas. But then I didn't, and now I can't help wondering if that was a joke the universe played on me. 'Guess I'm not gonna die after all,' and then *bam*—when I least expect it."

"Heywood, the universe doesn't decide when you die," Ellie said. "God does, and He doesn't play jokes. When's your birthday?"

"As luck—or lack thereof—would have it, I turn thirty on the thirtieth of April."

"Well, then we just have to keep an eye on you for a few more months," she said. "I believe you'll live to be a very old man. And I imagine when you're a hundred and ten, I'll still be asking you when I get to meet Claudette."

A smile broke across Heywood's face. He began laughing, and the more he did, the funnier Ellie's comment became until all three of them were laughing.

"Oh, Miss Fields," Heywood said when he finally caught his breath. "As my grandpa would say, you put the fodder where the calf can get it."

"I guess it's the teacher in me," she said. "We're direct. But seriously, Heywood, you can't spend your life expecting to die."

"Don't worry, Ellie. I promise you I live very much in the here and now. I just have to carry this little dark cloud around in the back of my mind for a while longer." He winked at her. "Perhaps my photography will be my legacy. I'll be leaving the world that shot of you tossing your hat into a trash can on Bourbon Street."

"The minute you're six feet under, I'm throwing that thing in the bayou," Ellie said, which made Heywood laugh again.

"I wouldn't put it past you," he said. "I really am okay, Ellie. Most o' the time, I'm aces. I'm just havin' a little trouble shakin' it lately. Reckon I need something to take my mind off it."

Raphe spoke up. "I believe I can help." He cranked the motor and sent them slicing through the water at a fast clip.

Ellie's hair blew away from her face, and now she really did shiver with the cool night air coming at them so fast.

Raphe reached under the seat and grabbed a flannel shirt. "It's clean. I keep it here for night trips when Remy stays with Kitty." He offered it to Ellie, who buttoned it over her dress and rolled up the sleeves to her wrists.

Heywood grinned and pointed at the shirt. "You know, most women would've put that around them like a shawl."

"Men's clothes are more comfortable than women's," Ellie said. "I used to steal my brother's hand-me-downs before Mama could give 'em away."

"No explanations necessary. You look lovely in flannel. Hey, where are we goin', Broussard?"

"You'll see," Raphe answered, the motor at full throttle. "We're not too far."

Up ahead, the river narrowed, making a sharp bend. Raphe steered them into the curve of the water, aiming the boat between two cypress trees right by the bank. He throttled way back and let the boat idle as they approached. When it looked as if he were about to steer them right into the bank, Ellie could finally see that the grass grew not on land, as it appeared from a distance, but in the river itself.

Once they cleared the grass, Raphe shut off the motor

completely and tilted it up out of the water, then took up an oar, moved to the center of the boat, and paddled them into a canal that soon became a dark, watery tunnel. It narrowed more and more as the branches of tall trees lapped overhead, blocking out the moonlight.

Heywood had moved to the front seat of the boat, turning his head this way and that—no doubt struggling to take in every inch of this eerie place, just as Ellie was. None of them spoke until Raphe broke the silence. "Until we get back out here, I need you to be very quiet," he said barely above a whisper. "And I need you to promise you'll never bring anybody here or tell anybody what you saw."

Heywood whirled around and looked up at him. "What is this place, Raphe—river or bayou?"

"Neither—and both," Raphe answered. "It's hard to say. But do I have your promise?"

"Absolutely," Heywood answered.

Raphe turned to Ellie. "And yours?"

"And mine," she said.

Raphe dipped the paddle into the water and began rowing. The farther they went, the more dense the tree canopy grew until Ellie couldn't see her hand in front of her face. All she could do was listen—to occasional splashes of water, the calls of owls and other night birds, and creature sounds she'd never heard before. Had she been on a dark journey through any other wilderness with anyone else, she would've been terrified, but her fascination with the bayou far outweighed any fear of it, and she knew deep down where it counted—had always known, really—that she could trust both of these men with her life.

On and on they glided, through trails of Spanish moss

that made her wonder what snakes might be hiding above, around first one bend and then another, until finally Ellie could see streams of moonlight piercing the leafy rooftop high above and the tiny canal spilled into a slough that had no other outlet. It was brilliantly lit, its glassy waters aglow.

Raphe guided the boat to a spot a few yards from the bank, where a fallen tupelo gum reached out into the water, and positioned them so that the boat was parallel to the tree. Apparently satisfied with the view, he silently laid down the oar and straddled the center seat of the boat. The three of them sat there like theater patrons waiting for the curtain to go up.

Heywood, like Ellie, was scanning his surroundings, marveling at this hidden patch of moonlight deep in the swamp. But then Ellie noticed that Raphe wasn't searching. His eyes were riveted on that fallen tree. She followed his gaze but saw nothing at first—just the remnant of a trunk, half in the water and half out.

At last, in the deep quiet, she heard movement in the swamp grass, a distinctive swishing that sounded like it came from something gargantuan. And then she saw it, gleaming like alabaster bathed in silver. The white alligator.

It climbed onto the tree and lay there like a sunbather. It had to be over twelve feet long and such a pure, brilliant white that you almost couldn't look directly at it. Light from the moon made the alligator's eyes gleam in the night. She could make out the texture of its snowy hide and a single ribbon of dark pigment twirled down its back. Its feet were enormous, like something prehistoric. Could it sense their presence? It seemed to be basking in its solitude, undisturbed by the light or the living.

Ellie tore her eyes away from the alligator and turned to Raphe, who was looking not at the breathtaking reptile but at her. He reached out to her, and she took his hand. Heywood looked at them, his eyes wide, his mouth open in awestruck silence. He and Raphe laid a hand on each other's shoulder.

The alligator remained still under the moon, drinking in soft light without the blistering heat of day until it had its fill. Then it followed the tree into the water, as if it had been sunning poolside and needed refreshment. It silently glided through the water, passing just a few feet away from the boat, crossed the slough, and disappeared into the tall grass where nothing and no one would ever find it.

Raphe and Heywood released each other. Ellie hadn't realized how tightly she was squeezing Raphe's hand until he said, "*Viens côté moi*, Juliet—come to me."

He pulled her toward him until she sat in front of him on the seat of the boat, shaking. He put his arms around her and held her against him as Heywood peered into the night, hoping, no doubt, for one more glimpse of the most extraordinary vision they would ever share together, fleeting but undeniably real. The three of them were joined now and always would be. Without uttering a sound, they all knew it.

SIXTEEN

RAPHE AWOKE TO THE SOUND OF THUNDER, and what a blessed relief it was to escape the phantoms haunting his sleep. The nightmares hadn't troubled him for a while now, and though he was grateful for the respite, their return caught him off guard, his defenses down. Now his brow was damp with sweat, his heart pounding against his chest.

The scenes passing through his mind as he slept had been all the more horrifying because they were once as real as he himself was. He had endured them all in the steaming bayou heat after the hurricane that changed his life and ended those of so many others.

His sisters had been spared the worst of the storm's aftermath, sleeping at the church and helping the surviving women in the community cook for their men, who faced the grisly task of recovering the dead. With so many gone, even a seventeen-year-old boy like Raphe had to help search for remains, kill the snakes scrambling into houses to escape the floods, and shovel his way through the muck and mire left by a twenty-foot wall of displaced water.

In reality, the bayou had been silent by the time he returned there after the storm. But in his dreams, all of the bodies floating in the water were screaming, their clothes ripped by the wind, their arms and legs bleeding. How would he ever explain such a thing to someone like Juliet? She felt the sadness of his loss—he could see it in her eyes and on her face—but she could never understand the sickening shock of pulling a body from the bayou only to discover it belonged to your brother, your nephew . . . your precious mother. He would never want her to understand such a thing.

Maybe that was what had summoned the dreams—his desire to protect Juliet. It was overwhelming, his need to keep her safe, but from what exactly? Deadly storms? The daily struggle to make a living and care for Remy? Raphe himself might be the biggest threat of all to her happiness. Choosing him would mean choosing a hard life, far removed from her family in Alabama. He would sacrifice anything for her, but in the end, would he be asking her to sacrifice herself for him?

The thought of a life without her made the hole in his heart so deep that nothing could possibly fill it. And yet he had to ask: Where does love end and selfishness begin? Or could it be possible for one to overcome the other if you loved somebody so much that their happiness *was* your own? All he could do was wait for an answer as he waited for daylight.

SEVENTEEN

ELLIE GASPED AND STOPPED IN HER TRACKS.

"You see a snake or somethin', Ellie?" Gabby asked, walking a couple of yards ahead of her.

"No, but can I talk to you and Bonita for just a minute?" They were on their way to the landing with all the children after school. "The first Monday of the month is a week from today, y'all."

"Woo, that's right!" Gabby said. "First Monday. Superintendent's comin', most likely."

Ellie considered her options. "Well, I guess there's no time like the present. I'll just tell him straight off that I don't believe in bullying children and I absolutely will not do it. And then when he fires me, y'all can help me find a job, because I'm not going back to Alabama with my tail between my legs."

"Is there some reason we gotta do this the hard way?" Gabby asked her.

"What do you mean?"

Gabby shrugged. "Mama always says you catch more flies w' honey than vinegar. 'Stead o' mixin' it with that superintendent, why not just let him think he won, and then he'll go on and leave us alone?"

"And how would we do that?"

"You leave it to me," Gabby said with a wink. "All you got to do is tell that man, soon as he gets here, that me and 'Nita's in charge o' keepin' French outta this school. You do that an' we'll handle the rest. Don't you worry none."

"You sure, Gabby?" Ellie asked.

Gabby gave a dismissive wave of her hand. "You fool with enough kids and enough men, you gonna learn how to keep both of 'em in line. Leave the kids and the men to us. You have a good night now."

"You too." Ellie was still unsure about Gabby's plan, but she didn't have a better one. She put her leather tote into the pirogue and pushed it off the bank, jumping into the bow just before the front of the boat went in. Then she began paddling.

The ride home was one of her favorite parts of the day. In the mornings, she was surrounded by a flotilla of school-children chattering away and calling out to ask her about the day's lessons or point to a heron's nest as they floated by it. But in the afternoons, they were all in such a hurry to get outside that most of them were long gone by the time she got to the landing. She had the bayou mostly to herself, taking her time and pausing as often as she liked. That was her gift to herself every weekday.

Today was no different except—except for what? Except just being in a boat on the water made her lonely for Raphe. And being lonely for him was scarier than any Rougarou. He wasn't what she had come here to find, yet there he was. Ellie wanted to focus on her work, her purpose, and Raphe had nothing to do with that. She conjured the image of a fiancé she had trusted turning into someone else across the dinner table, and told herself Raphe might do the same.

But deep down, she knew that was a lie. And she had to wonder what was more unsettling: searching for the one who can make you whole or finding him. Because anything found can be lost.

EIGHTEEN

ON SATURDAY MORNING, Ellie arose before daylight—the old habit of a farm girl, she guessed. But it worked to her advantage because she loved watching the bayou wake up. Actually, it never slept. What she experienced in those wee hours was the transition from night sounds cloaked in darkness—the call of an owl, the plop of a bullfrog leaping into the water, wings taking flight from somewhere high above—to the louder daytime chatter of the bayou as fish, fowl, mammal, and reptile hunted, mated, frolicked, and conversed.

Ellie made herself a pot of coffee and poured a cup, then wrapped Mama Jean's shawl around her nightgown, lit a lantern so she wouldn't step on a snake, and walked barefoot to the bench at the end of the dock. Dimming the lantern so it wouldn't rip the curtain of early morning darkness, she sat down, put her feet up, and pulled the shawl around her legs, resting her chin on her knees as she closed her eyes and listened to the bayou. The rhythm of chirping crickets and croaking frogs, the occasional splash of water abruptly disturbed, the low-flute hoot of an owl—to Ellie it was music, maybe the best there was, next to the sound of Raphe's fiddle.

She opened her eyes and sipped her coffee, waiting for the

first streak of light in the night sky. It came soon enough—first a faint silvery slit in the blackness that slowly lengthened before opening itself to sunrise colors of pale pink and coral. Before Ellie knew it, the sky was glowing with a watercolor wash of rosy orange, and she could see the singers of the swamp—the birds dotting limbs of cypress trees, the frogs on their lily pads.

Once the bayou was completely lit with sun, she was about to step inside for more coffee when she heard a sound off in the distance. She listened as it grew closer and closer—a boat chugging its way up the bayou until at last she could see it, first in the channel and then turning into the slough. It was, in fact, coming her way. She quickly grabbed her lantern and hurried inside, tossed off her nightgown as she ran into her bedroom, and threw on a T-shirt and her overalls.

She stepped onto her porch to see the boat pulling up to her dock. And then she watched a lanky figure tie up and climb the ladder.

"Heywood?" she called as she opened the screen door.

He strolled up the dock, took off his Panama hat, and bowed. "Your humble servant."

"What on earth are you doing on my doorstep this early in the morning?"

"I was out photographing the sunrise—which was a stunner, by the way—and I realized, upon completion of my artistic pursuits, that I am starving. Thought you might feed me, *non?*"

"Should I say *oui* or *d'accord* if I'm willing?"

Heywood thought it over. "Not sure. We'll have to ask my boy Raphe."

"Don't just stand there letting mosquitoes in my house—

come on in," Ellie said. "How'd you know I'd be up this early?" She went into the kitchen and took eggs, milk, and butter out of the icebox.

"Well, you're a country girl, so . . ."

"Up with the chickens?"

"Let's just say I took a chance and won," Heywood said with a smile as he joined her in the kitchen and built a fire in the stove.

"Hey, will you do me a favor and go grab some bacon and boudin out of the smokehouse? I'll pour us some coffee. Let me guess: black."

"Of course." He headed for the door. "There's still hope for hair on my chest."

By the time he came back, Ellie had the biscuit dough going. She rolled it out and cut the biscuits while Heywood started frying some bacon and boudin. Once she had a panful, he slid it into the oven for her and kept tending the smoky meats as he sipped his coffee.

"When did you get back to Bernadette?" Ellie asked him.

"Just last night. Mechanical problems on the rig shut us down early. Wish I could say I was sorry. Me and the *Whirlygig* lit outta Morgan City like a bat outta—well, in a hurry."

"What do you take pictures of this early—besides the colors in the sky?" Ellie started setting the table, putting a butter dish, cane syrup, and some of Florence's blackberry jam in the center.

"Oh, Ellie, you should see it." He took a plate from a kitchen shelf and loaded it with the bacon while he kept tending the boudin. "It's misty and mysterious and just so beautiful. The shape of the cypress trees against the sky when the sunrise first breaks through—you just can't imagine the shadows and the textures. And the color o' the water changes constantly from the first few seconds o' daybreak on. It's like lookin' into a kaleidoscope—if you could find a kaleidoscope filled with water and cypress trees and Spanish moss—and the occasional alligator waking up from a rough night." He moved the skillet off the heat and set the meats on the table.

"How do you like your eggs?" Ellie asked.

"Scrambled."

"Good, because that's the only way I cook 'em." She began cracking eggs into a mixing bowl. "How long were you out there?"

"Several hours, I guess. I couldn't sleep and got tired o' tossin' and turnin', so I figured I might as well do something constructive with myself. Hard part was wakin' up the *Whirlygig*."

"I take it the *Whirlygig* does not get up with the chickens?" Ellie said as she whisked the eggs and poured them into a buttered skillet.

"She does not," Heywood said.

"I didn't realize your boat was female."

"You don't think I'd waste my precious time on the bayou with a guy, do you?"

Ellie laughed. "No, I suppose not."

Once the eggs were done, she filled a bowl with them and took the biscuits out of the oven before joining Heywood at the table. She offered thanks, and they passed each other first one dish and then another.

Heywood buttered a biscuit and took a bite. "Miss Fields!" he exclaimed. "You can cook!"

"Of course I can cook. I was raised by Southern women. They insist that a girl know her way around a lard can."

"But you didn't want to cook for those Alabama suitors?"

"I don't want to cook for anybody who expects me to," Ellie said, dipping a piece of boudin into cane syrup.

"Good for you. For the record, I didn't expect you to cook for me. I just thought if I begged, I could persuade you."

"You could persuade anybody to do anything, Heywood, and you know it."

He dipped a biscuit in cane syrup and took a bite. "That's the best thing I ever ate."

"Better than Miss Ollie's po'boy?"

"Okay, second best," he corrected himself.

Ellie took a sip of her coffee. "You said you weren't sorry the oil rig had to shut down. Are you unhappy when you're working—when you're not on the bayou or pulling up to Miss Ollie's table in New Orleans?"

Heywood buttered a second biscuit. "I didn't used to be. But the rigs have gotten rougher, and I guess my patience has grown thinner. Kinda tired of spending any time doing something that doesn't mean anything to me. And believe me when I tell you—drilling for oil means absolutely nothing to me. I find the whole enterprise absolutely soul-draining."

"Think you might quit?" Ellie spread some blackberry jam on a biscuit.

"I want to. Just have to figure out that pesky business of making a living."

"Couldn't you fish with Raphe?"

"Wish that were possible. But Raphe's name is out there among the big shrimp companies, and he makes a lot more money working on their boats than he does fishing. I don't know if casting nets would keep me in the style to which I've become accustomed."

Ellie laughed and nodded. "I can understand that, given my own very high standards. Nothing but the finest scrub board for my washtub."

"How *do* the common folk live?" Heywood dug into his eggs.

Ellie sipped her coffee and looked at him across the table. "Heywood, I need to ask you something. Ever since last weekend, I've been thinking about it—the white alligator. It's practically all I think about. And I just wondered—what do you make of it?"

He sat back in his chair and shook his head. "Most amazing thing I've ever seen in my life. That gator was so white—so *pure* white—except for that one little ribbon o' charcoal down its back. And that tunnel we went through to get there and then the slough and the moonlight—I can't believe I didn't have my camera with me."

"Did seeing it . . . I don't know . . . *rattle* you at all?"

"What do you mean?"

"I'm not sure," she said.

"Were you scared of it, Ellie?"

"No, that's not how I would describe it exactly. I'm not making any sense."

Heywood gave her a playful nudge. "Maybe it was the shock of seeing a ghostly form after I upset you with news of my impending death."

"You are not allowed to talk about that ever again," Ellie said, shaking her finger at him. "I require you to live long enough to be my friend when I'm old and gray, and I will accept nothing less."

Heywood smiled at her. "You might go gray, but you'll never get old. You shall forever be my hat-tossing, po'boy-chomping, hurricane-swilling Miss Ellie Fields, even when you're walking with a cane and dipping snuff like my grandma."

That made Ellie laugh. "As long as I can have a truly stylish snuff box. Again, I do have my standards."

They ate their breakfast in silence for a minute before Ellie said, "I don't know why I can't stop thinking about it. I feel like there's something I'm supposed to understand, but I can't unravel it. It's like trying to see something through smoky glass. Everything's all shadowy."

Heywood took a sip of his coffee and smiled at her. "I swear, you and Raphe Broussard are dipped from the same bucket."

"How so?"

"You both have a troublesome tendency to dive straight past the surface and go deep right away. Me, I like to keep an observational distance."

"Not sure I follow."

"It's like with the alligator. You felt something on the spot and in the moment, and you let it take hold of you—both of you. I'd much rather see it through my camera lens. Then I can hold the picture in my hands and meet it on my terms."

"Something happened, though, didn't it? It wasn't just my imagination?"

"No, it wasn't your imagination. Raphe took us down a path, Ellie—all three of us. I guess we'll just have to wait and see where we end up."

HEYWOOD HELPED ELLIE WITH THE DISHES and thanked her for the leftover biscuits and boudin she packed for him, then headed out for the Atchafalaya to do some fishing.

Ordinarily, Ellie would relish a little time to herself on a Saturday. Mama Jean always said she had a "contemplative nature" and would "forever prefer the solitude to the clamor." But today Ellie felt oddly restless and decided to paddle to the landing and ramble around Chalmette's. She needed a few odds and ends for the kitchen anyway.

Paddling the bayou made her breathe differently. No matter what troubles might be swirling in her head, the simple act of gliding over the waters of the Teche calmed her spirit and eased her mind.

At the landing, she pulled the pirogue onto dry land and walked to Chalmette's. "Bonjour, Emmett," she said as she went inside.

"Ah, bonjour, Miss Ellie!" he said. "What can I do for you today?"

"You can let me roam aimlessly around your store. I'm afraid I might have a touch o' cabin fever."

"Ah, well, we can fix that fo' sure! Roam around my store much as you like. Buy ever'thing you see or nothin' at all."

"Merci, Emmett," Ellie said.

She picked up a basket from a stack by the front counter and meandered the well-organized aisles of Emmett's massive store, which held everything this community could possibly need: fabric, dress patterns, yarn, and thread; galvanized washtubs, seed, and shovels; shotguns, fishing rods, boat parts, and tackle; dry goods, soft drinks, and beer. There was even a toy section, she was surprised to discover.

Ellie smiled as she walked past metal trucks and spinning tops and paper-doll books. She lightly ran her fingers over the pink ruffled dress and white apron of a doll with brown eyes and long dark curls spilling from underneath a pink bonnet.

"Did you have such a doll as a little girl?"

Ellie turned to see Raphe at the end of the aisle. "Not exactly, but close." He came and stood next to her. "My doll's name was Suzy, and she had a navy-blue dress and bright red shoes that really buckled. I was pretty impressed with myself when I learned to buckle them without any help. Unfortunately for Suzy, when I was about five, I decided she needed a haircut. She was never quite the same."

Raphe smiled as he reached up and touched one of the doll's brown curls. "She looks a little like you."

"I wouldn't be caught dead in that bonnet," Ellie said, which made him laugh.

"Good, because it would cover your hair, and that would be a shame," he said, looking down at her. Then he frowned and asked, "Why are you here on a Saturday when you walk by Emmett's every day of the week?"

"Trying to cure the heebie-jeebies."

Raphe looked confused. "Heebie . . . *jeebies?*"

"You know—when you're anxious and worried and generally out of sorts, you've got the heebie-jeebies."

"What brought them on?"

"My mind won't stop turning around and around—" Ellie stopped herself and lowered her voice. "Around something you showed me not too long ago."

He laid his hands on her shoulders. "Will you come outside with me?"

Ellie followed Raphe to the back door and set her basket down. They went into a backyard of sorts, where Emmett had a big circle of benches, most of them just plank seats—

the kind you'd see with a picnic table—but there were two with backs like park benches.

"What's this?" she asked him.

"It's where the men gather to talk—to complain about a small catch or brag about a big one. And lie about both." Raphe motioned her to one of the park benches, where they sat down together. "You've been thinking about the alligator?"

"I have a hard time thinking of anything else." Ellie absently fidgeted with one of the buttons running down the front of her skirt.

"Was I wrong to take you there?"

"No," she said, looking up at him. "Not at all. I can't believe I got to see such a thing. Only now—"

"Now you don't know what to do with what you saw?"

Ellie nodded.

"It was the same for me the first time. And every time after that, I guess."

"I can't explain it," Ellie said, struggling to make sense of her own thoughts. "There was something about the tunnel we went through to get there and the full moon and then that gleaming white . . ."

"Maybe you crossed over something when you went through the tunnel. Now you can see something you couldn't see before, but at the same time, you can't go back."

"What is it that I'm seeing, Raphe—that *we're* seeing?"

"Something perfect trying to survive in a world that isn't. Something pure always in danger of ruin. Breaks your heart a little, *non*?"

She felt her eyes sting as she nodded.

He put his arm around her and covered her fidgeting hand with his steady one. "Mine too, Juliet. Mine too."

NINETEEN

THERE WERE NO CHILDREN on the bayou when Ellie paddled into Bernadette on Monday morning. Not a single pirogue or canoe. But when she arrived at the landing, there were all the boats. Approaching the school, she saw the older children gathered around Bonita and the younger ones circling Gabby in the schoolyard.

"Y'all ready now?" Gabby called out.

"Ready!" came the answer from all the students.

"Alright then, y'all go play till you hear the bell," Gabby called out. "Oh, hey, Ellie!"

"What are y'all up to?" Ellie asked her as the three women walked into the school together.

"We just gettin' 'em ready for the super," Gabby said with a grin.

"They ready, alright," Bonita agreed.

"Should I be worried?" Ellie asked.

"Naw, but that man oughta be," Gabby said.

Bonita laughed and shook her head. "I could feel sorry for him if I wanted to, but I don't."

Inside the younger kids' classroom, Ellie saw that Gabby and Bonita had covered the alligator with quilts and stacked the little "dreaming pillows" Ellie brought for the children

156

in a box hidden under her desk. Anything that might make learning look fun had been stowed away, and the interior shutters that normally opened onto the dogtrot were closed.

Ellie was unpacking her tote bag when two men came into her classroom. One didn't look much older than she was. He was tall and a little on the thin side. His light blond hair was neatly trimmed, and he was clean-shaven. He had pale blue eyes and a face Ellie would describe as kind if she didn't know better. His navy suit and tie looked very expensive. So did his leather shoes.

The other man was a different story altogether. He looked like a tough customer—that's what Mama Jean would say—with deep lines in his tanned face, khakis smeared with dirt, and a fedora. His dark eyes were cold, and he had a bowie knife strapped to his belt. The handle of the knife was blood-red, with silver rams' horns at the hilt.

He caught Ellie staring at the knife and laid his hand over it, sending a chill down her spine.

"Miss Fields?" the younger man said, approaching her desk.

"Yes?" She tried to gather her wits. "I mean yes, I'm Ellie Fields."

"I'm Boone Strahan, the superintendent of education." He extended his hand, which Ellie shook.

"Pleased to meet you," she said.

There was an awkward silence as Boone stood there, offering no information about his intended goal for the day.

"Is there . . . something in particular you'd like to discuss?" Ellie asked him. "Something you'd like to see?"

He seemed surprisingly nervous. Ellie had expected someone brash and arrogant. This man looked and acted more like a professor than a politician.

"I got things to do," said the other man, who was standing in the doorway, his arm propped against the frame.

Glancing at the bowie knife, Ellie calculated how quickly she could make it out one of the open windows. She wanted to keep the children away from him.

"This—this is my assistant, Mr. Gig Luetrell," Boone said. "He'll be surveying the, uh, the community surroundings while I evaluate the school. Please don't let us keep you, Mr. Luetrell."

As Luetrell turned to go, Ellie stepped into the corridor and looked out the front door to make sure he left the children alone. He showed no interest, hurrying past them to the landing. She immediately rang the school bell to bring her students inside, using the distraction to alert Gabby and Bonita about Boone Strahan and Gig Luetrell—one she believed to be a far greater danger than the superintendent.

"Boys and girls, take your seats and we'll get settled," Ellie said. "We have a special guest this morning."

They were all staring at the stranger, who took out an expensive-looking silver pocket watch and flipped open the cover. Perhaps he was on a tight schedule.

"That's a beautiful watch," Ellie said, trying to put him at ease.

He gave her a nervous smile and turned it around so she could see its luminescent face. "A gift from my mother. She always loved mother-of-pearl."

"So does Mama Jean—my grandmother," Ellie said. "Why don't you take a seat in the rocking chair and make yourself at home?"

Boone virtually fled to the sanctuary of the rocker, where he seemed painfully aware of the children's scrutiny, repeatedly adjusting his tie and brushing at nonexistent lint on his trousers. Here was someone who clearly hated being the center of attention.

Gabby had come into Ellie's class this morning, leaving Bonita with the older children. She stood in the back of the room as Ellie made the introductions. "Class, this is Mr. Strahan, our school superintendent. Can you say good morning?"

"Good morning, Mr. Strahan," they said in unison.

"Good morning." He forced a smile.

"Why don't we begin our morning lessons, Mr. Strahan, and you can just stop me if you have any questions or advice?" Ellie suggested.

"Very good," he said. "I believe my primary purpose is to monitor their English, to ensure that—that strong measures are—are taken to eradicate French in this school."

"We understand," Ellie said.

"I promise I won't—that is—interfere with your teaching. To tell the truth, I wouldn't know how."

Gabby cleared her throat to get Ellie's attention and gave her a wink.

"Oh, I forgot to mention, Mr. Strahan—this is one of my assistants, Gabby Toussaint," Ellie said. "She and her sister Bonita, who's with the older children right now, are in charge of keeping our lessons in English—using whatever measures they deem appropriate."

"My pleasure." Boone cast one of his awkward smiles in Gabby's direction.

Ellie didn't know what to make of this man. He seemed far too gentle a soul to be in politics at all, much less the rough-and-tumble kind his father was famous for. And he didn't appear to have any idea how to do his job. He was the last person on earth you would expect to see in the company of somebody like Gig Luetrell.

With Boone looking on, Ellie had the little ones practice writing their ABC's on slates while she began the morning history lesson with the older kids. They were studying Bayou Teche.

"Now, does anyone remember which Indian tribe named the Teche?" Ellie asked. She saw Gabby discreetly nudge Antoine Doucet, whose hand shot up. "Yes, Antoine?"

"*C'est la* Chitimacha," he said, wincing a little as if he knew what was about to happen.

"No French!" Gabby reprimanded him, grabbing him by the ear and leading him out of the classroom. Once they were outside in the corridor, everyone could hear what sounded like a paddle striking a backside, each time followed by a wail from Antoine. The older children were doing their level best not to laugh, while all of the younger ones, as if on cue, began to wail along with Antoine, though Ellie didn't see any tears.

Antoine returned to the classroom, bowing his head and rubbing his backside, with Gabby following behind, carrying a wooden paddle the size of a rolling pin. "Don't you worry, Mr. Strahan," she said, "we gon' beat the French out of 'em if it's the last thing we do."

A horrified Boone stood up from his chair. "Do you—do you mean to tell me—you *beat* children for speaking French?"

"It's the law," Ellie said, hoping Boone didn't notice that the first and second graders had grown bored with their wailing and were back to writing their ABC's.

"What law?" he demanded.

"Y' Papa's," Gabby said.

"The law says no French," Ellie added. "But my instructions from the school board said no French by whatever means necessary. This is what's necessary if you want children to forget a language their people have spoken for hundreds of years."

"Well, that just can't be," Boone insisted. "As your superintendent, I—I'll be back. I need to think about this."

Boone hurried out of the schoolhouse. Ellie went to the window and watched a brand-new Chevy speed away from the school. She wondered how Gig Luetrell planned on getting back to Baton Rouge.

"He's gone," she said.

"Antoine, honey, you did so good," Gabby said. "Step on in the broom closet and take them dream pillows out your britches."

The class howled as Antoine grinned and did a little dance to the broom closet at the front of the class, swishing his very poufy rear end back and forth.

"I tell you what," Gabby said, "Antoine just about had me believin' he was gettin' a whoopin'. That boy can holler fo' sure."

TWENTY

ELLIE RANG THE DISMISSAL BELL, waved goodbye to most of her students, and thanked the Toussaints for their help. Then she went back inside and spent a couple of hours giving extra help to Marceline Ardoin, who had confessed a dream of going to college. Ellie meant to do whatever she could to help her get there.

She and Marceline walked to the landing together before saying their goodbyes as Ellie climbed into Doc's pirogue. After that first day of school, she had left the bass boat tied to the dock, instead taking the pirogue, which she paddled up the Teche each morning with an armada of schoolchildren traveling in a similar fashion. The pirogue made her feel at home in the bayou.

About half the students had peeled off to their family cabins when Ellie waved goodbye to the others and paddled into Doc's slough. She waved to Tante Dodo.

"Bonjour, Eh-LEE!" called the old woman in her heavy French accent, briefly pausing the handmade broom she used to sweep her front porch.

"Bonjour, Tante Dodo!" Ellie called back. When she first came here, Doc had told her to go to Tante Dodo and Mr.

Hudie if she had any kind of problems at the cabin. That had proven sound advice, with Ellie and the elder Cajun woman becoming close friends almost immediately. It was Tante Dodo who had helped her master the pirogue, which Ellie now easily steered to the bank, then jumped from boat to land as naturally as she put one foot in front of the other.

She carried her schoolwork in a handsome leather tote Mama Jean had given her "because a professional woman should *look* the part." It seemed out of place in the bayou, but it made Ellie feel as if her grandmother were right there, watching over her.

Inside the cabin, she changed into a T-shirt and overalls. Her mother never could abide this particular outfit, but the worn cotton and denim were soft against her skin and the fit was wonderfully loose and comfortable. They were hand-me-downs from her brother, several years her junior but nearly a foot taller. She rolled the legs up to her knees and put her hair in a ponytail. It had grown too long to style much, but maybe the beauty parlor in town could do something about that.

After building a fire in the woodstove to warm a pot of chicken and rice she had made the night before, Ellie chipped off a few chunks from a block of ice in the icebox, put them in a glass, and poured it full of sweet tea, then went out on the porch to sit in her swing. Her mind kept drifting back to Raphe. Staring at the pirogue that rested on the bank, she pictured him standing in it, rowing in the moonlight. What would she do if he were to suddenly appear in the slough and row right up to her dock? What would she say to him?

Sudden movement on the edge of the slough caught her attention. It was Tante Dodo, in her usual cotton dress, white apron, and white bonnet, leading a parade of older ladies from her cabin toward Ellie's. They must've been waiting for her to come home. The ladies were taking their time, some walking strong like Tante Dodo, others hunched over and a little more feeble, leaning on walking sticks. Ellie watched as they slowly made their way around the water and into her front yard, if you could call it that—the banks here were far too shady for grass to grow.

Ellie opened the screen door to her porch. "*Bonjour, mes dames!*" she called.

"Bonjour, Eh-LEE!" the women called, waving to her.

Ellie welcomed them—five in all—onto her porch. "Would you like to come inside? Can I get you anything—a glass of tea, maybe?"

"*Non, merci,*" Tante Dodo said. "We sit?" She pointed to the swing.

"Of course." Ellie motioned for three of the ladies to sit in the swing and pulled her two porch rockers together for Tante Dodo and another woman who carried a long walking stick. Ellie grabbed a chair from the table inside and took a seat with them.

Tante Dodo folded her hands in her lap and began explaining their mission in halting English dipped in French. "*Maintenant,*" she said, "we come to ask you help, Eh-LEE."

"What can I do for y'all, Tante Dodo?"

"*Ils—*" Tante Dodo began in French. She paused, and Ellie watched the old woman's lips move as she silently translated to herself before speaking again. "*They* want learn the *anglaise*. They want you teach. I . . . would *like* . . . to get better."

"You ladies want to learn English?" Ellie asked.

Tante Dodo smiled and nodded, looking relieved to be understood. "Oui! Learn English."

"Can I ask why?"

"*Pour notre petits-enfants*," Tante Dodo said. "You say . . . grand . . . grand*children*. They talk the *français* at home—for us," she said, gesturing around the circle of women. "But they talk the *français* in school—" Tante Dodo slapped one of her hands with the other. "We talk the *anglaise*, they talk the *anglaise*, they no more—" Again she slapped one hand with the other.

Ellie felt a knot in her stomach. "You mean you ladies— you want to learn English so your grandkids can speak it all the time at home? So they won't slip into French and get punished at school?"

"Oui!" Tante Dodo smiled broadly and clapped her hands together. "You teach?"

Ellie nodded, unable to find her voice just now. To think they were willing, at their age, to try to learn a whole new language just so some stranger wouldn't hurt their grand-children in the name of good citizenship. And what kind of wrongheaded thinking had led school authorities into such nonsense in the first place?

There were smiles all around as the women squeezed each other's hands and spoke excitedly in French.

"I imagine Sunday afternoons would be the best time— when you ladies aren't busy?" Ellie asked when they had quieted down.

"Oui!" Tante Dodo said. "You come my house, Eh-LEE. We gather at *quatre*—at—" Tante Dodo held up four fingers.

"At four o'clock on Sunday afternoon?"

"Oui! Four o'clock. I cook. You teach. We pass a good time."

Ellie smiled at the group. "Alright then, ladies. Starting this Sunday, I'll meet you at Tante Dodo's at four and we'll pass a good time."

"We pay," Tante Dodo said.

"No, no." Ellie shook her head. "You don't have to pay me anything."

"We *pay*," Tante Dodo insisted. "What we pay?"

Ellie thought it over. "We'll trade. I'll teach you ladies English, and you teach me how to cook like you. Deal?"

Tante Dodo translated for the women. "Oui!" they all said.

As the women stood up to go, they hugged Ellie and kissed her on the cheek.

"Au revoir!" Ellie called after them, waving goodbye as they set out.

The cabin was quiet again, and the sun was going down. Ellie could hear the French chatter of Tante Dodo and her circle as they made their way along the bank and back to the little cabin beyond the trees.

As the last of the ladies vanished from sight, Ellie saw a motorboat turn into the slough and head in her direction. She stood on the screened porch, squinting to make out the lone figure. He was almost to the dock before she recognized, of all people, Boone Strahan. Have mercy. The superintendent of education, and here she stood barefoot, in overalls. She flew into her bedroom, unfastening as she ran, threw off the overalls, and slipped on a cotton dress and a pair of flats. There was no helping her hair. The superintendent was already knocking.

Ellie opened the door to find a very awkward Boone Strahan staring at her.

"Hello," she said. "Would you like to come in?"

"Yes—I mean—that is—could we sit out here?" Boone had taken off his suit jacket and was nervously fussing with his tie.

"Of course," Ellie said. "Make yourself comfortable. Can I get you some tea?"

"No, thank you. I'm sorry to just appear unannounced. I won't stay long. The town doctor told me where to find you."

Boone took a seat in the porch swing as Ellie pulled up a rocker across from him. There was a long silence, with only the late afternoon sounds of crickets singing and fish jumping, before Boone finally spoke again. "Do teachers down here really paddle these children for speaking French?"

"Not always," Ellie said. "Sometimes it's a slap on the hand with a ruler. Sometimes they make them stand in a corner in front of the class. Sometimes they make them write 'I will speak English only' over and over on the chalkboard during recess or deprive them of things they enjoy, like story time."

Boone rubbed his brow as if to wipe away the images Ellie was conjuring. "It just seems so cruel."

"It *is* cruel," she said. "And stupid."

"But we *have* to stamp out this French."

"Why?" Ellie said.

"To make sure Louisiana doesn't get left behind. To keep pace with the rest of America now that the war's over."

"But how does it hold us back to have schoolchildren who speak two languages instead of one?" Ellie countered.

"Well, because they prefer French to American English. We have to break the Cajuns of speaking French entirely— eradicate it from their daily life. If we don't, they'll slide back into their native tongue, and then we'll have a whole region of the state that can't communicate in the language of America."

"That's just not true, Mr. Strahan."

"Please—call me Boone."

"Okay, Boone. You call me Ellie and we'll talk this through. I just had a group of ladies—women past seventy—come here and ask me to teach them English so they can help their grandchildren speak it consistently and stop getting punished in school. The people here understand the importance of English. But you can't take away their native language. It's part of their culture. It's part of their heritage and their identity."

"Daddy says—that is to say, the *thinking* is—not only are they speaking French instead of English, but they're speaking an unusual dialect that isn't even standard. It makes us look backward."

"I expect there are people in places like New York and Chicago who would say the same thing about the way you and I speak English."

"True, but—"

"Tell me something, Boone. You and your family ever go overseas? Vacation in Europe maybe?"

"We did the tour when I was fourteen or fifteen, and then I went back with some friends after the war."

"Did you learn any other languages for your trip?"

"I already knew Spanish from the boys' academy. And then I learned a little conversational Italian and German."

"And did any native speakers in Germany or Italy or Spain hit you with a stick when you couldn't find the words in their language and slipped back into English?"

Boone stared at the floor. "Of course not."

"So why was it okay for you to fall back on *your* native language but it's not okay for these children to do the exact same thing? Why do we punish them for being bilingual when we should be praising them for it? Most of all, how can we sleep at night when we've made innocent children so afraid of school that they stop eating and sleeping and they cry all the way to class? How do fear and shame help us in the great march forward? How have fear and shame ever helped any child?"

Boone looked up at Ellie. She had struck a nerve. "Fear and shame can cripple a child," he said.

"I couldn't agree more."

Boone stared at her for a moment before he abruptly stood up. "I should go." Before she could answer, he was out the door and headed for the dock. She followed him as far as the bottom of the porch steps. He stopped a few feet away from her, turned, and said, "I'm really not an awful person, you know. Everybody can see my father put me in this job, for which I'm utterly unqualified. But as long as I have to be here, I want to help these children—if you'll show me how."

She smiled at him. "I believe that. Otherwise I would've run you off my porch with a broom."

Boone smiled back at her and gave a small bow. "Good afternoon, Ellie."

"Bonjour, Boone."

GIG LUETRELL WAITED LIKE A SNAKE hiding in the Spanish moss until downtown Bernadette was silent and vacant. He wouldn't even need to use his knife to break in. He knew from experience that nothing would be locked except the general store. And he didn't need what they were selling. What he wanted was information.

Walking right through the front door of the school, he stepped into the classroom where he was sure that pretty little morsel had completely fooled Big Roy's idiot son. Gig opened all the desk drawers, riffling through them for signs of French that might help his boss get his hooks into this two-bit town even more. Why did oil always have to be buried in nowhere places like this one? He found nothing useful.

But then, just as he was about to give up, something in the center of the room caught his eye. Those quilts. Why were they there? As he pulled them back to reveal what lay beneath, a smile spread across his face. The white alligator. He had found what he came for. Now the question was, what to do with it?

TWENTY-ONE

BY EARLY NOVEMBER, Ellie felt that she, Bonita, and Gabby had hit their stride with the students. Classes were running smoothly, the kids were engaged, and none of the little ones had cried since September, except for the occasional skinned knee on the playground.

On a Friday morning, Ellie had just given the older students their essay assignment for the day when Bonita came into the classroom. "You prob'ly need to let me stay with 'em and you go check on Remy," she said. "I think he's coming down with that awful stuff that's been goin' around."

"Oh no," Ellie said. "I'll go see about him. They have their assignment for the rest of the afternoon, so in case I have to take Remy to Doc, would you just keep an eye on things till it's time for the bell?"

"Happy to." Bonita took a seat at the desk.

Ellie found Remy lying on a pallet Gabby had made for him next to Ellie's desk.

"I b'lieve this baby's got a touch o' fever," Gabby said. "Thought I'd keep him away from the others, much as I could."

Kneeling beside him and laying her hand against his fore-head, Ellie could feel the heat coming from his skin. "You're right, Gabby."

Remy's cheeks were flushed, and he had developed a cough. "I don't feel good, Miss Ellie," he said. "My head hurts real bad."

"I'm so sorry, sweetheart. We should get you to Doc's." Ellie turned to Gabby. "Maybe we ought to let the older kids take the little ones on home so these rooms can air out a little. We can leave all the windows cracked over the weekend."

"That's prob'ly the thing to do," Gabby agreed. "You go on with Remy. Take your purse with you, and I'll leave your satchel on your dock when I pass by."

"You're a lifesaver, Gabby." Ellie helped Remy raise up and lifted him into her arms.

Unlike Raphe, who carried his nephew with ease, Ellie struggled to cover the short distance to Doc's office.

"Not another one." Doc shook his head as they came in the door. His waiting room was full of children, and he had apparently called for Minerva Richard, the local midwife, to come and help. Minerva was a formidable Creole woman who wore a stiffly starched, snow-white uniform when she worked for Doc, even though he didn't require it. She said that a woman giving birth wants the aid and comfort of another woman, so she delivered their babies in her regular clothes, but sick patients in a doctor's office want to see a nurse. Minerva was married to an accordion player named Lawyer Richard, whom Raphe often joined onstage at the dance hall. Their son, Freeman, carved all the white alligators for Chalmette's.

No sooner did Ellie sit down with Remy in her lap than Minerva was at her side with a thermometer.

"Open up, baby," she said to Remy, who immediately obeyed, like always. Minerva used her watch to check his pulse, then she read the thermometer and shook her head. She took a stethoscope from around her neck and put it in her ears. "Sit up for me just a minute, sugar."

Remy raised up as if it were all he could do to lift his head off Ellie's shoulder.

Minerva pulled his shirt up, listened to his heart, and then put the stethoscope to his back and had him take a few deep breaths. "Po' baby got this ol' virus been goin' around. Gets your respiration system all gunked up. Done hit near 'bout ever' family on the bayou, one way or 'nother. Won't kill you, but it'll make you wish the good Lord would take you. Seem to be more catchin' to the chillun' than the grown folks. I'll tell Doc what's goin' on."

Minerva disappeared into Doc's examining room and then came back out to check the next patient.

Remy was silently crying, as if even now he didn't want to be a bother. Ellie rocked him gently back and forth in her lap, wiping his tears away and stroking his hair, damp with sweat from the fever.

"I'm so sorry you feel bad, sweetheart," she said. She wished there were something she could do to make him more comfortable, but Doc and Minerva were moving as fast as they could, working the crowded waiting room. Then she had an idea. "Remy, would you like me to tell you the story of the white alligator?"

He nodded.

"Well . . . long, long ago, there was a boy named Jacques Babineaux who lived on the Atchafalaya . . ."

IT TOOK DOC OVER AN HOUR TO GET TO REMY. "Son, don't you worry," he said in his reassuring voice. "We'll have you feeling better before you know it."

"Yes, sir," Remy said.

"Does your head hurt?"

"Yes, sir."

Doc finished his examination and asked Ellie about the other children. He seemed relieved when she told him Gabby and Bonita had dismissed class. Maybe the virus wouldn't run through the school like wildfire.

Doc gave Ellie a bottle of aspirin and another of liquid medicine, which he said would help Remy sleep and ease his cough. "Unfortunately, a virus like this just has to run its course," he said. "Not much I can do but make sure the fever doesn't stay too high for too long and keep him comfortable."

"Doc, do you know how I can get hold of Raphe?" Ellie asked.

Remy had a coughing fit. When it settled down, he said, "Nonc's not home. He's helpin' Mr. Leo on his boat. I was s'posed to go to Aunt Kitty's till he gets back."

"Well, that won't do," Doc said. "Her kids will all catch this. Ellie, can you take Remy home with you? I'll call Florence and have her run over to Kitty's to let her know what's happened. Nobody over there has a phone."

"I'll be happy to. Would that be alright with you, Remy—to stay with me till Nonc can come and get you?"

"Yes, ma'am." Remy looked too sick to care who looked after him.

"Now, Ellie, you need to be careful yourself—wash your hands a lot," Doc instructed. "I left a first aid kit at the cabin. It has a thermometer in it—use that to watch his temperature. If it gets over 102, you get him to me quick as you can. Other than that, just give him the aspirin and cough medicine every four hours and keep him warm so he can sweat this off. Most patients start improving pretty quick once the last fever breaks—and he might have several before it's gone for good, so just get ready for that."

"I will."

"I'd help you more if I could, but there's just so many of them—"

"I know you're doing all you can, Doc. Is there anything I can do for you?"

He smiled and shook his head. "Just say a little prayer that this thing soon plays out."

Ellie helped Remy up and carried him to the landing. She laid him on an old quilt she kept in the pirogue for emergencies and then pushed off, jumping in and taking up the long oar that would paddle them home.

Remy coughed and wheezed all the way to Doc's cabin, and Ellie had never been more relieved to get home. The sky was slowly turning gray, and the wind was beginning to gust. Rain was coming, maybe even a storm.

She carried Remy inside and laid him on the iron bed next to hers. Rummaging around in her closet, she found a stack of her brother's old T-shirts—more thefts from her mother's giveaway bags. She took off Remy's shoes and socks, then helped him undress and put on a T-shirt, which fell below his knees but was clean and soft, and he could sleep comfortably in it. Then she found Doc's thermometer and checked his temperature—99.9 degrees. She gave him the aspirin and cough medicine and helped him drink as much water as he could before tucking the covers around him.

"Try to go to sleep, sweetheart," she said. "I'll be right in the next room if you need anything at all. Want me to leave the door open?"

"Yes, ma'am," Remy said.

Ellie went into the kitchen and made herself a strong pot of coffee, preparing for a long afternoon. She would write her brother and Mama Jean to pass the time, alert to any change in the little boy's breathing as she listened and longed for the sound of an approaching boat.

TWENTY-TWO

IT WAS SIX IN THE EVENING before Remy's fever stopped rising and finally broke. Ellie had gone through two more of her brother's T-shirts and as many pillow slips, trying to keep him warm and dry as he sweated it off. Remy wouldn't touch a bite of food, but Ellie was able to persuade him to sip a little tea with honey in it. She had moved him from one bed to the other, changing the sheets on the first while he sweated in the second, hoping she didn't run out of clean linens before he got better. He kept asking for Raphe, and she assured him that his uncle would be there soon, but the truth was she had no idea when he would come.

Around nine, with Remy sound asleep, Ellie finally heard a boat, traveling at what sounded like full throttle until it turned into the slough and slowed down. Stepping onto the porch, kerosene lamp in hand, she saw Raphe quickly striding up the dock. She held the screen door open for him and led him into the cabin just as the rain that had been threatening all day started pouring down.

"I'm so sorry," he said. "This should not have fallen on you."

Studying him with the lamp, Ellie could see that his hair was wet and his shirt was buttoned wrong. "It's alright. You couldn't help it. But where on earth have you been?" She pointed to the lopsided shirt.

"Out on the water helping Leo." Raphe hurriedly unbuttoned his shirt and tried to right it, but he kept misaligning the buttons. On his third try, Ellie set down the lamp, pulled his hands away, and took over. "His motor quit on us right as we started in, and I had to fix it." Raphe watched her as she unbuttoned his shirt, straightened it, and closed it again. "I jumped in the river because I had grease all over me. Didn't get home till just now. Kitty sent one of her kids to tell me Remy was sick. Can I see him?"

"He's in here."

Ellie led Raphe to her bedroom, dimly lit by a small lantern so Remy wouldn't wake up in the dark and feel afraid. She stood in the doorway as he went inside and knelt by the bed. Putting his ear against Remy's chest, Raphe listened to his breathing, ragged at times, then laid his hand on his nephew's forehead.

Ellie stepped away to give him privacy and built a fire in the woodstove, where she began warming a chicken bog Tante Dodo and the other ladies had taught her to make. She had tried unsuccessfully to persuade Remy to have some.

With the pot of chicken and rice heating up, she pulled a log from one of the fireplace bins. The days were still warm, but nights were growing chilly, especially with the rain. Raphe came into the front room and took the log from her, then gathered a few more and built a fire to warm the cabin. Rain was pelting the roof now, and thunder was rolling in.

He sat down on the floor and leaned against the hearth. Ellie had never seen anyone look so exhausted, not just from work but from the weight of responsibility for Remy, which he shouldered mostly alone—likely his own choice, since Kitty seemed willing enough to help. But there was something more. Raphe didn't just look tired—he looked neglected, from his rumpled clothes to his uncut hair to the hint of dark circles under his eyes.

"I know we need to get out o' here and give you back your home," he said. "But could Remy stay until it stops raining? His face feels so warm. I could leave and wait for the rain to stop. Then I could come back and take him home."

Ellie sat down next to him on the floor. "That oughta keep you busy till around midnight. When's the last time you ate?"

Raphe shrugged. "Sometime this afternoon."

"Why don't you let me fix you some supper, and then you can sleep on that bed under the window? I'll stay in the room with Remy—I'm already used to giving him his medicine and checking his temperature every four hours. We'll all feel better in the morning."

"I couldn't do that."

"Why not?"

"Because it's not fair to you. You taught school and then you took him to Doc's and you've had him all day and night. We need to go and let you get back to what you want to do."

"And what exactly could I be doing at nine o'clock in the middle of a bayou when it's pouring rain?"

He smiled at her. "Good time to catch frogs."

"I'm all stocked up."

Raphe ran his fingers through his wet hair.

"Let me get you a towel," Ellie said, but he put his hand on her shoulder.

"Don't get up," he said. "The fire'll dry it. You're as tired as I am."

179

"I doubt that. I'll be back." She went into the kitchen and came back with a towel, a plate of chicken bog with crusty bread, and a glass of tea.

"I have to eat your cooking if I want to stay?" He grinned at her as he ran the towel over his wet hair.

Ellie sat back down next to him. "Eat it and brag on it."

"Then I guess it must be done."

Raphe tasted the dish, then took a second bite. "Is this Tante Dodo's chicken bog?"

"She taught me how to make it."

"Maman used to say that if you want to learn one of Tante Dodo's dishes, you'd better hide under her table and watch her make it, because when she gives you the recipe, she always leaves one thing out."

"I guess I'm special," Ellie said. "She gave it to me straight. I'm trading some of the older ladies English lessons for cooking lessons. We meet at Tante Dodo's on Sunday afternoons."

"How long you been doing that?"

"A little while now. It's important to them to help their grandchildren speak English at home. And I figure y'all won't let me stay in Louisiana if I can't cook your food. I didn't want the ladies giving me what little money they have, so a trade seemed in order."

"This is very good."

"Merci. And you could sound a little less surprised."

"I'm not surprised that you can cook," he said, looking at Ellie. "I'm just surprised that you would take on such a thing, with all you have to do already. Nobody but you would give up your own time to help the ladies like that."

"I think I'm the one getting the most out of it," she said. "What those women know—not just about cooking food but

about really *feeding* people, making them feel good inside—
that's what I wish I could learn."

"I think you already did."

Ellie smiled at him. "My food's not as good as theirs."

"Your food is very good. But that's not the point, is it?"
He took a bite of the bread and had a long drink of tea.

"Raphe, how on earth do you manage all of this? I mean,
the mechanical work on the shrimpers and the fishing with
Leo and looking after Remy . . ."

He took another drink of his tea. "Some days—like today—I don't. I guess I just do the best I can to take care of
Remy and hope it's enough."

"But who—who takes care of you?"

Most of the vets Ellie had dated back home had looked
at her like they were picturing her raising their babies. And
here was Raphe raising one on his own, with just occasional
help from his sister. Ellie found herself wondering what it
would feel like to be the one he leaned on.

Raphe turned to look at her. His lips were parted as if he
we were searching for words. "I don't have any—"

"Nonc! Nonc!"

Raphe jumped slightly at Remy's panicked call. He and
Ellie hurried to the bedroom.

Remy's face was flushed a deep red, and his eyes looked
glassy. "My head hurts, Nonc," he said as Raphe laid his
hand against Remy's face.

"He's burning up," he said to Ellie, who was already shaking the thermometer.

"Here, sweetheart, let us check your fever, and we'll figure
out how to make you feel all better." Ellie slipped the thermometer into Remy's mouth, trying her best to mimic Doc's

reassuring voice. She and Raphe impatiently waited as they gave the thermometer time to do its work. "It's 103," Ellie said as she read it. "We have to get him to Doc's."

"It's pouring rain," Raphe said.

"Do we have time for you to go get Doc and bring him here?" Ellie knew the answer but thought it best to let Raphe come to it himself. She watched as he studied Remy's face and calculated the distance.

"No," he said.

Ellie headed for the wardrobe in her bedroom. "You douse the fires, and I'll gather up some quilts to try and keep Remy as dry as we can."

Raphe hurried into the front room and took care of the fires. When he returned, Ellie had Remy wrapped in one quilt and was preparing another. Raphe helped her cover his nephew and picked him up as Ellie grabbed more covers on the way out the door.

At the porch, Raphe stopped her. "You can't go out in this."

"I can't *not* go—I couldn't stand it." She covered her head and shoulders with Mama Jean's wrap and draped a quilt over Raphe's head and shoulders to try to protect him from the rain. They ran for the dock, where Raphe carried Remy down the ladder on his shoulder, laid him in the boat, and then reached up for Ellie and helped her down.

Raphe sat on the back seat to steer, quickly starting the motor and guiding them into the bayou, as Ellie sat at his feet and pulled Remy onto her lap, holding him tightly against her. Raphe took off the quilt she had draped over him and covered her with it.

They raced down the bayou to the same channel Raphe and Heywood had used to show Ellie the Atchafalaya. Raphe quickly snaked through it to the open water, where Ellie could see lightning in the sky and prayed it wouldn't strike the boat before they could get to shelter. The wind was picking up, making the river choppy. Now and again the bow of the bass boat would rear up out of the water, forcing Raphe to slow down to keep them steady. Just as the channel of the river narrowed, a bolt of lightning struck a tree on the bank, splitting it in two and setting it on fire. Ellie cried out and felt Raphe's hand squeeze her shoulder through the quilt.

Finally, the river narrowed still more, and Raphe pulled up to a long dock jutting into the water. The homes here had electricity, but the storm had apparently knocked down a power line because the bank of the river was dark. Raphe tied up the boat and took Remy from Ellie, laying his nephew over his shoulder. Then he reached for Ellie's hand and pulled her up, helping her onto the ladder before climbing up himself. They ran to the porch of a two-story house, which Ellie could barely make out until they were right in front of it. She knocked as loud as she could.

Soon Florence, wearing her nightgown and robe and holding a kerosene lamp, opened the door. "Oh my goodness! Come in out of the weather! Is that Remy?"

"He's really sick, Florence," Ellie said, her voice shaking with worry. "His fever's 103."

"Hurry in and let's get him dry!" Florence said. "Take this lamp and carry him upstairs to that first bedroom on the left. I'll get Doc."

Raphe and Ellie ran upstairs with Remy and carried him into the bedroom Florence had directed them to. Ellie pulled back the covers and helped Raphe remove the wet quilts around Remy before they put him into bed. His T-shirt was still dry, thanks to all the cover. They could hear Doc hurrying up the stairs as they stood helplessly, looking down at the flushed child in the bed.

In a minute Doc came into the room, his medical bag in hand. "You two look worse than Remy."

Raphe and Ellie glanced at each other, both of them soaking wet, their clothes clinging to their bodies and dripping water on the floor.

"I'm sorry we dripped all over your house!" Ellie said to Florence, who was just joining them. She had brought in a stack of towels.

"I'm not a bit worried about this house," Florence said. "But if y'all don't get dry, you'll catch the pneumonia, and then you'll be sicker than poor Remy here." She handed towels to Raphe and Ellie, who began absently drying off as they watched Doc examine Remy.

"Doc, he keeps c-c-complaining about his h-head," Ellie said. "Nothing seems to-to help it." She was shivering uncontrollably.

Raphe wrapped another dry towel around Ellie and put his arms around her, trying to warm her. They looked on as Doc listened to Remy's heart and lungs, then took some pills out of his medical bag and helped Remy swallow them. Doc gave him two spoonfuls of a liquid medicine with water before tucking the covers tightly around him.

"Raphe, could you start a fire for me?" Doc asked him.

Raphe looked down at Ellie, still shivering in his arms. "We'll get you warm soon," he whispered to her before letting go to build a fire.

As he finished, Florence, who had stepped out for a few

minutes, came back into Remy's room. She pointed to Ellie and Raphe. "You two, come with me."

"But, Florence—" Ellie began.

"No buts. You won't be any good to Remy if you're in the hospital. Both of you, follow me." Florence led Raphe and Ellie to two bedrooms at the end of the hallway. "Ellie, you're over there." She pointed to the room in the left corner. "Raphe, that's you on the right. My nephew is about your size, and he left some clothes the last time he stayed in that room. You put those on and hang your wet things by the fire to dry. Ellie, you'll have to make do with my old-lady clothes, but at least they'll keep you from freezing to death while your things dry. You can come back in and see Remy when you're done."

"We c-can't th-thank you enough," Ellie said.

"Merci, Florence," Raphe said.

Ellie was shaking so hard that her muscles hurt. She peeled off her wet clothes and spread them over a rocking chair in front of the fire Florence had built and then put on the long nightgown and thick floral cotton robe spread out on the bed.

She gave herself a couple of minutes to warm her hands over the fire and then opened her bedroom door to find Raphe about to knock on it. Ellie gasped, not just from surprise at seeing him there but also at his attire. Florence had assigned him a pair of khakis and a pink camp shirt.

Ellie shook her head and smiled. "I may never be the same."

They hurried down the hall to Remy's room, where Doc was labeling two vials of blood. Remy had fallen asleep and was sweating.

"I'll get these to the hospital lab in Lafayette first thing in the morning," Doc said, sealing the vials in white boxes, which he carefully labeled.

"Why the blood?" Raphe asked him.

Doc stood up, took off his glasses, and cleaned them with a handkerchief. "I'm just being extra cautious. Some of my other patients also complained of a headache, but none as severe as Remy's." He put his glasses back on. "Occasionally, a virus like this can turn into meningitis—"

"*Meningitis?*" Ellie had heard horror stories of what it could do to children.

"Now, now," Doc said, "it's perfectly treatable when it's viral. The bacterial kind is what you really have to worry about. If Remy has it, I'm ninety percent sure it's connected to this virus going around, so we can manage it, but it *is* more serious. Meningitis would account for his ferocious headache. Then again, that might just be his reaction to the same thing everybody else has, but I want to be sure."

"You must be exhausted, Doc," Ellie said.

He gave her a weary smile. "I knew what I was getting into when I hung out my shingle. It just pains me to see so many sick children in our community. And you two look like you're about to fall over. Remy ought to sleep through the night—what's left of it anyway. We'll leave a lamp burning low so he won't be scared if he wakes up, and let's keep his door open. Y'all leave yours open too, and you'll be able to hear him if he cries. Everybody try to get some rest. Tomorrow might be longer than today. Good night."

"'Night, Doc," Ellie said.

"Bonsoir, Doc," Raphe said.

They went to Remy's bedside and stood there, watching him breathe and listening for sounds of distress, but he was peaceful now. Without taking his eyes off Remy or saying a word, Raphe reached for Ellie's hand, lifted it to his mouth, and kissed it.

TWENTY-THREE

"NONC! I CAN'T WAKE UP, NONC! HELP ME!"

Ellie sat bolt upright in bed. Remy. She grabbed Florence's robe and hurried down the hall just in time to see Raphe rush into his nephew's room, sit down on the edge of the bed, and wrap his arms around the boy.

"It's alright, Remy," Raphe was saying. "You're not dreaming. You're just in a strange place. See? Miss Ellie's here."

Ellie knelt down on the floor next to Raphe so Remy could see them both. "How do you feel, sweetheart?" she asked Remy, who still seemed confused.

"You sure I'm not still dreaming, Nonc?" He rubbed his eyes and looked around. "I dreamed I went home with Miss Ellie, and then you came and we went out on the bayou in a big storm."

Raphe felt Remy's face. "You weren't dreaming, Remy. We just didn't know you were awake because your fever was so high."

Remy looked from Raphe to Ellie. "Where are we?"

"We spent the night at Doc's," Raphe said. "You remember getting sick at school?"

"No, Nonc."

"Well, you did. And Miss Ellie carried you to Doc's office

and then took you home with her. You were very sick when I got there, and we had to bring you here even though it was storming out."

Now Remy's eyes were wide. "You mean I really went on the bayou at night in a big storm?"

Raphe smiled at him. "You did. We all did."

"Miss Ellie too?"

"Miss Ellie too."

Remy stared at her, squinting, as if he were piecing it all together. Suddenly, he pointed at her. "You told me the story of the white alligator!"

"You did?" Raphe said.

"I tried," Ellie said. "But I'm not as good at storytelling as Nonc, am I, Remy?"

"You did fine," he assured her.

"Thank you for that." She reached up and stroked Remy's forehead. "We had to do something to pass the time in that waiting room, didn't we, sweetie?"

"Yes, ma'am."

Doc and Florence came into Remy's room, still in their nightclothes and robes. Ellie and Raphe got out of the way so Doc could examine Remy.

"Still got a touch of fever," Doc said as he read the thermometer. He listened to Remy's heart and lungs with his stethoscope. "There's some congestion. How's your headache, son?"

"Just about gone," Remy said.

"Well, that's a good sign," Doc told Raphe and Ellie, who were standing by the fireplace, anxiously looking on. "But I still think we need to get his blood samples to Lafayette just to be on the safe side."

"You gotta stick me with a needle?" Remy's eyes were wide with alarm.

"I already did that, Remy, while you were sleeping," Doc assured him. He joined Raphe and Ellie at the fireplace. "Let's go downstairs and have some breakfast, and then I'll leave right away."

"Doc, I think I should go," Raphe said. "You been up half the night, and your office is gonna be full today."

"No!" Remy cried from his bed. "Don't leave me, Nonc!"

Raphe sighed and rubbed his forehead. Ellie realized he must have been torn like this a million times, trying to figure out how to be in two places at once.

She went to the child's bedside and sat down. "You know, Remy, we both missed an awful lot in school yesterday. I was going to tell all you boys and girls a story about a Chitimacha Indian chief whose people once lived all along the river. He was such a great warrior that they say even the alligators were afraid of him!"

"*Vrai?*"

"Absolutely," Ellie said. "Tell you what. Let's have some breakfast, and then we'll let Nonc go to Lafayette so Doc can rest up to look after any of our neighbors who get sick like you did. While Nonc's gone, I'll tell you the story of the Indian chief, and then you can tell him all about it when he gets back." She leaned in and whispered so only Remy could hear: "Nonc really needs our help today. Let's do what we can to make this easier for him."

Remy smiled at her and nodded.

"Good, that's settled!" Florence said. "Let's have some breakfast."

ELLIE HELPED FLORENCE wash the breakfast dishes as Raphe told Remy goodbye. He came back downstairs wearing his own clothes, dried by the fire, and thanked Florence again for her hospitality. Ellie walked him to Doc's car, where he laid the small cooler holding Remy's blood samples on the front seat and then turned to her.

"I don't know how to thank you," he said.

"You don't have to thank me. I want to be here for Remy, and—and I want to be here for you."

Raphe stepped closer to her and held one of her hands between his. He started to speak but, seeming unable to find words, bent down and softly kissed her, lingering for only a moment before he released her. Then he got into Doc's car and drove away, leaving Ellie to wonder if what just happened had really happened at all.

TWENTY-FOUR

ELLIE KEPT REPLAYING RAPHE'S GOODBYE, lightly touching her fingers to her lips while she climbed the stairs at Doc's house and went to Remy's room to keep him company. She found him sitting up in bed, frowning at a book in his hands.

"What you got there, Remy?" She stopped to stoke the fire before kicking off her shoes and climbing under the covers with him, the two of them leaning on pillows against the headboard.

"I don't know," he said. "I found it on the table by my bed, but I can't read any of the names in it."

"Let me have a look." She reached for the book and read the cover. "Well, no wonder! This is a book of Greek mythology. Those names are hard for *anybody* to read."

"What's Greek myth . . . myth . . . ?"

"Myth-ol-o-gy." She sounded it out for him. "That's a pretty big word all by itself, isn't it?"

"What's it mean?"

"It's a group of stories that people thousands of years ago told each other to try and explain the world around them. The ancient Greeks lived on an island between the Aegean and the Ionian Seas—far away from Louisiana. They believed in a god of the sun, a god of the wind, a god of the sea—"

"Instead of the one God of everything?"

"Exactly. Instead of the one God of everything. And the stories they told each other to try and explain things like the sun, the wind, and the sea—those got retold over and over again, from one generation to the next, and eventually somebody wrote them all down. That's what this book is about."

Remy looked down at the book and pointed. "What's this name?"

"That's Poseidon."

"And this one?"

"Zeus."

Remy turned a couple of pages and pointed to a picture of a mighty warrior in battle. "What about this one?"

"That's Achilles," Ellie said.

"What did he do?"

"According to their legends, he was a fierce warrior who had one weak spot near the heel of his foot. When wise men began studying the human body and naming its parts, they named that part of the foot the Achilles tendon. We still call it that."

"*I've* got one?"

"Sure do. See?" Ellie pulled the covers back enough to show it to Remy on his own foot. "How about that? There's a very important part of your foot that's named after a make-believe warrior from a story that's been told for thousands of years. A story's a powerful thing, *non?*"

Remy grinned at her, rubbing his nose as he thought it over. "I think the Indian chiefs are more interesting."

"Well, that's because they were real, and they lived right where you do. It's always interesting to hear stories about the people who came before us and lived in places we've been—places we've seen for ourselves, like the Teche or the Atchafalaya. Want me to tell you about the chief?"

Remy nodded and smiled.

Ellie checked her watch and felt his face, which was a little warm but nothing like the night before. "Tell you what. Let's take your medicine and get you all snuggled in, and I'll tell you the whole story."

A WRECK ON THE HIGHWAY had made the trip to Lafayette long and tedious. Raphe returned to Doc's house late in the afternoon, road weary and ready to get home. The air was chilly, the sky gray. Inside the house, he climbed the stairs to Remy's room, wondering if his nephew would be able to travel the short journey back to their bayou cabin—and if the weather would hold off long enough for them to get there.

In the doorway to Remy's room, Raphe stopped and stared silently at the bed. Juliet and Remy were both asleep. His head was on her shoulder, his face pressed against her neck. Her arms were on top of the bedspread, one hand against Remy's back, the other against his hair, as if she had fallen asleep stroking it, with no thought to whether holding him might make her sick. They both looked so peaceful.

The scene stirred long-suppressed memories of a mother's touch, of comforting arms wrapped around him in a storm, of childhood hurts "kissed well," of rosary beads drawn through loving hands and prayers softly spoken in French. Looking at Remy and Juliet, Raphe suddenly envisioned a child who had been wandering, lost and alone in the bayou, finally seeing the lights of home. And he had to wonder: Was Remy lost or was he?

TWENTY-FIVE

IT WAS THE END OF ELLIE'S FIRST DAY BACK with her students after she'd closed the school for two weeks on Doc's recommendation.

"Are you comin' to the dance hall on Saturday night, Miss Ellie?" Remy asked as he fell into step with her. As it turned out, he didn't have meningitis, thank goodness, though he had still been very sick when Raphe took him home from Doc's.

"Well, I'll try to, Remy," Ellie said. They were walking with the Toussaints and a group of students, headed for the landing.

"I'm comin' with Aunt Kitty," Remy said. "I have to stay with her for a while."

"Really? Why?"

"Nonc had to go to Morgan City to work on a whole bunch o' boats. He says I'm his business partner, 'cause he couldn't work on boats if I wouldn't stay with Aunt Kitty. He says I'm really helpin' him out."

"That's very grown-up of you, Remy. I'm sure Nonc appreciates your help."

Remy ran ahead to catch up with his cousins. Ellie had to

admit that her heart sank. She had seen Raphe only briefly when he returned from Lafayette and took her home. There was no time to talk, with a sick little boy in the boat needing the warmth of his bed. For the past two weeks she had been expecting to see Raphe any day, any minute. But he had left without saying goodbye.

Now here she was with someone she had known only a short time occupying all of her thoughts, while back home was another, one she had dated for months and promised to marry, who never crossed her mind. How was that possible? Ellie knew the answer even as she asked the question: She loved one man, not the other, and time had nothing to do with it.

RAPHE WAS SO TIRED HE COULD BARELY MOVE. For two weeks, he had repaired one boat after another, helping a big shrimping operation get repairs done for the next season. He had worked twelve-hour days without stopping for weekends ever since he got to Morgan City, and he still had one more boat to go. All he wanted was to go home.

As much as he'd tried to fight it, all he really wanted was Juliet. It wasn't fair. Being with him would mean a life spent in the bayou, sharing her gifts with one little community, when she had so much to offer and so many prospects. She could go anywhere, do anything—and she deserved that. He should leave her alone. But he knew he couldn't.

TWENTY-SIX

ELLIE HAD RISEN EARLY, EATEN HER breakfast, and put on her brother's overalls. She was sitting on the dock, sipping her second cup of coffee and watching a roseate spoonbill perched on the bank, when the bird suddenly took flight, its bright pink feathers electrified against the blue sky. Over the flapping of its wings, she heard the noise of a boat motor. Within a few minutes, the *Whirlygig* came chugging into the slough.

She stood up and waved as the boat approached the dock. "Captain Thornberry, I presume?"

"*C'est moi!*" Heywood shouted back over the engine noise. He tied up his boat, climbed the ladder onto the dock, bent down on one knee, and kissed Ellie's hand. "Your humble servant."

"Oh, get up and shut up," Ellie said.

Heywood laughed and hugged her, then stepped back and looked her up and down. "You really do like men's clothes, don't you?"

"What can I tell you? The cotillion got canceled."

"It suits you," Heywood said. "But you have to go change because we're goin' to New Orleans for lunch—in your car, if that's okay."

197

"I can't go to New Orleans for lunch!"

"Why not? It's Saturday—no school."

"Well, because normal people don't do that."

"No, but *we* do. C'mon, Ellie. Let's go to New Orleans and have ourselves a lunch befitting our social station."

Ellie had to laugh. "Did you just rob a bank or something, Heywood?"

He shook his head sadly. "Why must you always attribute my activities to nefarious pursuits?"

"Alright, alright, I'll go! Come on up while I change my clothes. How's Claudette?"

HEYWOOD TOOK ELLIE TO LUNCH at Ollie B's, where they visited with Miss Ollie, and Ellie again watched him slip her some money. Then they set about roaming the French Quarter, Heywood's camera in hand. It was a new one, he said, a Kodak developed for combat photographers during the war.

Ellie was fascinated by the things that caught his eye, things she might never have noticed. On Royal Street, she would've taken pictures of a passing carriage or maybe a street vendor, but Heywood looked past all of that, through open double doors of an old brick building across the street, and took a picture of a woman—an artist—sitting on a stool before an easel. She was working on a painting, her long, flowing red hair lit by sunlight streaming in from tall windows. It was an absolutely perfect New Orleans moment, but without Heywood, Ellie would've missed it. There were so many distractions swirling around the woman and her painting. How had he found her?

Ellie watched as he captured light and shadows against the

cracked stucco and centuries-old brick, then photographed the elegantly scrolled wrought-iron and courtyard gates. She saw him aim his camera at the chipped paint and brass knob of an old door, bypassing the flowers growing right beside it, and knew full well that once the film was developed and an image appeared, Heywood's choice would prove to be the right one.

Along the way, they stopped for chicory coffee and beignets, indulging in pecan pralines from the French Market. Eventually they made their way to a park bench overlooking the Mississippi River, sipping lemonade Heywood bought on the street.

"This has been the best day," Ellie said with a smile.

He took a sip of his lemonade. "I was afraid you'd think I brought you here on false pretenses."

"Why? Because you needed a ride to New Orleans, so you invited me to lunch to get the keys to my car?"

"It sounds so calculated when you put it that way."

Ellie laughed and dabbed her forehead with her cold cup. "Tell you what, Heywood, if it means I get to ramble around New Orleans with you all day, you can consider Mabel at your disposal."

"I'll keep that in mind."

They were silent—a rarity when they were together—as they watched a tugboat push a barge upriver.

"Heywood," Ellie finally said, "how do you know? What to take pictures of, I mean?"

He held his camera up and pointed it at Ellie. "There. I just look for beauty and fire away."

"I'm serious," she said.

"So am I."

"The woman sitting at that easel on Royal Street—she wasn't a pageant-girl beauty, but . . ."

"But there was beauty *in* her. And that made *her* beautiful."

"Yes. You're absolutely right. But how did you see it when I would've walked right by?"

Heywood thought it over. "Part of it's just light and shadow—when you see 'em come together in an interesting way. But then part of it has to do with what's inside a person—something they sort of give off. I can sense it, and the camera can see it. You have it, by the way, Miss Fields. So does Raphe."

"You take pictures of Raphe?"

"Don't you dare tell him. He'd hate it. But I manage to capture a few shots of him now and then when he's focused on something else, like his fishing line or his fiddle. He has to be really distracted, though. Never saw anybody as annoyingly alert as he is." Heywood stood up and looked at the angle of the sun, which was casting the golden light of late afternoon on the river and on Ellie. "Hey, do me a favor, Miss Fields. Close your eyes and turn your face toward the sky." He propped one foot on the edge of the bench and brought the camera in closer.

Ellie gave a dismissive wave of her hand. "I'd feel silly, Heywood."

"C'mon—just one time? Close your eyes and tilt your head back a little."

Ellie sighed but gave in. She could feel the warmth of the sun on her face and the river breeze in her hair.

"Now," Heywood instructed, "think of the single most amazing moment in your life."

Immediately Ellie had a vision of the white alligator, of the three of them together, of Raphe's arms around her and his face against her hair. She heard the click of the shutter button. Opening her eyes, she turned to Heywood, expecting him to be laughing at her for being persuaded to do something so foolish in broad daylight. But he wasn't laughing. He was looking at her with—what was the word—adoration? How strange to think she could spark such a thing in someone like Heywood.

"Thank you, Ellie," he said. "That's one I won't soon forget."

"Now it's my turn. Let me take your picture."

He grinned at her, clearly trying to bring some levity into a weighty moment that had taken them both by surprise. "Sure you won't break my camera?"

"I'm a professional, remember?" Directing him to sit on the end of the park bench and look out at the river, she photographed him in profile, his Panama hat shading his face.

He smiled at her when the shutter clicked. "No turning back now, Miss Fields."

Had she captured his handsome features and tender expression? Would the viewer see, in Heywood's gaze, the love of a time and place he feared were slipping away from him? It seemed intrusive to capture such a thing, yet tragic not to.

"Wouldn't dream of it," she said, watching him take off his hat and fan his face with it. "Heywood—you really are gonna be okay."

"Promise?"

"Promise. I feel it in my bones. It's a terrible thing that happened to all those cousins of yours. But it doesn't have to happen to you. Ever heard of a self-fulfilling prophecy?"

He raised his eyebrows. "Did somebody take psychology in college?"

"Got an A. I'm practically a doctor."

"Practically." He leaned over and kissed her on the cheek. "You are my very dear Miss Ellie Fields. And I feel a little better about the world, knowing that you're in it, worrying about me. I give you my word I will not self-fulfill a dadgum thing."

Ellie gave his hand an affectionate squeeze. "I appreciate that. Now I can sleep at night."

They sat together, watching the sun sink low over the Mississippi.

"I saw him, you know." Heywood kept his eyes on the water.

"Who?"

"My boy Raphe."

Ellie turned to face him. "When?"

"Couple o' nights ago."

"In Bernadette?"

"No, in Morgan City."

"Oh." She felt an unexpected, unwanted stinging in her eyes and fixed them on a barge slowly gliding upriver, a tugboat pushing it along.

Heywood put his arm around her. "You can't fool me, Miss Ellie Fields. Not one bit."

She looked up at him and stopped fighting the tears. He held her tight and let her cry on his shoulder.

"Some people," he said, "have a very hard time admitting how badly they want something. I know at least two of them."

Once her tears subsided, she took the handkerchief he offered her and blotted her face. "He didn't even say goodbye, Heywood."

"For which he should be shot. I've told him as much."

Ellie smiled even as she dabbed at her eyes. "Will you personally see to the execution?"

"Already on my calendar. 'Have lunch with Ellie. Shoot Raphe. P.S. Use a really big gun. Scoundrel's got it coming.'"

Ellie laughed in spite of herself. "I appreciate your attention to detail. You really think he's a scoundrel?"

"Of course not. And neither do you."

She sat up and looked out at the Mississippi. "It's never still, is it? One boat passes out of view and a different one comes in to fill the space. It's always changing."

"True, but it's also constant—strong river currents flowing in their ordained direction to the Gulf of Mexico."

Ellie brushed her hair back from her face and tilted her head. "Are we boats or rivers, do you think?"

"Hmm. Good question." Heywood rested his chin in his hand as he thought it over, then turned to her. "I am most assuredly a boat. Raphe is a river if ever there was one. And you, Miss Ellie Fields—you have touches of both."

"Leave it to me to land in between," she said with a sigh.

"I didn't say you weren't either. I said you were both."

"Is there a difference?"

"Most definitely."

They watched the muddy water swirl as one boat after another passed by.

"I guess we'd better start back?" Ellie finally said.

"I suppose." Heywood stood up and offered her his hand. "May I escort you to your limo, which some would describe—most uncharitably, I think—as a jalopy?"

"They're just jealous of my refined tastes in classic automobiles." She took his hand, and they began walking along the river.

"Tell me something, Ellie. Do you ever long for New Orleans when you're tucked away in your bayou cabin?"

She thought it over. "No. Not really. I love New Orleans, but in the way you love that eccentric aunt who comes to visit at Christmastime—the one with the big jewelry and a little too much Shalimar. She's fascinating for a couple of days, but who could live with that much drama on a regular basis?"

"How about that," he said, swatting at a mosquito as they strolled through the fading light of early evening. "You couldn't live with her, and I don't think I could live without her."

Ellie stopped walking and turned to him. "We've always known that, haven't we?"

He smiled down at her. "I guess we have, Miss Ellie Fields. I guess we have."

TWENTY-SEVEN

A WEEK LATER, Ellie was on her way to Bernadette's beauty parlor, run by Leta LeJeune and open only on Saturdays from five in the morning till five in the afternoon. The Toussaint sisters had advised her to get there early because every woman in town would eventually show up, and Leta didn't take appointments. Also, she "put her last head in the bowl" at three because she had to get to the dance like everybody else, Gabby had explained. You had to bring your own curlers and bobby pins so you could go home with your hair set. Leta didn't have time to comb anybody out, but she would give you strict instructions on how to do it yourself.

It was around seven when Ellie tied up at the landing and walked downtown to a small brick building with "Beauty" painted in big pink swirly letters on the picture window. Four women with curlers peeking out from under head scarves were standing around a piece of plywood on two sawhorses, set up in the middle of the street, drinking steaming cups of coffee from a pot in the center of the table. There was no traffic in Bernadette, especially this early on a Saturday, and anybody who might come along could just drive around. Clearly, Saturdays at the beauty parlor weren't just about hair. This was woman time.

"Morning, Miss Ellie!" they called to her as she started for the door of the beauty parlor.

Ellie smiled and waved to them but then stopped, turned, and walked toward the coffee table. "Ladies," she said, propping her hands on her hips, "every time y'all call me *Miss* Ellie, you make me feel like my grandma. You think I could just be Ellie?"

The women looked at each other, and then one of them— Marceline Ardoin's mother—raised her coffee cup. "To Ellie!" she said. The others followed suit.

"Thank you, ladies!" Ellie laughed. "Y'all save me some coffee. I'd better go get in line."

The minute she opened the front door, a tidal wave of conversation hit her in the face. The beauty shop was full, and the women of Bernadette had a lot on their minds.

Gabby had schooled Ellie in beauty shop protocol. She took a seat and waited for Leta to wave her to the shampoo bowl, where she handed the beautician her money and a sack that held her curlers, comb, and pins.

Leta put her hands on Ellie's shoulders and held her at arm's length, studying her face and her hair. "You got a *fine* head o' hair, girl." She turned to the other women. "Ain't she got some fine hair, y'all?"

"That's fo' sure."

"Look at the color. Got them pretty gold streaks in the brown."

"That's some good hair on that girl."

"You don't need much, but you need a little," Leta said.

"You sit down there and lemme shampoo you—get my hands in that hair and see what we got."

As Leta shampooed her hair, Ellie tuned in to the conversation in the beauty shop.

"Y'all not gon' b'lieve what that man o' mine come at me with last night."

"Tell it, girl."

"He says, 'Aw, dahlin', you makin' the best syrup cake they is. You oughta cook up a bunch and we sell 'em at Chalmette's!' I look at him and I says, 'Clyde Toups, I'm keepin' y' house an' cookin' y' meals an' raisin' y' seven boys—when you think I got time to sell syrup cake? Ain't a woman on this bayou can't make one!' An' he says, 'Aw, my Marie, I just so proud o' y' cookin', y' can't blame me for wantin' to show you off!' Men! Can't live with 'em, can't feed 'em to the alligators."

Ellie smiled, listening to all the women laugh at the lovable foibles of husbands as Leta lathered her hair for a second time.

"How long you and Clyde been married, Marie?"

"Goin' on twenty-five years now."

"You still think he's handsome?"

"Girl, I still think he's the purtiest man I ever seen!"

Again the women laughed as Leta wrapped a towel around Ellie's hair and raised her up.

"It's somethin', ain't it?" Marie smiled as she opened her purse and pulled out a stick of gum. "You do all that courtin' when you're young, an' then all of a sudden outta nowhere, one o' them boys just gets under your skin." She unwrapped the gum and popped it into her mouth. "When that happens? Girl, you done for."

Ellie watched as Leta made the first snips with her scissors.

"You best watch out, Miss Ellie!" Marie called. "One of these bayou boys might hook you in the heart before you know it!"

Ellie laughed with the other women. "I'll be on the lookout. And I'll tell y'all what I told the ladies outside—if you don't quit callin' me 'Miss' and making me feel like my grandma, I'm gonna keep every one o' you after school."

"Alright, Ellie," Marie said. "We gon' mind her, ain't we, girls?"

The women laughed together and agreed.

Ellie watched as small, wet clumps of her hair fell to the floor. Leta was cutting it shorter than she had ever worn it—just below her chin. Ordinarily it made Ellie anxious to have her hair cut, but today she felt oddly excited and eager. It was as if, with every snip of her scissors, Leta was releasing the weight of tired old expectations, the leaden burden of disappointment and frustration she had been carrying for the past few years. This was a fresh start. Ellie smiled into the mirror.

"That's what I like to see!" Leta exclaimed. "A happy woman. Can't no woman be happy till she got the right hair. You got to like who you see in that mirror, girl."

"You're right, Leta," Ellie agreed. "You're absolutely right."

She suddenly remembered what Raphe had said that night on their boat ride from his cabin to hers—that he wasn't happy, but he was home. On this cool morning, Ellie knew exactly what he meant. She might not be happy, but she had found her home. Maybe happiness would follow her to it.

TWENTY-EIGHT

STANDING BEFORE THE MIRROR at her washstand, Ellie removed all the curlers and pins. As Leta had predicted, she looked like Shirley Temple at first: "You got the natural wave, so don't you be scared when you see them ringlets after you take out the curlers. Just keep a-brushin' back like I showed you, an' you gon' be amazed. You gon' look like one o' them women in the picture show."

Ellie had never had a haircut like Leta's, with some shorter layers on top of longer ones. As she vigorously brushed through the curls, her hair did indeed look a little glamorous, with a side part and long bangs that swept over her eye. She first smoothed the curls and turned them under, then tousled them with her fingers like Leta showed her. Leta had freed her hair—and freed Ellie at the same time. Mama Jean would approve.

Though she had no desire to go to the dance hall tonight, she knew Leta—who had made her promise to wear something pretty to show off her new hair—would be disappointed if she didn't come. She would put in an appearance, stay for an hour or so to please Leta, and then come home, where she would build a warm fire, put on her nightgown and Mama Jean's shawl, and sip a cup of muscadine wine. And she would try very hard not to think about the reason she cared nothing about dancing tonight.

TRUE TO HER PLAN, Ellie was back from the dance hall by seven thirty. She had arrived early so she could visit with everyone before the music started. She accepted a couple of invitations to two-step and then, once the dance floor was filled with couples, slipped out. Her heart wasn't in it, but she was glad she went. Leta was thrilled with her hair and proud to show it off to the other women.

Ellie tied up at the dock, lit the porch lamp, and went inside, lighting a couple of other lamps as she made her way to the back bedroom, where she got undressed. But instead of her nightgown, she reached in her wardrobe for her brother's overalls and one of his old cotton tanks. She might not feel like dancing, but she wasn't yet ready to give up the night.

Grabbing some wood from one of the bins by the fireplace, she laid a fire but didn't light it just yet. She poured herself a cup of Florence's wine, grabbed Mama Jean's plaid woolen wrap and a kerosene lamp, and walked down to the bench at the end of the dock.

The night was crisp but not too cool to enjoy. Ellie set the lamp down beside the bench, where it made a soft glow around her. Then she wrapped up in the shawl, took a sip of wine, and listened to the nocturnal sounds of the bayou, an unruly choir of crickets chirping and frogs calling, now and again interrupted by a hooting owl—their conductor, making a futile attempt to bring the singers into harmony. She could hear water lapping against the dock below.

Pulling the shawl a little more tightly around her, she thought about Mama Jean, who was due a letter. Ellie would write one tonight or maybe tomorrow after Mass. The nearest Baptist church was twenty minutes away, and while Ellie knew she would miss the familiarity of services there, the thought of worshiping with strangers so far from home made her feel lonely. She'd rather attend Catholic Mass with her neighbors than go to the Baptist church by herself. She had been to Mama Jean's church enough not to embarrass herself.

Ellie had closed her eyes, breathing in the night, when she heard a sound off in the distance—a boat motor. It was unusual this time of the evening, though not unheard of on Saturdays, when even the elder Cajuns were at the dance hall and no one went to bed early. She opened her eyes as the tip of the boat came into view and then, to her surprise, headed into the slough. In fact, it was coming right toward her dock. Ellie squinted into the darkness to make out the shadow sitting in back to steer the boat. The closer it got, the more familiar the shadow became.

Ellie stood up, her gaze following the path of the boat until it was only a few yards away. She knew she should say something or at least wave, but all she could do was stare, her lips parted, searching for words.

At last Raphe arrived at the dock, where he tied up the boat and stood there, unsmiling. If she didn't know better, she would say he looked fearful, his brow slightly furrowed, his hands at his sides.

"Bonsoir," he said, looking up at Ellie.

"Bonsoir," she answered, her voice a little breathier than she would've liked.

He nodded toward the dock. "Can I sit with you?"

"Of course."

He climbed out of the boat and scaled the ladder, standing just inches from Ellie. She could see tired lines around his eyes and a bandage covering one hand. His hair had grown longer while he was away. It was touching the collar of his white shirt, which was unbuttoned at the neck, with the sleeves rolled up. His clothes were wrinkled, as if he had traveled in them.

"Heywood said you'd be angry with me," he said, staring intently at her. "He came to visit me in Morgan City and took me to supper."

"He told me he saw you." Ellie was finding it difficult to formulate a thought with Raphe standing close enough to touch.

"He said it was wrong of me to leave Bernadette without telling you," Raphe went on. "But I had to. I didn't want to see you."

"Oh." Ellie took a step back. She felt a little sick.

"That came out wrong." He closed the distance between them. "What I meant was, I was afraid that if I saw you, I wouldn't be able to leave."

"Oh?" Ellie felt like an idiot. *Oh, oh, oh, oh* . . . Why couldn't she form words right now? She heard something jump in the water, but it didn't matter. Nothing mattered. She couldn't take her eyes off Raphe.

"I don't think I could stand it if you went back to Alabama," he said.

"I'm not going back to Alabama."

"How can you be sure?"

"Because you're in Louisiana."

His eyes traveled from her face to her hair. "You changed it," he said, reaching out and running a strand of it through his fingers.

Ellie nodded, her eyes on the white bandage as he let his hand fall to his side. "You hurt your hand."

"It's very pretty," he said, ignoring his injury and looking at her hair the way you would admire an especially fine seashell on the shore.

"Do they hurt?" Ellie was too concerned about his hands— one wrapped in white cloth, the other covered with small nicks and cuts—to think about her hair.

"I believe you have released Juliet," he said with a smile.

"Do they hurt," she repeated, gently lifting his hands, studying the bandage and abrasions.

He laid his palms against her face. "Not so much. Not now."

"I missed you," she whispered.

For a fleeting second, Ellie had a vision of the photograph Heywood would take right now: a Cajun fisherman passionately embracing a schoolteacher in overalls, lit by lamplight on a dock in the bayou. But then Raphe's wounded hands were in her hair and his breath was on her face, and Ellie stopped thinking anything at all.

TWENTY-NINE

FROM THE BIG SOFA IN DOC'S CABIN, Ellie watched a crackling fire as Raphe lay with his head in her lap. She was slowly running her fingers through his hair with one hand and resting the other on his chest. They had finally brought themselves to part long enough for her to warm up leftover chicken and dumplings, feed him supper, and make him lie down to rest.

"Have you always gone away to work?" she asked him.

"Not always." Raphe covered her idle hand with his. "When I was a boy, nobody had to leave the bayou to work. But the storm tore up all the boats. Wrecked the small docks. Everybody had to start over from nothing—started taking jobs outside. I was lucky that Papa taught me a trade so I could go to work for the big boats as soon as they were back up."

"What's it like down there—in Morgan City, I mean?"

"Lonesome. And dirty. Not the town but the docks. When I'm home, everywhere I look, I see something beautiful—the cypress trees, the water, the birds . . . the schoolteacher."

Ellie smiled, leaned down, and kissed him.

"But down there," he continued, "it's all machinery and noise on the boats. Can't smell nothing but fuel and fish."

"Do you have to go back?" Ellie could see his eyes getting heavy as she kept stroking his hair.

"I should. There's another shrimp company wantin' its boats tuned up before spring. Lot o' work. Lot o' money."

"There are more important things than money."

"Yes," he said, lifting her hand and kissing her palm. "Much more important things."

"If you could do anything in the world to make a living—along with fishing, of course—what would it be?"

He smiled up at her. "Cook. I'd spend my days fishing and stirring the gumbo pot. And I'd spend all my nights with you."

Raphe closed his eyes. Ellie stopped talking but kept running her fingers through his hair. She watched the easy rise and fall of his chest beneath her hand as she listened to the crackling fire and his deep, relaxed breathing. Ellie heard in those rhythms—for the first time in her life—the sound of pure contentment, flowing over her like creek water on smooth rocks. And she knew without a doubt that she could listen to it forever.

THIRTY

ELLIE AWOKE TO QUIET. Her bedroom was chilly. She freshened up and tied a long, warm robe over her nightgown. Quietly cracking the door to her room, she peeked outside. The pillow she had carefully slipped under Raphe's head was still on the sofa. So was the quilt she had covered him with. His shoes lay on the floor where she had slipped them off, but he wasn't there. Her heart did a momentary dip before she looked out one of the tall front windows and saw him standing on the front porch, taking a sip of coffee.

Raphe turned and smiled when she joined him. Without saying anything, he kissed her, then put his arm around her and handed her a cup of coffee with sugar and milk. How did he know how she liked it?

They stood together, listening to the bayou wake up.

After a long time, Raphe said, "You never told me which you feel—Ellie or Juliet."

Ellie took a sip of her coffee and rested her head on his shoulder. "I don't mind being everybody else's Ellie. But I believe I am your Juliet."

"In that case, Juliet," he said, "I think the next time we fall asleep under the same roof, we should do it as husband and wife. *Es-tu d'accord?*"

She didn't hesitate. "*Oui, je d'accord.* I've never d'accorded with anything so much in my life."

ON A BRIGHT DECEMBER AFTERNOON, with her family summoned from Alabama, Ellie married Raphe in the Bernadette dance hall. Mama Jean declared the groom "practically Scottish." Heywood said it was the happiest wedding he had ever photographed. Claudette couldn't make it.

THIRTY-ONE

Spring 1950

"HERE'S YOUR MORNING MAIL, SENATOR." Lura Poteet
fanned the envelopes vertically along the edge of Big Roy's
desk at the statehouse. "Not much worth reading today, but
you might want to take a look at these."

"Thank you, Lura," he said as she quickly and quietly
made her way to the door the way she always did. It was
one of many things Big Roy admired about her: Lura did
what needed to be done and then left him in peace. Pity he
couldn't say the same about his latest wife.

"Say, hold up for a minute, Lura," he said. "I need to ask
your advice on something."

She immediately returned and took a seat in one of the
guest chairs across from his desk. "Yes, Senator?"

"I thought I had a plan for that bunch o' Cajuns on the
bayou, but it's not working. That crazy preacher I bank-
rolled was supposed to distract 'em with his alligator hunt,
but none o' the locals went after the money, and they just
ignored all the outsiders that came down there—waited 'em
out till they gave up. I was hopin' to kick up a little skirmish
between the Cajuns and the other hunters, but I reckon that

218

bayou bunch knew nobody from the outside would ever find a needle in a haystack like that white gator—which prob'ly don't even exist. What you reckon I oughta do?"

Lura adjusted her glasses and cleared her throat. "It would seem to me, Senator, that all Brother Lester succeeded in doing with his alligator hunt was to give the Cajuns a common enemy. He pulled them closer together, when what you want is division. I would suggest removing him from the picture, upping the ante considerably on that alligator—say, $20,000—and making the hunt open to local residents only. White trash would hunt their own mama for that kind of money."

"That's a *lot* of money, Lura."

She smiled and nodded. "Yes, Senator, it is—which is why no one but you will collect it. I'll find out who the best hunters are down there, and your mad dog Luetrell can tail them, do what needs to be done to make sure that once they find the alligator—if *anybody* finds it—he'll collect the reward and return it to you for whatever fee you deem appropriate."

A smile broke across Big Roy's face as he leaned back in his chair and lit a cigar. "Why I ever listen to anybody but you is a mystery even to me, Lura. I thank you. Just take this mail back with you and do whatever you see fit. You can sign my name well as I can. And when you get back to your desk, pop open the safe and grab yourself a fistful. Just put it on my expense report under 'Miscellaneous.'"

THIRTY-TWO

"HEY, FOOTSIE."

"Hey, Remy."

"You catchin' anything?" Remy sat down on the cool ground underneath an oak tree where Footsie Taylor was fishing with a cane pole and cast his own line a few feet to the right of his friend's cork, which was bobbing along in the water.

"Ain't caught *nothin'*," Footsie said, shaking his head. "Sho' is a purty mornin', though. Reckon I could find me some worser things to do than chase after fish on a day like today."

Footsie was the youngest of ten children in a Creole family who lived a few miles down the bayou from Bernadette. His father worked the cane fields during the harvest, and he caught crawfish to sell at Chalmette's the rest of the year. He often played guitar at the dance hall on Saturday nights, with Footsie and Remy skipping rocks on the creek out back while the adults danced inside.

All of Footsie's clothes were hand-me-downs and a little too big for him. The straps of his overalls were forever slipping off his shoulders, and he had to roll the pants way up so he wouldn't trip over them. He also had rolls of cotton fabric around both arms, where he had turned up the too-long sleeves of his shirt. Footsie never wore shoes. That's how he got his nickname. His wide-brimmed straw hat—his fishing hat—was frayed around the edges, but he had a nicer one—his "go-to-town hat"—that he saved for special occasions.

"You sure are lucky, Footsie, you know that?" Remy said, scratching his jaw.

"You outside yo' mind, Remy?" Footsie tugged his line to the left a foot or two. "I'm po', I'm colored, I got no schoolin', an' I ain't never put on nothin' that wasn't wo' out when I got it. What you think lucky 'bout that?"

"I'm sorry," Remy said. Footsie kept staring out at the water. Remy put a hand on his friend's shoulder. "Really, Footsie. I mean it. To me, we're the same. But I reckon we ain't. And I'm real sorry I forget that sometimes."

Footsie shrugged and smiled at him. "I know you don't mean nothin' by it."

"That don't make it right. I just meant that you know where you belong. You got a mama and a papa and a bunch o' brothers and sisters. Ain't no doubt where you belong."

"You got folks, Remy."

"Not like you," Remy argued.

"That schoolteacher mean to you at home?"

Remy shook his head. "No. She's real nice. Always wants to know what I'd like for supper and if I'm worried about anything."

"What 'bout yo' Uncle Raphe? Don't he want you no mo'?"

Remy frowned as he watched his cork go under but then pop right back up. "He ain't changed at all. We still do all the things we used to do together. But I don't see how that's gonna last. Won't they have kids like Aunt Kitty and Uncle Nick?"

"If they was colored, I'd say yeah, but you can't never tell *what* white folks gon' do."

"I reckon I just gotta own up to it, Footsie. I ain't nobody's kid and I ain't never gonna be."

RAPHE CAME HOME LATE IN THE AFTERNOON and found his house empty. He could smell jambalaya in a covered cast-iron pot on the stove. Remy was likely playing with Footsie. But if his wife wasn't here to greet him when she knew he'd be coming in from a long day on the river, that meant she had a problem she wasn't ready to tell him about and had sought Tante Dodo's counsel. She was homesick for her mother and her Mama Jean, which happened only when she was very upset about something. He quickly washed up and changed his clothes, leaving the dirty ones outside in the washtub. Then he sat in the porch swing and waited.

Eventually he saw Juliet paddling his grandfather's pirogue into the slough. She looked startled to see him when he walked down to the bank to greet her.

"I thought you wouldn't be home till later," she said.

He smiled and pointed to the sun dipping low in the sky. "It's later."

She shook her head as if she could shake her troubles out of it. "I'm sorry. I'll get supper on the table." She tried to hurry past him, but he put an arm out, caught her around the waist, and gently pulled her against him.

He held her as he felt her relax into his shoulder, first sniffling and then sobbing against his shirt. Raphe patiently waited for her to cry until she didn't want to anymore, then wiped her tears with his fingertips, took her by the hand, and led her to one of their favorite spots on the bank, a sandy clearing beneath a tall, shady cottonwood. Raphe would always sit against the tree. Juliet would sit between his legs and rest her back against his chest. He would put his arms around her, and they would make any big decisions they needed to make.

Late this afternoon, his wife didn't so much rest against him as collapse into him. "Tell me why you cry, Juliet."

She took a long, deep breath. "I'm such a failure, Raphe."

"That's a pretty big thing to say." He twirled a strand of her hair through his fingers. "What makes you think so?"

"Remy."

"Did he give you trouble today?"

"No. Remy never misbehaves. It's just—I can't seem to get through to him. It's my job to get through to children, Raphe. I do it all day, every day. I get through to the children of people I barely know, but I can't reach Remy. I can't make him believe he has a home with us."

"Ah, that." Raphe sighed and nodded, tightening his arms around her.

She turned so she could wrap her arms around his waist and rest her head on his shoulder. "I've been doing everything I could think of—learning to cook his favorite foods, reading to him, spending some time with him when it's just the two of us, making sure I stay out of the way and give him time with you . . . But today—just when I thought we were having a great talk—he looked up at me and said, 'It's okay if you want me to leave when you start having babies.'"

Raphe winced, feeling his wife's pain and his nephew's all at the same time.

"And the thing is, Raphe, he wasn't whining or complaining

the way most kids his age would. It was so matter-of-fact—like he was pretty sure it would happen and he needed to start making arrangements or something. And when I tried to assure him that he was part of our family and this was his home . . . he just smiled and said he'd like to go play with Footsie. He didn't believe me. I at least know enough about kids to know when they're not buying what I'm selling."

He leaned down and kissed her on the forehead. "And what does Tante Dodo advise?"

"She says making a child feel secure, '*ca demande un tas de patience.*'"

"Did she know who she was talking to?" Raphe asked.

At last Juliet laughed. "Are you suggesting I'm no good at things that *demande* a lot of patience?"

"I would not say you are impatient. I would say you are determined."

"And I would say you've been married long enough to become a really great liar. It's a quality I admire, by the way. Sometimes the truth is just too blooming hard to hear."

"In that case, I think your gumbo is delicious."

"Stop it!" She was laughing again.

"Remy has to find his own way, Juliet," Raphe said. "We can try our best. We can give him all the love in the world, but if he can't accept it . . . I've been trying so long. I've done all I can think of."

She raised up and smiled at him. "We'll just have to think a little harder."

THIRTY-THREE

ELLIE WAS LOADING A PICNIC BASKET on her table when she looked out the front window and saw a familiar but long-absent sight: the *Whirlygig* chugging into the slough.

She put her fried chicken—one of Remy's new favorites, she was proud to say—into the basket before hurrying down to the dock. "State your name and state your business!" she shouted over the loud engine.

"Thornberry's the name, picnicking's my game!" Heywood shut off the engine and pitched Ellie ropes from the bow and the stern.

She tied up the *Whirlygig* while he collected a couple of sacks from the boat and climbed up. He set them down on the dock and hugged her.

"Miss Fields—I mean, Mrs. Broussard—you are a sight for sore eyes on this fine spring morning! Where's the mister?"

"Where do you think?"

"On the river."

"Exactly. He and Remy had to make just one quick run before the picnic."

"Good!" Heywood said. "I'm glad he's gone. It'll give us an opportunity to talk about him."

"Want some cold lemonade, New Orleans style?"

Heywood clutched his chest. "Be still, my foolish heart. I would love some." He grabbed the two sacks and followed Ellie into the house. "I come bearing Gambino's."

Ellie leaned over the sacks as he set them on the table and took a deep breath. "Heavenly days, I love that bread. Too bad it's not full o' Miss Ollie's shrimp."

"If I coulda figured out how to keep those delectable crustaceans hot and fresh, I would've procured some."

"Well, I'm not complaining," Ellie said. "I'll take Gambino's any day. Let's sit on the porch where it's cool." She poured them lemonade from the icebox as Heywood pulled off two pieces of bread from one of the French loaves he'd brought.

They carried their bread and lemonade to the porch swing. Ellie took a bite and sighed. "This makes up for any flaws in the entire state of Louisiana."

"Found many?"

Ellie tilted her head sideways as she thought about it. "Aside from the snakes and the mosquitoes, nothing much comes to mind. But then I haven't been through the heat of a Louisiana summer yet. I hear they're dreadful. Right now I'm just glad it finally stopped raining, or we would've had a soggy picnic."

Heywood smiled at her. "I would ask how married life suits you, but I can see it on your lovely face. It suits you quite well. And I'm ashamed to admit it, but I am completely jealous of you and Raphe. Each of you ended up with one of my favorite people on this whole dadgum planet. I am green with envy."

"Heywood Thornberry, you've never been jealous of anybody in your life, and I can tell you why. Want to hear?"

"Do tell."

"Because, deep down, you know you shine a little brighter than the rest of us."

Heywood gasped. "Mrs. Broussard, are you suggesting that you find my boy Raphe dull in comparison to moi?"

"Actually, the mere sight of your boy Raphe makes my heart flip-flop, even when he's hot and sweaty from a day on the river, but he thinks you're way more interesting than he is, just like I think you're way more interesting than I am. Neither one of us could ever keep up with you, Heywood. That's why we're always so glad to see you."

"I am deeply flattered and wholly undeserving."

"By the way, you're staying through your birthday. That's final and nonnegotiable. You can share Remy's loft if you don't want to sleep on your boat."

"You two don't have to babysit me until the ill-fated thirtieth birthday," Heywood said.

"No, we don't. But you're here, and I don't see any reason why you can't share your birthday with us. It won't hurt you to hang around and fish with Raphe for a couple of weeks." Ellie grinned at him. "Claudette's welcome to come."

Heywood clasped his hands together and shook his head sadly. "Alas, she has accompanied her family on a spring trip to Grand Isle. Lest the death knell toll for me."

Ellie smacked him on the back of his head. "Quit spouting that nonsense. You're gonna live long enough to make Methuselah look like a spring chicken."

Heywood was laughing. "Now that's old."

"Oh, look—they're back!" Ellie pointed to the dock where Remy was tying up the bass boat and Raphe was climbing the ladder with their fishing rods.

"Mind your manners, boys, we've got company," Ellie said as Raphe and Remy came onto the porch.

"Mr. Heywood!" Remy exclaimed, giving him a hug and grinning up at him. "Got anything special on the boat?"

"I do indeed, you little mercenary! Go and fetch it from the captain's seat."

Remy took off as Heywood got up to shake Raphe's hand and clap him on the shoulder. "In your absence," Heywood said, "I attempted to steal your bride, but she would have none of it."

"Pretty sure I'm supposed to feed you to the alligators for that," Raphe said.

"Can it wait till after lunch? I'm starving."

"Oui," Raphe said with a shrug. "Remind me to end you after we eat."

"Looks like y'all didn't have much luck on the river," Ellie said as Raphe propped the fishing rods in the corner of the porch.

"I think Remy scared 'em away," Raphe said. "Couldn't stop talking about the picnic. I'll go clean up real quick."

Raphe went inside as Remy came running onto the porch. "Mr. Heywood, it's a beauty!" He was holding a bone-handled pocketknife.

"Come over here and show me you know how to use it right." Heywood sat down in the swing next to Ellie, who was shaking her head at the thought of a boy with a knife.

"Remy, you know you have to be very careful with that," she said.

"Yes, ma'am, I know," he said as he opened the knife the way Raphe had shown him.

"That's good," Heywood said. "Show me how you close it without cutting your hand."

Remy safely closed the knife.

"Outstanding. Now I'll tell you what she's thinking." Heywood nodded toward Ellie. "Never run with it open, never throw it at anybody, and remember it's a tool, not a toy. Got it?"

"Got it!"

"It really is a beautiful knife, Remy," Ellie said. "What do we say?"

"Merci!" he said to Heywood.

"You're more than welcome."

Ellie reached out and combed through Remy's hair with her fingers. "Remy, honey, I filled the pitcher on your washstand. Run upstairs and clean up so we'll be ready to go, okay?"

"Okay, M'Ellie!" He ran up the porch stairs to his loft.

"M'Ellie?" Heywood said.

Ellie glanced up toward the loft and smiled. "It's something he started a few months ago. After we married, I told Remy he didn't have to call me 'Miss Ellie' at home. He tried 'Tante Ellie' for a while, but that never seemed to suit him. I think he's just shortening 'Miss Ellie' to something a little more familiar."

"Or maybe he's shortening Maman Ellie to something a little less familiar till he's sure it would be welcome."

Ellie shook her head and sighed. "I wish."

Heywood gave her a gentle nudge with his elbow. "Is this my rebellious Miss Ellie Fields, the one who would not be corralled, longing to be Maman?"

"Yep," she said with a smile. "I would love to be Maman

to Remy. I'd love for him to feel that secure with me. As for being corralled—Raphe doesn't make me feel hemmed in at all. I guess it's because he wants me to do whatever makes me happy. And what makes me happiest is making Raphe and Remy happy. Heavens to Betsy, I sound like a sap, don't I?"

"Yes, but a highly sophisticated one."

Ellie giggled. "Oh, I am the picture of sophistication with my cast-iron skillet and my pirogue, chalk dust in my hair half the time."

"But you're happy."

"I'm very happy, Heywood. And I want you to be too."

He put his hands up in protest. "Stop! Don't say it! Married women always think everybody else needs to be married."

"Because you do!" Ellie was laughing the way she always did when they were together.

"He does what?" Raphe said as he came onto the porch.

Ellie got out of the swing and put her arms around her husband. "He needs to get married so he can be happy like us!"

Heywood hung his head. "Broussard, what have you done? Ellie was my friend, my confidante. Now she's one of them! The meddlesome married women."

Raphe looked down at Ellie and smiled. "I like meddlesome married women."

"Gabby's gonna be at the picnic," Ellie said.

"I keep telling you, I am betrothed—wait, is Gabby the curvy one with the dark eyes, the curly black hair, and legs clear to Texas?"

"The very same," Ellie said.

"Well, I will of *course* be *polite*," Heywood said.

Ellie rolled her eyes. "You're hopeless."

"Ready to load up?" Raphe asked her.

"Why don't you and Heywood get started, and I'll go shake Remy out of the loft."

Raphe and Heywood started loading the boat with Ellie's picnic basket, blankets, and jugs of tea and lemonade as she climbed the porch stairs into Remy's loft. She found him with his face washed and his clothes changed, frantically searching for something between the two twin beds in his room.

"Uh-oh, what have we lost?" she asked him.

"My new tennis shoes! I can't find 'em anywhere!"

"Well, let's think about this a minute." Ellie sat down on the bed and patted the spot next to her, where Remy took a seat. "I know you had them on when you left this morning, but I believe you were barefoot when you came back. Hold up your foot and let me have a look."

Remy crossed one leg over the other so she could see his sole.

Ellie frowned and shook her head slowly. "That's a mighty dirty foot to have spent much time in a shoe. Did you maybe take your sneakers off in the boat?"

Remy thought for a minute and then smacked his forehead. "I did! I took 'em off in the boat!"

Ellie went to his basin and poured water onto a washcloth. "Here," she said as she handed it to him. "Carry that with you to the dock and see if you can't wipe off at least a layer or two of dirt before you put your new shoes back on, okay?"

"Okay." Remy started down the stairs as Ellie picked up the dirty clothes he'd left on the floor. Then she heard him coming back up.

"Forget something else, honey?"

Remy paused at the door and shook his head. Then he came inside, put his arms around her waist, and hugged her. Before Ellie could say anything, he ran out of his room, down the stairs, and out to the dock. She could hardly breathe as she watched him out the window.

Ellie could never explain how or why it happened, but in that fleeting instant she felt it deep down in her soul: She had just become a mother, as surely as if she had given birth.

THIRTY-FOUR

BOONE STRAHAN PAUSED OUTSIDE THE DOOR to the oak-paneled study. It was open, as usual. His father had no need for privacy in his own home because he controlled everything and everybody in it. His commanding voice came drifting out.

"Here's your money. I don't want you coming anywhere near me or my office once you clear that land."

Another voice, cold and familiar, replied, "You mean when I burn down those cabins."

"You're a real cur dog, Luetrell," Boone's father said. "Lucky you're good at what I need done, or I'd let Lura's bunch put an end to you—which I will absolutely do if you even think about taking my money without holding up your end. That annual picnic in Bernadette will go on way into the night. Perfect time for you to take care o' business so I can buy out those Cajuns before they figure out what they're sittin' on. Hang the placards on the dance hall once they're all in there. The prospect o' that prize money oughta occupy 'em while you get things done, and the fight for it'll occupy 'em after, once they realize how easily their shanties can be taken away. Do what I told you to do in town. Now get outta my house."

Boone heard his father's leather chair slide on the tapestry rug beneath his desk and knew that he had just stood up—the signal for anybody who knew him well to get out and get out fast. Boone hurried upstairs and watched out the front window as Luetrell crossed a carpet of grass to the parking court, where he climbed into his pickup and drove away.

That vicious man was on his way to Bernadette—for all Boone knew to destroy Ellie's house. Few people had ever been as kind to him as she had. Few had taken the time to even get to know him. He was just "Big Roy's boy." He owed it to her and the families she worked so hard for to try to save their homes from Luetrell. Then he would have to find a way to save them from his own father.

THIRTY-FIVE

FOOTSIE TAYLOR WAS WAITING FOR REMY on the bank when Raphe steered his bass boat to the landing. The boy ran to the water's edge and caught a rope Heywood tossed to him, then tied the boat to a tupelo gum as Remy climbed over the bow and jumped out.

"How goes it, Footsie?" Heywood called out.

"Fine, Mr. Heywood!"

"Got something for you. Catch!" Heywood reached into his pocket and tossed a brand-new pocketknife to Footsie, who caught it and stared at it wide-eyed.

"What do we say, Footsie?" Ellie said as she gathered up a couple of quilts. "Your mama would want me to remind you."

"Thank you, Mr. Heywood! Thank you very much!"

"You're mighty welcome!"

"Look, Footsie, yours is just like mine!" Remy exclaimed, pulling his knife out of his pocket. "Let's go down to the creek and carve some sticks. We can be warriors like Achilles!"

"Who in the Sam Hill is that?" Footsie said.

They took off before Ellie could remind them it was almost lunchtime. "Now we'll never see them again," she said to Raphe as he helped her out of the boat.

"Sure we will." He bent down and kissed her. "Soon as they get hungry."

"You two are Mushville!" Heywood picked up two jugs filled with sweet tea and lemonade. "Absolute Mushville!"

"There's no call for jealousy," Ellie said with a grin. "Go ahead, Raphe, give Heywood a kiss too."

Raphe grabbed Ellie's picnic basket and his fiddle case. "I'd sooner kiss ol' Miss Ernie down at the post office."

"Ha! I'll remember that next time I need somebody to help eat my oyster catch," Heywood said as the three of them fell into step and headed for the dance hall.

"What possessed you to get Footsie a knife?" Ellie asked him.

Heywood shrugged. "They play together all the time, and it's no fun sharing one. Where did Remy learn about the illustrious Greeks?"

"From a book at Doc's when he was sick back in the fall," Ellie said. "I can't believe he still remembers. How do you know about the illustrious Greeks?"

"Combat training. Uncle Sam taught us anything and everything to stop a German, from the ankles up."

"And yet you have given two boys knives?"

"They're good boys," Heywood said. "And they're joined at the hip. I figure Footsie doesn't get a whole lotta presents. I just hope his older brothers don't take it away from him. I didn't think about that till now. I had sisters, and even they took my stuff."

"Don't worry," Ellie assured him. "Footsie leaves all his treasures with Remy for safekeeping."

"He does?" Raphe asked her.

"Mm-hmm," she said. "By my calculation, we are currently

boarding three nickels Footsie found under the porch at Chalmette's, a quartz rock, an arrowhead, and soon, I'm sure, a pocketknife. For a couple of days there, he had a bullfrog in a shoebox under Remy's bed, but I persuaded the boys that frogs aren't happy inside."

"They bought that?" Heywood said.

"Well . . . I also gave them each a dime."

"Ah! The truth comes to light!" Heywood grinned. "Child bribery!"

They followed the flow of basket-laden families laughing and talking as they strolled through town and on to the dance hall. The men had set up two long serving tables made of sawhorses and plywood, which were quickly covered with platters of fried chicken, barbecued ribs, and boudin; cast-iron Dutch ovens overflowing with jambalaya, deer chili, and maque choux; a mountain of boiled crawfish and corn on the cob; potato salad, baked beans, and dirty rice; fried peach and apple hand pies, layer cakes, hand-turned ice cream, and crusty French bread. A huge iron pot was simmering chicken and andouille gumbo over a fire behind the tables. Quilts were spread all over the grounds. The women of Bernadette uncovered their dishes as the men loaded them onto the serving tables.

Ordinarily, the Creole families along the bayou had their own house dances. Their musicians played at the dance hall alongside Cajuns all the time, but the only time all the dancers came together was at the annual picnic. Ellie had no idea why. But it was typical of small Southern communities. Things went on as they always had, with nobody ever questioning the reason why.

Over all the chatter and laughter, musicians could be

heard tuning up inside the dance hall. Ellie saw Raphe casting glances toward the open doors of the hall as he lifted all of her dishes out of the picnic basket.

"There!" she said as he finished. "You're all done. Now take your fiddle and get on in there before you explode."

Raphe picked her up and twirled her around. "Save me a dance?"

"You know I will."

He kissed her, grabbed his fiddle case, and headed for the dance hall, stopping at the door to turn and wave to her.

Ellie waved back and smiled as he disappeared into the hall. She helped the women finish arranging the serving tables and then stepped back a little so she could take in the whole scene. This time last year, she was alone and unhappy, trying to decide whether to accept a job in a tiny Louisiana town she had never heard of and searching for the courage to leave her whole life behind. Now Bernadette was her home—and her life. She was happily married to a man she loved more every day, and they had a little boy to raise together. Not only that, but they had a wonderful community of friends and neighbors. Ellie had an overwhelming sense of belonging— the kind she had wished for so long ago, watching Doc escort Florence to the dance hall that first time.

She heard a click and looked up to see Heywood holding his camera.

"Unless I miss my guess, Mrs. Broussard is feeling a tad on the wistful side," he said.

Ellie smiled at him. "You don't miss much, do you?"

"I try hard not to miss the good stuff."

They started making their way to the dance hall, stopping now and then so Heywood could aim his camera and capture a moment: Tante Dodo fanning herself with her bonnet; Doc and Florence holding hands; Minerva Richard bouncing a toddler on her knee, one she had no doubt delivered.

"Yet another reason I love Bernadette," Heywood said as he pressed the shutter button. "In this little burg, food and music trump everything, including all the race nonsense. Folks here don't care if you're black, white, or purple as long as you can sing, dance, play, or cook. Too bad it's not that way all over Louisiana."

"Too bad it's not that way everywhere—especially at the school board," Ellie said. "They'd have a fit if I tried to bring the local colored children into our school."

"What they don't know won't hurt 'em." Heywood snapped a picture of Gabby, who was leaning against a tree and staring straight at him.

"Now that the weather's warming up, I've been finding little tidbits outside the window of the classroom—things like an apple peel or a candy wrapper," Ellie said. "One morning, I put a tablet and some pencils in a box just outside the window and laid a candy wrapper on top. The box was gone by recess. The next day, I found a little white alligator carving in its place. I'll bet you anything Freeman Richard's been sitting outside, trying to learn through the window. Breaks my heart to think about it—a child cruelly deprived of the education he's so hungry for, grasping for scraps from the table. If you ask me, it's no less despicable to deny a child knowledge than to deny him food."

"My guess is that you, Mrs. Broussard, are already scheming your way around the long arm of the law—and the foolishness of the school board."

Ellie smiled. "I might have a few ideas. Let's forget about all that and go listen to Raphe play."

"Absolutely. And while we listen, perhaps you might invite Miss Gabby Toussaint over for a little chitchat?"

AFTER LUNCH, with the whole town inside the dance hall waltzing to "*Plus to Tournes*," Heywood and Gabby slipped down to the creek bank for a little privacy.

"Now, lest I mislead you, Miss Toussaint, I must confess that I am betrothed to a certain Claudette Sonnier—"

"Shut up, Heywood," Gabby said just before she planted a kiss that made him forget all about his alleged betrothal.

When they came up for air, he looked down at her and said, with none of his usual bluster, "Gabby . . . there's something you should know—"

But she silenced him with another kiss. Heywood had his arms around her, holding her close against him, when he heard a hammering sound—muffled by the music coming from the dance hall but still audible.

"You hear that?" he asked her.

"Fo' sure," she said.

They followed the sound to the west side of the dance hall, where they saw a man hammering placards to the wall. He was too busy to notice them. Heywood took one look at him and quickly pulled Gabby back, out of sight around the corner.

"You look like you seen the Rougarou," Gabby said.

"Rougarou don't come close."

THIRTY-SIX

WITH THE MUSICIANS ON A BREAK, all the dancers came out for a late afternoon meal, eager to make another round at the serving tables. But the placards stopped them. Ringing the dance hall, they read them together:

WHITE ALLIGATOR HUNT
$20,000 *Reward*
LOCALS ONLY. NO TEAMS. CONTEST ENDS APRIL 30.
DELIVER GATOR HIDE TO SENATOR ROY STRAHAN, LOUISIANA STATEHOUSE, BATON ROUGE

"They'll never find it, Raphe," Ellie whispered as she watched her husband read the placard. He looked ashen. "Let's go find Heywood."

Just then she and Raphe spotted him, huddled with Gabby and Leo near the entrance to the hall. Leo climbed onto one of the picnic tables and stood on top of it, calling out for the crowd to gather around. It took a few minutes over all the chatter, but the families of Bernadette eventually circled the picnic table and grew quiet.

"Y'all come on over here and listen to what Heywood's got to say," Leo said loudly.

Ellie stood in front of Raphe, his arms wrapped around her waist, as they waited for Heywood to speak. He was climbing onto the picnic table with Leo as Gabby looked on from below.

"Y'all know I'm generally full o'—well, full of it," Heywood began. The crowd laughed. "But right now, I'm as serious as I know how to be. Gabby and me, we saw the man hanging those placards. And I know him—from the oil fields. His name's Gig Luetrell, and he's about the meanest excuse for a human being I've ever met. There truly is nothing he wouldn't do for a dollar, or for spite, or if he just happens to be bored. I know that placard says there's a whole lotta money up for grabs—money that'd help whoever wins it do all kinda things for your family. But believe me when I tell you—if that man's involved, no good'll come of it. And if he has anything to do with it, you'll never see a dime o' that money. Meantime, if the white alligator really does exist . . . why, I can't imagine killin' him. That's all I have to say."

A murmur went through the crowd as Leo spoke again. "Hold on, ever'body. The women been cookin' for days, so let's go on with the picnic. Men, come to Chalmette's at nine in the mornin' an' we'll figure out what we gonna do."

Heywood jumped off the picnic table. Leo followed him, rubbing his knee as he stepped down. "I'm a-gettin' too old for this," he said.

"CAN I GO EAT WITH FOOTSIE?" Remy had a fried chicken leg in each hand.

"You sure you won't run out o' chicken before you get there?" Ellie said with a grin.

"No, ma'am."

"Well, alright then. Tell Miss Davinia I said to run y'all over here if you start to get on her nerves."

"I'll tell her." Remy ran to the back side of the dance hall, where Footsie's family had laid their blankets.

"Heavens to Betsy, that's all Davinia Taylor needs is one more kid to look after," Ellie said.

Gabby dipped a spoon into a cup of homemade ice cream. "Once you get past four, another one don't make a bit o' difference. You an' Raphe want a big family?"

"I don't know if I'd say we want a *really* big family. But we definitely want more kids."

"More kids? You think o' Remy as your own now, don't you, *cher*?"

"I didn't at first. I mean, I wanted to—I just didn't think he'd ever let me. But I feel more hopeful now, Gabby, like we've crossed a bridge or something, you know?" Ellie smiled at her and brushed a leaf off her skirt. "So what's the scuttlebutt on you and Heywood?"

"Aw, we gettin' married," Gabby said. "I hope he figures that out before I have to tell him."

THIRTY-SEVEN

RAPHE AND ELLIE DUCKED OUT the back doors of the dance hall and walked down to the creek. With the musicians on break, Ellie could hear the water flowing over rocks and fallen logs. Raphe held her hand as they followed the bank around a bend to the limestone "dance floor" he had first shown her not so long ago.

"*C'est belle, non?*" she asked, mimicking what he had said to her that night.

"*Oui, c'est belle*, if *belle* means 'beautiful,'" he answered, repeating her response.

"I think this is the part where you ask me to dance with you to a sad, happy song," Ellie said. "Too bad the fiddle player's taking a break."

He slipped his arm around her waist and took her hand. "You can't depend on a fiddle player. We'll just sing it ourselves."

Ellie sang it with him as they waltzed around the giant rock in the babbling creek: "*Parlez-moi d'amour . . .*"

They sang and danced through a verse and chorus before Raphe stopped and held Ellie's face in his hands. "Are you still sure, Juliet?"

"About what?"

"About me. About Remy. About living in a cabin with no electricity. About washing clothes on a scrub board."

Ellie smiled up at him. "Let me tell you something, mister. The minute Louisiana gets power to the bayou, there will be a washing machine on my porch."

"You know what I mean. You have an education. You could've found your own way."

Ellie laid her hands over his. "No, I couldn't. I could get a job. I could make a living. But I couldn't make a life by myself—not one that meant anything. For that I needed you—you and Remy."

"No regrets?"

"None. What about you? Are you sure you want to spend your life with an impatient, bossy schoolteacher who still hasn't mastered gumbo?"

He bent down and gave her a soft kiss. "I can make my own gumbo."

Raphe was still smiling down at Ellie when something suddenly caught his attention, and his expression changed. He was looking over her head toward the bayou.

"Juliet!" he said, turning her in the direction of an unnerving sight. The sky was glowing orange, not just in one spot but several, scattered down the bayou on either side of the water. And now Ellie could smell smoke drifting through the air.

Without another word, they went running hand in hand back to the dance hall, where everyone had gathered inside as the musicians began tuning up.

"*Non!*" Raphe shouted. "Don't play!"

The crowd parted, and the musicians stared openmouthed as he and Ellie ran to the stage.

"Remy, come here!" Raphe shouted. "Everybody! Bayou cabins on fire!"

As the crowd rushed the front and back doors of the dance hall, Raphe and Ellie anxiously searched the crowd, looking for Remy and hoping the slight elevation of the stage would help them spot him. The dance hall quickly emptied, but there was no sign of Remy. They ran outside, toward the landing, and were relieved to see Remy and Footsie scrambling up the bank nearby. Heywood was helping Gabby into a boat with her parents.

"Remy!" Raphe called out.

Remy came running, with Footsie close behind him.

"What's happening, Nonc?" Remy looked terrified.

Raphe picked him up and held him tight before explaining their situation. "We'll be alright, but some of the cabins in the bayou are on fire. We don't know which ones, so we need to get home right away."

Footsie seemed frantic, looking right and left, scanning the landing for his family. Ellie put her arm around him. "Honey, why don't you stay with us till we find your mama, okay?"

He was speechless. All he could do was nod and cling to Ellie's skirt as Heywood joined them.

Heywood took one look at the distraught boy and tried to distract him. "We need a lookout! Climb up, Footsie!" He knelt down and helped Footsie climb onto his shoulders. "You hold on tight and let us know if you spot your mama or anything else we need to know about, okay?" He grasped Footsie's legs to keep him steady.

"Okay, Mr. Heywood," Footsie said.

They hurried to the landing with everyone else. Those with motors let the pirogues tie onto them so they could move faster down the Teche. Raphe tied the Richards' pirogue to his boat and pulled out into the bayou, going as fast as he could while keeping both boats steady and steering wide around any snags to make sure the pirogue cleared them as Lawyer helped guide it with a paddle. Remy and Footsie sat next to Ellie in the center of the boat. She grabbed a quilt from beneath the seat and wrapped it around them as the night air brought a chill.

The first fire they came to appeared to be on the same tributary as Doc's fishing cabin, Ellie's first home in the bayou. As Raphe steered them toward the glow in the sky, they saw a heartbreaking sight: Tante Dodo and Mr. Hudie, clinging to each other as they watched the roof cave in on the cabin they had shared for sixty years. The little house was engulfed in flames.

Doc and Florence pulled up beside Raphe's boat. Watching the old couple, beloved by the whole community, lose their home, Florence burst into tears.

"Raphe," Doc said as he put his arm around his wife, "you all keep going and see who else needs help. We'll take Tante Dodo and Mr. Hudie home with us for the night. Everything's so wet from all the rain we've had, I doubt we have to worry about the fire spreading."

"Okay, Doc." Ellie heard Raphe's voice break as he said it. She turned and reached out for his hand. He took hers and kissed it before turning his attention back to the motor while Heywood kept a lookout from the front of the boat.

Soon they could see that Raphe's cabin and his sister's were both fine. They traveled on toward the next glow in the sky and found it at the house of Leta LeJeune, the town beautician. All that remained was a corner of her front porch and one post with a white alligator—now charred—nailed to it. Leta and her husband were climbing into a boat with some of their neighbors.

Raphe kept going farther down the bayou, where most of the Creole families lived. Ellie saw tears rolling down Footsie's cheek and reached across Remy to pat the boy's hand. "Don't you worry, Footsie," she said. "Everything's gonna be alright."

"Looks like Lawyer's place is okay!" Heywood called out. They heard a shout go up from the pirogue in the back and a "Thank you, Jesus!" from Lawyer's wife, Minerva.

Raphe towed them to the bank and waited as Lawyer helped his family out of the pirogue. On the bank, Free-man Richard turned and looked at Ellie. He raised his hand goodbye. She forced a smile and waved back.

"I thank you, Raphe," Lawyer said.

"I'm glad for you, *mon ami*," Raphe said.

Lawyer untied the pirogue. "Be careful. Fires don't start by theyself, 'specially in wet weather."

Once Lawyer had freed the boat, Raphe steered back into the Teche, down the main channel to the last fiery glow on the bayou.

Ellie watched Footsie point as they passed the houses be-tween Lawyer's and the fire. When he realized his own house was burning, his face crumbled and he began to cry. Remy put his arms around his friend. Neither child said anything. They just held on to each other as the boat drew closer and closer to the fire.

Near the bank in front of the burning cabin, Ellie could hear the terrified voice of a woman calling out, "Footsie! Footsie, baby, where are you? Footsie!"

"We've got him!" Heywood shouted.

Footsie's mother came tearing through the crowd of relatives watching her house go up in flames and ran down to a rickety dock. "Footsie!"

Heywood picked up the boy and handed him to his mother.

She knelt down and held him tight against her, saying over and over, "Oh, my baby. My sweet baby."

"You find him, Davinia?" a man called out.

"He's alright!" she answered as Footsie's father ran to the dock and picked him up.

Her child safe, Davinia collapsed. Her sobs echoed over the bayou, piercing through the roar of the fire as it devoured her home. One by one, the timbers supporting the roof of the cabin fell into the flames. What had once provided this family shelter, humble though it was, quickly disintegrated into a fiery heap of rubble, leaving them exposed, covered only by a blanket of smoke.

"Where's a family this size gonna go?" Heywood asked.

"They could sleep at the dance hall," Raphe suggested, "till we can find 'em something better."

"That's not a bad idea," Heywood said. "The women already made a bunch o' pallets for the children at the picnic—should be enough to keep the Taylors warm and dry for the night."

Remy had climbed onto Ellie's lap and put his head on her shoulder. She covered him with the quilt and rocked him back and forth. "I'm worried about Footsie," he whispered in her ear.

"He'll be alright, sweetheart," she whispered back. "Nonc and Mr. Heywood will make sure o' that."

"Lemme run up here and see if Virgil and Davinia agree

to the dance hall," Heywood said. "If they do, y'all can take me back to your house and I'll go get their family in the *Whirlygig*. It'll be tight, but it oughta hold everybody, and we don't have to travel far."

Raphe nodded. "Sounds good."

Heywood hurried out of the boat. They watched him relay the plan to Virgil, who stood still for a moment, then shook Heywood's hand. Within minutes, Heywood was back in the boat and they were under way.

As they journeyed back up the Teche, the smell of smoke and charred wood filled the air. Ellie kept rocking Remy, who was falling asleep in her arms, as she thought about the first time she had traveled the bayou with Raphe and her sweet boy in a pirogue, slow and peaceful. Back then she wondered if this Louisiana waterway would carry her to a new life. It had. Speeding across the Teche now, its banks marred by homes destroyed, Ellie remembered what Raphe had told her about the white alligator—something perfect trying to survive in a world that wasn't, like a home in a blaze, like a loving community assailed by hate or greed or just plain meanness.

"Raphe, look." Ellie saw Heywood pointing at yet another horrifying glow in the sky and a pillar of smoke much higher than any they had seen on the bayou. She gasped at the sight of it. Remy stirred but didn't awaken. Raphe opened the throttle, speeding up the bayou as fast as he safely could until they reached the landing and saw what they knew they would see yet desperately hoped not to. St. Bernadette's Catholic Church was ablaze, its roof disintegrating, its soaring steeple toppled onto the ground and in flames.

Heywood jumped out of the boat and tied it up. Raphe

climbed over Ellie's center seat and knelt down beside her. "Juliet? Will you be alright here? Do you want to come with us?"

Ellie could hardly form a thought, let alone speak. She just stared helplessly at Raphe and shook her head.

He kissed her on the cheek. "I won't be long." He followed Heywood up the street.

RAPHE AND HEYWOOD PASSED CHALMETTE'S, where they could see the windows of its double front doors had been broken. A pile of Freeman's white alligators were burning in front of the store. Up ahead, they saw Father Timothy, pastor of St. Bernadette's, watching the church collapse. The men who had tried in vain to save it were now pumping water from the creek to hose down Doc's office and the dance hall, safeguarding them from the fire. There was nothing else anyone could do. The church was gone.

"It was fine when we left," Heywood said, never taking his eyes off St. Bernadette's.

"Nothing that big burns so fast without some help," Raphe said.

Heywood nodded in agreement. "I'd bet the *Whirlygig* there's fuel on that fire. And I'd bet my next birthday I know where it came from."

THIRTY-EIGHT

SOMETHING WAS WRONG WITH JULIET. She had stayed at the cabin to put Remy to bed while Raphe and Heywood went back for the Taylor family and ferried them to the dance hall. Leo and his wife were there to help Virgil and Davinia get their children situated for the night. Heywood told Raphe he needed to be on the water tonight to clear his head. He promised to be there for the morning meeting at Chalmette's.

Now Raphe was pulling up to his own dock, thinking over and over about the strange expression on his wife's face as they watched the church burn, and again as she said goodbye when he carried Remy up to his loft before returning to the dock to join Heywood. It was as if she were in a trance, unable to fully hear him or see him or feel his touch. He was so worried that he asked Doc about it. Doc said it wasn't unusual for some people to go into shock after a tragedy and urged Raphe to get home as soon as possible.

He quickly secured the boat and hurried up the dock to his cabin, which was completely dark except for a dim light coming from Remy's window. Juliet always left a lamp burning for him.

Raphe quietly ran up the stairs and peeked into Remy's

room. He was sound asleep. Back downstairs, he stepped inside the silent cabin and felt his way to the lamp and matches that stayed in the center of the table. Even a little glow from the lamp was reassuring.

"Juliet?"

She didn't answer.

Raphe carried the light into his bedroom and found his wife in her nightgown, sitting on the floor against the back wall, her arms wrapped tightly around her knees. He went back into the kitchen, pumped cold water onto a dish towel, and then knelt down beside her, placing the towel on the back of her neck. She seemed startled by the chill.

"Juliet?" he repeated, blotting her face with the towel.

She looked at him—he could tell she was finally seeing him now—and squinted as if she were trying to recall his name.

"Juliet, it's me."

She nodded and laid her hand against his face, but then she grew agitated. "Remy? Is he alright?"

Raphe kissed her forehead. "He's fine. I just checked on him."

She nodded and attempted a smile. But then tears were flowing down her cheeks. He lifted her off the floor and carried her to their bed, lying down next to her and holding her as she wept and sobbed what was surely the worst shock of her life into his shoulder. And it broke his heart to know—as a great storm had taught him long ago—that this was just the beginning.

IN THE WEE HOURS OF THE MORNING, well before dawn, Ellie awoke to the sound of rain. It was accompanied by the peaceful rise and fall of Raphe's breathing, his skin warm against her face as she rested her head on his shoulder. She tightened her arms around him—gently so he wouldn't awaken. But the slightest movement from her always drew his attention. He opened his eyes, turning on his side to face her. He ran his fingertip down her cheek.

"Are you alright?" he whispered.

"No." She felt the tears coming again.

"Come to me, Juliet."

THIRTY-NINE

"BOONE! BOONE! YOU BETTER ANSWER ME, BOY!"

Big Roy was fit to be tied. Boone was supposed to help him work a fundraiser at the River Club tonight, but he never showed. He wasn't there for cocktails at six, and he wasn't there for dinner at seven, and he wasn't there for Big Roy's speech at nine. It was flat-out embarrassing, that's what it was, to have your own son—one you had worked mighty hard to get placed just right—skip out in front of some of the richest donors in Louisiana. Boone might hold a special place in his heart, but enough was enough. For this, he would answer.

"Boone!" Big Roy charged into his son's apartment in the east wing of the kind of mansion only oil money could buy. "What the—"

He was locked and loaded, ready to lay into his son, but Boone wasn't there. His bed was still made, and his lunch—uneaten—still sat on the silver tray that had been brought up for him. Now anger turned to concern as Big Roy looked around the apartment. Finally, he saw it—an envelope on

Boone's desk, the one Big Roy had imported from Italy. The envelope was addressed simply "Daddy" in Boone's precise hand.

Ripping open the note, Big Roy expected some lame apology for missing the dinner but instead found something that made his blood run cold. Boone had overheard his conversation with Luetrell. He had gone into the bayou to try to stop the fires. And once this was over, Boone wrote, he would resign his position and go out on his own.

Big Roy sat down at his son's desk and ran his hand slowly back and forth over the fine wood grain. Boone had likely left right after Luetrell did. It was now well past midnight and his son hadn't come home. There wasn't a doubt in Big Roy's mind that his son would never come home.

He picked up the phone and dialed. "Lura? I'm sorry for calling so late, but I need your help . . . It's time to do something about Luetrell . . . No, not jail. I want him gone . . . That's right . . . And Lura, tell those cousins of yours he took something that belonged to me. No mercy."

FORTY

ELLIE WAS SETTING THE TABLE when Remy came down-stairs and took his seat. Raphe had insisted on cooking break-fast for her, and he was busy at the woodstove as she readied the table.

"Morning, honey," Ellie said as she set butter and a small pitcher of cane syrup on the table.

"Morning." Remy yawned and rubbed his eyes.

Ellie poured him a glass of milk and was putting the bottle back in the icebox when she realized he was intently watch-ing her. "Something the matter, Remy?" She sat down next to him at the table.

He looked down, apparently embarrassed that she'd caught him staring at her.

"It's okay—you can tell me," Ellie assured him.

Remy looked up at her. "You were different last night."

Once again, Remy had observed what they thought he'd slept through.

"Yes. You're right, I was."

"How come?"

"Did you ever feel so sad or so scared that all you could do was cry?" Ellie asked him.

He nodded.

"Well, last night I think I was so sad and so scared that I couldn't even do that. You might believe grown-ups can handle anything, Remy, but that's not true. Sometimes we get scared and sad too. Sometimes we don't know what to do, even though we think we're supposed to. That's why I was different last night. Did I frighten you?"

"No, ma'am," he said. "I was just worried about you."

Ellie smiled at him and held her arms out. Remy climbed onto her lap and hugged her. "You're my special boy, you know that?" She kissed the top of his head and held him tight.

Raphe set a platter of biscuits and boudin on the table. He looked at her and laid his hand against her cheek. The kettle on the stove whistled. The morning went on like so many others. But it wasn't.

FORTY-ONE

AT THE TOWN LANDING, Raphe helped Ellie out of the boat and carried the large basket of biscuits and boudin they had made for the Taylors. Remy ran ahead to find Footsie as Raphe and Ellie followed the same crowd that just yesterday had joyfully gathered for the town picnic. But today's procession had taken on a somber, funereal air.

Some stopped to hold their loved ones close and stare at the charred remains of St. Bernadette's. Others, like Ellie and Raphe, went straight to the dance hall to carry the Taylors their breakfast.

Though this gathering space was big enough to accommodate the whole town, Footsie's family had huddled together in one corner of the building, the spot where the Creole families had clustered the night before, leaving undisturbed the pallets of their Cajun neighbors. The younger children, excited by the breakfast baskets streaming in, seemed to temporarily forget that they were sheltering, not celebrating. Virgil and Davinia sat quietly on a quilt with their two oldest daughters.

Emmett Chalmette came into the dance hall and greeted Raphe and Ellie. "They's so many people comin' out this mornin', I figure we might as well meet here," he said. "I don't think my store'd hold 'em all. Reckon we oughta start pullin' in some chairs?"

"Probably so." Raphe kissed Ellie before he went outside to help Emmett gather the chairs that had been left outside during the picnic. Virgil followed him and helped put the chairs in a circle as they brought them in.

Virgil joined the men gathering chairs, and the older Taylor girls went to the food tables to help their younger siblings as Ellie sat down with Davinia. "How'd y'all do last night?" she asked.

"Pretty fair, I reckon," Davinia said. "The young'uns think they on some kinda 'venture. The older ones, though—they know we ain't got no place to live."

"You and Virgil plan on placing the kids with your friends and family till you can rebuild, or do you want to try and keep everybody together?"

Davinia shook her head. "I want to keep my kids with me, but how we gon' do that with so many of us?"

Ellie sighed and put her hand on Davinia's shoulder. "We'll help any way we can."

Davinia fidgeted with a pulled thread on her skirt. She kept her eyes on it as she spoke. "Most o' my kids is stair steps. Had 'em one right after the other—had two sets o' twins, even. Oldest turns twenty this year. They all close together—all 'cept Footsie. They's four years 'tween him and the one that come ahead of him. All my other chillun, they can look after theyselves and look after one 'nother. But Footsie, he needs a lot more. And right now . . ."

"Why don't you let him stay with us?" Ellie asked. "Doesn't have to be for long—just a few days till you get settled someplace besides this dance hall."

Davinia looked at her and frowned. "White folks don't shelter colored chillun."

"Well, no, not usually, but—"

"What 'bout Raphe?"

"Those boys do everything together but sleep as it is. I don't think Raphe will see any difference between letting them play together on the creek and letting them sleep together in Remy's loft."

Davinia thought it over and nodded. "We can try it, I reckon. If he was to go to cryin' for me—"

"We'll get him back to you right away."

As the families of Bernadette gathered inside the dance hall, Ellie joined Raphe and told him about Footsie. "You don't mind, do you?" she asked him.

"They do everything together but sleep as it is."

Ellie had to laugh despite the trauma they were enduring. "I knew you'd say that. I knew you'd say *exactly* that."

They were about to take their seats when Heywood came into the dance hall with Gabby. Ellie nudged Raphe and nodded in their direction. He smiled and said, "Claudette better watch out."

Leo stepped onto the small stage and held his hand up to quiet the crowd. "Bonjour! We was s'posed to talk about the white alligator, but last night done give us somethin' worse. Ever'body that lost y' home, tell us how you doin'."

Doc stood up. "Tante Dodo and Mr. Hudie were too shaken up to come this morning, so I'll do my best to speak for them. They'll be staying in our bayou cabin for now—or from now on, if they want to. It's right there close to their place, so hopefully they'll feel at home. And it has some conveniences that'll make things easier on them. We'll consider them situated for now. If they decide they don't want to stay, why, I expect we'll all pitch in and build them something on their old cabin site." Doc took his seat.

Leo pointed to the town beautician and her husband. "Skeeter, how 'bout you and Leta?"

Skeeter put his arm around his wife. "We gon' live up 'bove her beauty shop till the boys can get down here from Lafayette and help us rebuild the cabin. We gon' be alright."

Leo grinned and nodded. "That's good to hear, *mon ami*. My Lanelle done told me if Leta leaves town, she's leavin' too, 'cause can't nobody else fix her hair. I'm mighty glad I ain't got to find me a new woman."

Laughter rippled through the crowd.

"That just leaves the Taylors," Leo said. "Virgil, you and Davinia got any idea what you might like to do till you can rebuild?"

Virgil shook his head.

"Anybody got a idea?" Leo looked around the dance hall, where a wave of murmuring could be heard as the community tried to find a way to quickly house a family of twelve.

"Raphe," Ellie whispered as it dawned on her, "what about the upstairs of the school?" She watched him mentally work through her idea and nod approval.

"You should tell them," he said.

Ellie raised her hand and stood up.

Leo gave her the floor. "Yes, ma'am?"

"Well, it just occurred to me that we've got the whole upstairs of the schoolhouse sitting vacant—two really big rooms, and both of them have woodstoves for heat. We'd just need to outfit one o' those so Davinia can cook on it.

If everybody pitches in a little bit, we should be able to set up a kitchen and beds for everybody. Wouldn't that work?"

"Kind o' you to think so, but no," Virgil said. "Ain't no way that school board gon' let colored people live in a white schoolhouse."

"Sorry to say it, but he's right," Leo said.

Ellie thought for a minute. "Well, the board doesn't own the schoolhouse—the town does, right?"

"That's true," Leo said.

Virgil shook his head. "I still think they'll say we in their school."

"What if the top floor weren't part of the school?" Ellie countered. "Everybody here trusts Doc. What if we vote to sell him the top floor for a penny? Then it becomes his property and he can do whatever he wants to with it. I think we all know we can trust him to sell it back to us for the same price when we need it again."

"Seems like it oughta work, far as I see," Leo said.

Everybody else agreed.

"Virgil," Leo said, "what you think?"

"Reckon we can give it a try."

"Good, that's settled," Leo said.

Heywood stood up. "Leo, can I say something?"

"Go ahead, Heywood."

"I think I've 'bout had enough o' oil rigs. I'd like to stick around here for a while and make myself useful. Y'all haven't got a sawyer to run your mill, and I know how to do that. It's what my family does back in Illinois. I figure the folks needing to rebuild could get going a lot quicker and cheaper if they could pay or trade to have their timber milled right here instead o' going all the way to the mill in Morgan City."

"Anybody oppose?" Leo looked around the room. "Alright then. Heywood, we thank you. And now, well, I reckon we got us some sorry business to talk about. Anybody besides Heywood see anything suspicious last night? Maybe somebody you didn't know hangin' 'round or stoppin' by your place to ask directions?"

Nobody had seen anything.

"Heywood, what about the man you saw with those alligator signs? You said his name was Luetrell?"

"That's right." Heywood came to the stage with Leo. "This man—Gig Luetrell—he's dangerous. They said he'd just got outta prison when he came to work on the rig I was assigned to. I don't know if that's true, but I do know he picked fights for his own amusement and put I don't know how many men in the hospital. Anybody that got crossed up with him tended to end up in the emergency room—a few of 'em disappeared. Some o' the fellas said the oil comp'ny kept him around—and paid him more'n anybody else—because he could sniff out crude oil like a bloodhound. After a coupla weeks, I decided lookin' over my shoulder all the time wasn't worth the aggravation and quit. Found myself a different job in Lafayette till I heard he moved on."

"What you reckon he's got to do with that senator's alligator hunt?" Emmett asked.

"Don't know," Heywood said. "But I can tell you this: If Luetrell's connected to that hunt in any way, you don't wanna be. I know there's folks around here could sure use that money, especially now. Money like that would change your life—buy all kinda advantages for your kids. But you won't ever see a dime of it, not if Luetrell's got his hands on it. And you might get yourself killed—sorry, ladies, but that's the honest truth. I've fooled with some tough customers in my time, but that one—he's different. And I'd bet you anything he set those fires."

"What about Brother Lester?" Emmett asked.

"You really think a preacher would set fire to people's houses, Emmett?" Doc asked.

"I don't know. But he despises the Catholic church. And of all the things he coulda stole from my store, he didn't hurt nothin' but Freeman's white alligators, which he thinks is some kinda idol we down here worshipin'. Just seems odd that somebody'd break in and bypass rifles and shotguns for a bunch o' wooden alligators. That don't make no sense."

"No, it don't," Heywood said. "I agree with you there. And you got me thinkin' about something else. Why would somebody like Luetrell be connected to a big-time senator's alligator hunt? Only thing they got in common is oil."

"What you gettin' at, Heywood?" Leo asked him.

"I'm not sure. But you folks that got burned out—Doc, maybe you can do this for Tante Dodo—next time you go back to your place, spend a little time in the water around it. Shut off your boat motor, and pole or paddle so you don't disturb the surface o' the water too much. Look for small pools of little, tiny bubbles. I'm not talking about the kind of random bubbles fish make. These would be tiny and steady and clustered in one spot, like there's a fountain underwater spewin' 'em to the top. Those can mark underwater oil deposits. I might be completely off the beam, but it couldn't hurt to check. If everybody that got burned out has bubbles, that could tell us why an oil man might want you gone. 'Course, that don't explain the church or Emmett's alligators. In any case, I think I've run my mouth enough, so I'm gonna shut up and sit down." Heywood abruptly left the stage and took his seat next to Gabby.

"I don't reckon we need to keep the ladies and the young'uns here any longer," Leo said. "The men can head down to Emmett's and make a decision about the alligator. Ellie, you and some o' the ladies mind walking over to the schoolhouse with Davinia—take stock o' what's needed and give the men a list?"

"Nothing we like better than giving men a list," Ellie said, which made everybody laugh.

The front door opened, and they turned to see Father Timothy come into the dance hall.

Leo invited him onto the stage. "Father Tim, come and join us. Would you like to say a few words?"

"That's a dangerous invitation to offer a priest," Father Tim said, trying to smile.

Leo shook his hand as he stepped onto the stage. Father Tim was young, fresh out of seminary when he came to Bernadette five years ago. He looked completely drained—of energy, of hope, of everything.

"As the shepherd of St. Bernadette's, it is my duty to offer this flock consolation and comfort in time of trouble," the priest said. "But I find myself lacking. I have faith in the healing power of God. But the truth is, I'm just too wounded this morning to seek it out. I imagine some of you might be feeling the same way. I know the physical structure of St. Bernadette's is just a building. The true church is sitting right here. But I would be lying to you if I said I didn't mourn the loss of our house of worship—the place where I've had the honor of christening your babies and officiating your weddings and grieving with you over your dead. Today I don't even have the host and the wine to offer you Holy

VALERIE FRASER LUESSE

Communion. Could we—could we at least pray together, do you think?"

Father Timothy and Leo stepped off the stage and joined hands as the families of Bernadette formed a circle. Together they prayed, "Our Father, who art in heaven . . ."

267

FORTY-TWO

ON SUNDAY AFTERNOON, Raphe was napping in a hammock that Heywood brought him from Morgan City. They had strung it on one end of the porch, opposite the swing. Ellie was getting ready to go to Tante Dodo's. She thought the ladies might want a break from their lessons, but no—they said they needed to be together today.

Ellie was packing her book bag when she heard suspicious noises overhead. She quietly climbed the stairs to Remy's loft, opened the door, and saw two little heads pop up between the twin beds. The boys looked so guilty that Ellie couldn't help but laugh. "If y'all aren't up to something, I'll pay for lying."

Remy and Footsie looked at each other, then back at Ellie, then back at each other before Remy shrugged and said, "C'mon, Footsie, she'll find out anyway. She always does." They stood up, Footsie cradling a brown baby rabbit.

"Ohhhh!" Ellie cried. "He's just a baby!" She hurried to the bedside where the boys were hiding. "Can I hold him?"

Footsie nodded and handed her the rabbit, which was trembling. Ellie cupped her hands around it and gently stroked its fur.

"He looks real scared, don't he, Miss Ellie?" Footsie said.

"Sure does," Ellie answered. "Where'd you boys find him?"

"Right by the porch," Remy said. "All by hisself—I mean *him*self—like he was lost or something. Can we keep him?"

"You boys know how I feel about penning up wild animals." Ellie kept petting the rabbit. "They belong outside where they can roam free."

"But he's so little!" Footsie objected. "He ain't nothin' but a baby, an' them alligators and snakes out there—they gon' eat him up fo' sure! Way I figure it, him bein' without his mama and me bein' without mine, maybe we s'posed to look out for one 'nother."

Ellie looked down at the rabbit, which was growing calmer in her hands, and sighed. "I know when I'm licked."

The boys started jumping up and down.

"Sh-sh-sh," Ellie said, putting her finger over her lips. "Like you said, he's just a baby and he's really scared, so you need to keep it nice and calm up here for him."

"Yes, ma'am," Remy said.

"Yes'm," Footsie agreed.

"I have to get on over to Tante Dodo's, so for now, you boys are in charge," Ellie said, handing the rabbit back to Footsie. "Remy, you go down to the kitchen and get some of the carrots I cooked for lunch. Mash them up and see if the bunny will eat some. He'll need some water too, in a saucer or something that's low enough for him to reach. Footsie, you get a quilt out of that wardrobe over there and make him a bed—maybe in the corner. Pull the sides up around him so he has a bed to snuggle into. And if he does his business on my floor, you boys had best clean it up."

"Thanks, M'Ellie!" Remy said as he took off downstairs.

"Footsie?" Ellie said.

"Yes'm?" He cradled the rabbit against him, stroking it gently as Ellie had done.

"I know this is hard. I know you miss your mama and your daddy and all your brothers and sisters. Must seem mighty quiet around here to you. But it's just for a few days. I want you to know you can come to me or Mr. Raphe if you get scared or lonesome or just need to talk to somebody. And if you get to missing your family too bad, just let us know and we'll take you back to them. Okay?"

He nodded and hurried to the wardrobe, no doubt hiding from her sight in case the tears should come and betray the sadness of a frightened little boy trying hard to find his courage.

FORTY-THREE

"Y'ALL NOT GON' B'LIEVE WHAT'S HAPPENED!" Gabby hurried to the bench where Bonita and Ellie were sitting to watch the children during recess.

"Couldn't much happen at the post office, unless Miss Ernie got some new dirt on somebody," Bonita said.

Gabby shook her head. "Not there—Chalmette's. Just as I was droppin' my letter in the box, I looked up the street, and I swear every man in this town was filin' into that store."

"Even Heywood?" Ellie said with a grin.

"Heywood and Raphe and Doc, *le conseil* and Lawyer and Virgil—even sweet ol' Mr. Hudie," Gabby said. "Wasn't no way I was gonna let that slide without findin' out what they doin'. You can't turn that many men loose for too long. So I went down there and found out the sheriff's done arrested ol' Brother Lester for settin' the fires!"

"You got to be kiddin'," Bonita said as she got up to help a first grader who had fallen down playing Duck, Duck, Goose.

"The men said they never seen nothin' so quick," Gabby went on. "Fires set on Saturday and here it is just Friday mornin'. But there's more. The superintendent's gone missin'."

"You mean Boone Strahan?" Ellie was astounded.

"Oui," Gabby said. "Nobody's seen him since last Saturday. Emmett said that's how come Brother Lester's in the jailhouse. The senator says nobody but Brother Lester woulda burned the Catholic church and Freeman's alligators on accounta he's the one that hated 'em both. Boone's papa also says whoever set the fires knows what happened to his boy. I wouldn't wanna be in that preacher's shoes right now, that's fo' sure."

Ellie felt nauseated. She didn't know Boone well, but she believed he had a good heart. And she knew his father had put him in an impossible position. She was happy to have an afternoon with her students to take her mind off what might've happened to him.

Bonita rang the school bell while Ellie and Gabby herded the children inside for the afternoon. Ever since the fires, Ellie had made sure to give them ways to talk about that night and bring their fears out in the open. This afternoon Bonita, who had decided she wanted to teach school like Ellie, would help the older kids write about the fires, while Ellie and Gabby let the little ones draw pictures. Then they would dismiss school early to give the children extra time with their families till everything got back to normal.

The Taylors had settled into the second floor of the school. Some of the men in town built them a separate entrance to ensure that the school board had no claim on their comings and goings. While they were at it, Ellie had the volunteer carpenters run a large pipe between the two floors in one corner of each of her classrooms, with a flue she could open and a cap Davinia could close to shut out the noise from below. When the flue and the cap were open, sound would easily carry from the schoolrooms to any of the Taylor children who wanted to listen from above. During recess, Ellie told Davinia, they could come outside and ask her any questions they had. She'd be happy to grade their lessons just like all the other students'.

Florence brought the children crayons, slates, and paper and pencils for their schoolwork. Today was the first day they had tried it out. So far none of the Taylors had come down to ask questions. Ellie didn't even know if they had listened in. She would just need *un tas de patience*, as Tante Dodo would say—a lot of patience.

FORTY-FOUR

ON SATURDAY MORNING, Raphe, Heywood, Doc, Emmett, and Leo arrived at the parish jail, where Brother Lester was being held without bail. As much trouble as he had caused in Bernadette, the men in town agreed that a preacher deserved the benefit of the doubt.

Inside the jailhouse, they were met by the lone deputy on duty. He was an old friend of Emmett's, and while the senator had ordered no visitors, the deputy said he would allow them to talk with Brother Lester through the bars of his cell, provided they agree to swiftly slip out the back door if they heard anybody else come in.

Raphe had never cared for Brother Lester and his constant interference in matters that were not his concern—things he didn't even understand. Still, there was something about the way the swift hand of so-called justice was moving that made him uneasy. The fires, the senator's son, the sudden appearance of this Luetrell from the oil fields—something about it didn't add up.

Inside his cell, Brother Lester looked small and alone. He was sitting on a cot, his black jacket and necktie folded neatly on the other end, his wide-brimmed black hat resting on top of them. The sleeves of his white shirt were rolled up to his elbows. His legs were crossed, his arms folded in his lap, his head bowed. Raphe and the other men looked at each other, wondering if he might be praying.

Finally, Doc cleared his throat and Brother Lester looked up. When he spoke, the fire was gone from his voice. "Are you my accusers? 'Thou shalt not bear false witness against thy neighbor.'"

"We're not your accusers," Doc said. "We've come to seek the truth."

"You'll not find it in this place," Brother Lester said.

Doc stepped closer to the preacher's cell. "You have to admit, Brother Lester, you've been mighty vocal about your opposition to the Catholic church."

"And you preached against the white alligator—which, if you really got a interest in the truth, don't nobody in Bernadette worship," Leo added.

Brother Lester looked confused. "I was told differently."

"You were misled," Doc said. "Hanging that alligator on their door doesn't mean any more to Cajun people than hanging a picture on the wall. I'm afraid you're the one who's been bearing false witness against your neighbors. Now about those fires and the senator's son—"

"'Thou shalt not kill!'" Some of Brother Lester's old ferocity crept back into his voice. "I have harmed no man. To do so would be an abomination."

"What about the fires?" Leo asked.

"'Thou shalt not steal!'" Brother Lester answered. "To burn a man's house is to take it from him. It's stealing. I would not commit such a sin against God."

Now Emmett had more questions. "The only thing damaged

from my store the night of the fires was the white alligators. Why? You *did* turn over my display that time."

"Like the tables of the money changers," Brother Lester countered. "I believed I saw evil in your community. I had to act. I had to make you see. But I destroyed nothing."

"That's true," Emmett said. "You made a big mess, but you didn't destroy anything."

"Brother Lester," Doc said, "Freeman Richard's been carving those alligators for a good while now. What made you suddenly decide they were graven images?"

The preacher stood up and came to the door of his cell, as if he needed a closer look at the men in order to see the truth. "The senator, of course. He believes in my ministry. He persuades the lost to come to my tent services and supports our crusade with his tithes and offerings. He told me himself he had seen an ugly scourge of alligator worship rising in the bayou. I was honored that he trusted me to vanquish such an abomination."

"But it's not true," Raphe spoke up. "It's never been true."

Brother Lester looked disturbed. "It *must* be true. Otherwise—"

"Otherwise, you've been wrong about us," Raphe said.

Heywood stepped up to the cell door beside Raphe. "Otherwise, the senator is a liar. Otherwise, he used you to turn half of Louisiana against decent Cajun families—decent Christian families."

The preacher was shaking his head and running his hands through his hair. "But why? I don't understand. He seemed so devoted to the Word, so committed to my ministry."

Doc reached through the bars to put his hand on Brother Lester's shoulder. "I'm afraid he's a wolf in sheep's clothing. You're not the first to be fooled, and I doubt you'll be the last."

"Why involve me, though?" Brother Lester pressed on. "Why involve my ministry?"

"We suspect the senator's after oil rights in the bayou and would do just about anything to get them," Doc said. "He lied to you so you'd help him turn everybody else against the Cajun families who own those rights—isolate them—and then he tried to use that alligator hunt to pit them against each other. He wants their property, plain and simple. And he doesn't care how he gets it."

Brother Lester turned away, sat down on his cot, and put his head in his hands. When he finally looked up at them, he said, "I have followed a false prophet. I have led others astray."

"You just trusted the wrong person," Heywood said. "Everybody's done it at least once."

Doc tried to reassure the distraught preacher. "You may have been wrong in what you taught them about Cajuns, but you never led anybody away from God. That's the important thing."

"Thank you for that, brother," the preacher said. "I just don't understand why I'm here. If I did the senator's bidding, why does he want me here?"

"To hide who really set the fires—and their connection to him," Doc explained. "You ever run across a mean sort named Luetrell?"

Brother Lester thought about it and shook his head. "No."

"Well, if you ever do, run like h—that is, get away from him quick as you can," Heywood said.

"What happens now?" Brother Lester asked.

"We'll do what we can to find Luetrell and clear your name," Doc said. "But it won't be easy. I don't think I have to tell you that."

"No, you don't. But there is something you *can* tell me: Why would you help one who persecuted you?"

"Because we're supposed to," Doc answered. "But while we're on the subject of persecution, before you go around calling Catholics idol worshipers, don't you think you ought to have a sit-down with Father Tim and find out what he actually believes?"

"But he bows down to statues—worships their images," Brother Lester argued.

"No," Raphe said. "No, he doesn't. And neither do we. Why would you say something like that without making sure it's true? You can't just accuse people—" He was too frustrated to finish.

"Anybody you want us to contact?" Doc asked.

"Yes, if you would be so kind," Brother Lester said. "My wife. I'll give you her number in Lafayette. Please tell her I'm alright. Please tell her—tell her we shall meet again by and by."

FORTY-FIVE

ELLIE AWOKE BEFORE DAYLIGHT. She didn't need to turn over to know that Raphe's side of the bed was empty. She could sense it. And she smiled, knowing exactly where he was.

The cabin was cool this early in the morning. Ellie swathed herself in Mama Jean's wrap and went onto the front porch, where Raphe was sipping his coffee and looking out at the darkened bayou.

He smiled and handed her cup to her. "What took you so long?" He put his free arm around her.

She stood on tiptoe and kissed him on the cheek. "I guess I'm getting old and slow."

For a while they stood silently together, listening to the bayou slowly wake up as hints of light began breaking through the darkness above.

"Raphe, remember when you first told me about the hurricane?"

"Yes."

"You said that you can lose your life or save it just by choosing where to be when the sun rises. I think that's true some days more than others. And I can't help thinking this is one of those days."

"Why?"

"I don't know. Maybe it's Heywood's birthday coming tomorrow—knowing what he thinks might happen. And the fires and who set them and the preacher in jail—it all has to stop somewhere. Or lead somewhere. Doesn't it?"

"Oui, Juliet. It does." Raphe set their coffee cups down and wrapped his arms around her. They held each other silently, listening to the fading nocturnal calls.

"Is that a new owl?" Ellie asked. "It sounds different from the one we usually hear." A familiar *hoo* floated across the water. "That one right there."

"Maybe he found a mate," Raphe said.

"I hope so. Sounded lonesome with just the one."

Raphe kissed the top of her head. "Don't tell me you're taking on the hurts of owls."

She smiled up at him. "I can't help myself."

"Neither can I." Raphe smiled, picked Ellie up, and gave her a lingering kiss. He carried her back inside as the owls kept calling and the sun kept rising and the night met the first light of day.

AT CHALMETTE'S, Raphe and Heywood said goodbye to Ellie and Gabby, who were on their way to Leta's beauty shop in a show of support from all the women in town. They followed the other men to benches out back at Chalmette's, stopping to pour themselves some coffee from a steaming fresh pot on a table by the back door.

Of course, *le conseil* was there. Leo waved to Raphe and Heywood as they came outside. They sat down on a long bench with Leo and his brother, Andre. The brothers' alligator-hunting cousins Binkie, Clifton, and Clayton were seated nearby. The five of them had their own elaborate system of winks, glances, and hand signals to communicate what they thought of any given proceeding. This morning's discussion had already begun.

"What worries me is the way that preacher feels about the white alligator," Lawyer Richard was saying. "My boy carves 'em—everybody knows Freeman been doin' that for a long time now. What if this Brother Lester was to take it in his mind to hurt my chile?"

"I don't think you gotta worry about that, Lawyer," Raphe assured him. "We went to see Brother Lester last weekend. I don't think he'd ever hurt anybody. And I believe we finally got through to him about that alligator-worshiping nonsense."

Lawyer didn't seem convinced. "Hope you're right, Raphe. Ain't fair for a ten-year-old boy to be goin' 'round feelin' scared in his own community on accounta some crazy firebug preacher."

Doc spoke up. "Well, that brings us to something else. We don't think he set the fires either."

"What you talkin' about, Doc?" Virgil asked.

"He's a preacher. And while he might be completely misguided about us, I believe he's sincere in his conviction. In his mind, setting fire to a man's house is the same as stealing it, which he says he'd never do because it violates the Commandments. Same with killing another human being. That's a line he won't cross."

Skeeter LeJeune joined the debate. "Don't nobody else around here hate the Catholic church, though, Doc. What about *that* fire?"

"I don't profess to have all the answers, Skeeter," Doc said. "And I don't know what to tell you about the church fire. But he said he didn't do it, and I believe him because he's a man who will do what he thinks is right, no matter what. If he *had* burned down the church, I think he'd be proclaiming it from his jail cell."

Raphe sided with Doc. "Y'all know I never thought much o' Brother Lester. He almost had me believing I needed to give up Remy. But when you talk to him straight on—I'm not saying I'd want to fish with him, but I don't think he's a liar."

"Neither do I," Heywood said.

"Me neither," Leo agreed.

"Where's that leave us?" Virgil wanted to know.

"Bein' mighty careful," Leo answered. "If Brother Lester didn't set those fires and didn't have nothing to do with the Strahan boy's disappearance, then whoever did—prob'ly that Luetrell fella—is still on the loose. And here's somethin' else: The preacher told us it was the senator convinced him we was all bowin' down to the white alligator."

"What for?" Binkie asked.

Leo took a sip of his coffee. "I reckon to stir up trouble. Maybe distract us while he looked for oil in the bayou?"

"You think there's any danger to our families?" Skeeter asked.

"Yes," Heywood said. "Luetrell is dangerous. And somehow he's tangled up in all o' this. He's the reason I still say the senator's alligator hunt is rigged. And he's the reason everybody needs to be on their guard till we know he's gone."

Binkie got up and walked over to the coffeepot, topping off his cup with a hot splash as he made a case for the hunt. "Speakin' o' the alligator, that's a cool fortune to wave on by. And it ain't just *that* money—it's all the other money a hunter could bring in once word gets 'round that he's killed L'esprit Blanc. Ever'body from shoemakers in New Orleans to cafés up and down the river would want you huntin' for 'em."

"I know, Binkie," Heywood said. "I can't imagine killing that alligator myself, but then I don't have kids to feed and I don't make my living on the bayou. I wouldn't fault you for going after it if I thought you'd actually see any o' that money, but I'm telling you, if Luetrell's tied up in it, you won't. And if he's working for the senator—well, that's a pretty dangerous pair, what with one man's power, the other man's spite, and not a ounce o' conscience between 'em."

Doc joined Binkie at the coffee table. "Heywood's right. My personal opinion is that the hunt was intended to set us all against each other—have us fighting over the alligator and all that money. Long as we don't give in to that, Binkie, I think every man here ought to do as he sees fit. We can't tell you whether to hunt or not. We just want you to go into it clearheaded so you know what you're in for—so you don't get tempted to do things you normally wouldn't because you're blinded by the thought of all that money, which we don't think any of us will ever see. Fair enough?"

"Fair enough," Binkie agreed.

Just then three men no one recognized stepped out of the store and into their circle. They were wearing jeans and cowboy boots. Two had on Western hats while the third wore a straw fedora. All of them were tall and muscular, with scruffy beards and tanned skin.

"Those three look rough as Luetrell," Heywood whispered to Raphe.

"Mornin'." The man in the fedora held up a fifty-dollar

bill and a photograph. "Lookin' for this man. Gig Luetrell. You seen him?"

"You all work for the sheriff?" Doc asked.

"No," the man said. "You seen Luetrell?"

Doc shook his head.

"Anybody else?"

No one answered. And no one looked in Heywood's direction.

"We'll be around," the man said. "You see him, you find us." The three men turned and walked back into the store.

Emmett stepped around the corner and watched them, then reported back to the others. "Looks like they pullin' a boat to the landin'."

"'Preciate y'all keepin' quiet," Heywood said. "Don't believe I care to get mixed up with those three."

Leo got up and poured himself some more coffee. "We'll handle our business ourselves, same as always. Let's all have us another cup. By then, it oughta be late enough for a beer, and I could use one."

REMY AND FOOTSIE STOOD on the sandy creek bank taking turns throwing their pocketknives at X's in the dirt. They had drawn a series of them—a big one just a few feet away, a smaller one about five feet away, and the smallest nearly ten feet away. Remy took aim, threw the knife, and hit the smallest X dead center.

"Dadgum it, Remy!" Footsie exclaimed. "I ain't never seen nobody throw a knife like you. I bet I got brothers way older'n you can't hit that target."

"Thanks," Remy said with a smile.

"How you get so good?"

"Mr. Heywood taught me. I *never* seen nobody could throw like him. I practice a lot when I'm by myself."

"You got the steadiest hand I ever done seen! Will you show me how you take ahold o' yo' knife?"

"Sure," Remy said. "First you lay it on your palm like this . . ."

FORTY-SIX

ELLIE SPOONED A BIG DOLLOP of chocolate icing onto the three-layer cake she had baked for Heywood. He was spending this afternoon with Gabby but told her he wanted to come over and help Remy make short work of any leftover frosting. He was uncharacteristically late for food, which Ellie attributed to Gabby's charms.

Raphe had held Remy off as long as he could, but the call of the river on a Saturday afternoon proved overpowering, and Remy just wouldn't give up. With Heywood surely on his way, Ellie persuaded Raphe it would be perfectly safe to take Remy out in the pirogue for a couple of hours while she baked.

As the icing cascaded over the sides of her cake, she heard the distinctive sound of the *Whirlygig* coming into the slough. Ellie had always thought there was something joyful about the chugging noise made by Heywood's boat. Or maybe the joy came from knowing she and Raphe were about to spend some time with their friend.

She kept smoothing the rich chocolate with a spatula. The birthday boy would have to let himself in, because chocolate icing wouldn't wait. It would set in big clumps if she didn't work it the way her mother had taught her.

Ellie found it soothing to bake, especially when she was worried about something or missing her family. Those two generally went hand in hand—a worried mind and a homesick heart. It didn't happen often, but when it did, Raphe would always offer to stop whatever he was doing and drive her to New Orleans to catch the train to Alabama for a visit. But the thought of being separated from him and from Remy was even worse than separation from her own kin. And their cabin was too small to invite her family here.

Right now, what Ellie felt was an unfamiliar mix of homesickness and fear—not just worry but outright fear. Mama Jean once told her that the worst thing about getting scared is forgetting how to get yourself un-scared. Everything that had happened to her community, from the fires and displacement of neighbors to the disappearance of someone she barely knew and yet felt an odd connection with—Ellie realized she had let it all get the best of her. It was time to take control of her fears and move on, if only long enough to bake a cake.

She turned it to make sure the icing was smooth all around and poured a little extra for the top. This was a big birthday, and she wanted it to be special for Heywood. The extra icing went into a bowl for Remy. She had turned to set it in the icebox when she heard the screen door open.

"Well, it's about time," she said. But when she turned back around, she saw not her dear friend but the very root of all that terrified her: Gig Luetrell standing just inside her cabin.

He grinned at her. "You look like you seen a ghost. Or maybe a white alligator."

"What do you want?" Ellie tried not to let her voice shake. She was as frightened as she had ever been in her life.

"You, of course," Luetrell said. "Need me a little help gettin' outta this bayou, and I figure you'll do fine."

"What are you talking about?"

"Need me a escort. A little insurance card in case some lawman takes it in his head to stop me. You're gon' get me outta this rat-riddled swamp. Seen your man leave, by the way. No need in tellin' me he's out back or anything."

"He's not. But a friend of ours—"

"Fella in that tin can of a boat out there? Oh, he's not gonna make it."

Ellie had to steel herself just to breathe. Surely this wouldn't be Heywood's path to an early grave, at the hands of one so vile. Luetrell had to be lying. He just had to. She heard water dripping and noticed for the first time that Luetrell was barefoot, his pants rolled up above his ankles, and he was soaking wet.

"I do apologize about your floor," he said. "Had to jump under the dock when I heard your comp'ny comin'."

Before she could stop herself, her eyes drifted to the knife holster on his belt. It was empty.

"See now, that's what gets people in trouble. Noticin' things they shouldn't. I'll miss that knife. But I put it to good use. Thought it best to let it sink with the departed." Luetrell shook his head. "You shoulda seen the look on that boy's face. He never saw it comin'. I'll never understand backstabbers. What's the point o' knifin' somebody if you're gonna miss the look on their face? That split second before the pain sets in when they get this little shocked expression—and then it hits 'em they're fixin' to die. I wouldn't miss that for all the booze on Bourbon Street." He pulled a silver pocket watch out of his shirt pocket and popped it open so Ellie could see the mother-of-pearl face. "Reckon what I could get for that?" He tossed the watch onto the table.

Ellie's heart was pounding. Forcing herself to stare at Luetrell and not let her eyes wander, she mentally ticked off her possible defenses—all out of reach. The cast-iron skillet overhead. Raphe's gumbo pot hanging on the fireplace. A shotgun in the bedroom. She'd never make it to any of them before he stopped her. She stood perfectly still, afraid to blink, afraid to breathe.

RAPHE LAID HIS FISHING ROD DOWN and watched Remy reel in his line. The bayou was unusually quiet. Raphe's mind was anything but. He and Remy were barely out of sight of the cabin when he got the unshakable feeling that he had made a mistake. What if Heywood got distracted? What if he was late? What if Juliet had been left alone by circumstance, isolated and endangered?

A hawk screeched overhead. Something wasn't right. He could feel it.

LUETRELL SAT DOWN at Ellie's table and tipped back his chair, propping his dirty feet on another one. He looked around the cabin. "This place ain't much to look at, is it? Your man must be Cajun trash."

Ellie held her tongue and stared at him, thinking about how she could defend herself if he should make the slightest movement.

289

"Ain't nothin' trashy about you, though, is there?"

Ellie tried to take slow, steady breaths. She felt sick, which she couldn't afford to be right now.

Luetrell pointed at the birthday cake. "Bring that here and cut me some. Second thought, I'll cut it myself. Behave yourself or I'll cut you too."

Ellie stared at the cake.

"Well, what you waitin' on? Get your tail over here with that cake."

She picked up the cake and slowly walked to the table, standing as close to Luetrell as her nerve would allow.

He looked up at her and grinned. "If you're real good, I'll let you set on my lap while I eat it all up. Then I might just gobble *you* up."

"Promise?" Ellie said. Then she slammed the cake into his face as hard as she could, so hard that he fell over backward. But as she tried to run away, he grabbed her ankle and tripped her.

Both of them scrambled to stand as Luetrell wiped cake and warm frosting from his eyes. Ellie lost her balance and fell toward the fireplace. Before he could see, she grabbed the gumbo pot and swung it at his head with all her strength before running out the door and down the dock, screaming, "Heywood! Heywood!"

Jumping into Raphe's bass boat, she pulled on the starter again and again, all the while staring in terror at the front door of the cabin. Just as the motor finally cranked, she saw Luetrell stumbling down the steps. His head was bleeding and he was still wiping cake off his face. Ellie saw him trip and fall just before she pulled alongside the *Whirligig*, screaming Heywood's name and praying he would answer.

When he at last stood up, he was holding his bleeding head and staggering.

"Heywood!" Ellie screamed. "Jump!"

Heywood jumped off his boat and into hers, almost tipping them over. He took the throttle from her and had the boat almost in the main channel when Luetrell pulled himself up and stumbled his way into a boat Ellie didn't recognize, tied to a tree on the bank. Luetrell was trying to pole his boat away from the bank. He had one foot on the front seat and one on the bow, leaning into the oar he was using to push against the bank, but the boat wasn't moving. The motor must've been mired.

Heywood suddenly changed course and steered straight for him. A few feet away, he stopped, stood up, pulled a knife out of his hip pocket, and threw it.

Luetrell screamed and grabbed the back of his ankle, dropping like a sack of potatoes the minute the knife hit its target.

Heywood took the throttle and steered them back out into the bayou, where he turned to see whether he had stopped Luetrell. "Unbelievable."

Ellie looked back and saw Luetrell, unable to free his boat or to stand, hurl himself into the water and start swimming toward them.

"Blood in the bayou," Heywood said, just before they both spotted an alligator slicing through the water toward the thrashing noise. Heywood grabbed Ellie and pressed her face against his shoulder so she wouldn't see. And then the bayou grew still.

FORTY-SEVEN

ELLIE AWOKE TO BLURRED VISION and unfamiliar surroundings. A dark figure was hovering over her, but she
couldn't make it out. She knew only that it made her feel safe.

From far off in the distance, she heard Raphe's voice calling to her. "Juliet? Can you hear me, Juliet?"

She kept staring at the shadowy figure and blinking her
eyes until slowly it came into focus. "Raphe?"

"*C'est moi*," he said with a smile, bending down to kiss
her, hold her hand, and gently stroke her hair.

"Where—where am I?" She looked around, struggling to
get her bearings.

"I'd think you might recognize this old room by now,"
another voice said.

Ellie looked up to see Doc standing behind Raphe. She
squinted at him. "Is this where we brought Remy?"

Doc smiled and nodded. "Yes. When he was sick with the
virus."

"But—but why—why am I here?" She looked at Raphe.
"How did you get here?"

"We were almost home—Remy and me—when we spotted
you and Heywood," Raphe said. "You both looked bad. I
tied the pirogue to the bass boat and brought you to Doc's

house. He bandaged Heywood and gave you something to help calm you down, but you had a reaction to it. We've had a hard time waking you up."

Ellie blinked at him as she struggled to get her senses back. "Where's Remy? Is he alright?"

"He's fine," Raphe assured her. "He's outside fishing on the dock."

"Good. That's good." Then she was anxious again. "And Heywood? Is he alright?"

Raphe smiled at her. "I don't know. See what you think." He nodded toward the corner of the room, and Heywood came and sat down on the other side of her bed. A clean white bandage was wrapped around his head.

"We got ourselves into a real pickle, Mrs. Broussard," he said.

She reached out and took his hand. "Are you okay?"

"Never better."

"That man—he wanted me to think he killed you, but something told me it wasn't true. I just couldn't believe that."

Heywood rubbed the back of his head. "I can't say he didn't try—clocked me from behind before I could get off my boat. Unfortunately for Luetrell, I have quite the hard noggin."

"So awful . . ."

Heywood winked at her. "As they say on the tombstones, he's gone but not forgotten. The sheriff's department recovered . . . well, what they could."

Ellie kept working her way through the fog as her head cleared more and more. "Boone—Luetrell told me he killed Boone with his knife."

"You sure about that, Ellie?" Doc asked. "You've been through a lot."

"I'm sure," she said. "That first time I saw him—Luetrell—when he came to the school, he caught me looking at that knife—a red handle with silver ram's horns at the hilt. Then at the cabin, he realized I noticed it was missing. That's when he told me. He pulled out Boone's pocket watch and threw it on the table to prove it—to scare me."

"If it's at the cabin, it's not going anywhere," Raphe said, running his fingertips over Ellie's brow. "Mighty glad you were there, Heywood. Mighty glad."

"So am I," Ellie said.

Doc brought a glass of water to Ellie's bedside. "Raphe, see if she can drink a little bit. Fluids'll help move the drug on out of her system."

Raphe lifted her up and held her while he gave her as much water as she could drink.

"I should go," Heywood said. "I have promised a certain Miss Toussaint Sunday supper on my luxurious yacht."

"Today is Sunday?" Ellie asked.

"Late afternoon," Raphe told her. "You slept through last night and most of today."

A smile spread across Ellie's face. "If it's Sunday, that means you made it, Heywood. You're thirty years old. Happy birthday."

"How 'bout that," he said. "Happy birthday to moi."

DOWNSTAIRS, FLORENCE POURED Doc and Raphe a cup of coffee at her kitchen table and excused herself to take food to the Taylors. Juliet had gone back to sleep, and Doc predicted she wouldn't be fully alert till tomorrow.

He gave his coffee a splash of cream and stirred it. "Mind

if I talk to you about a few things, Raphe—even if it's none of my business?"

"Much as you've helped us, I don't see how we could say anything's none of your business."

Doc smiled and took a sip of his coffee. "Ellie is a strong young woman, Raphe, and an optimistic one by nature. But she has been through a serious trauma."

Raphe nodded and slowly turned his coffee cup on the table. "Never shoulda happened. I never shoulda left her all alone with that—"

"Now, hold on." Doc put up his hand. "This is not your fault. You had every reason to believe that your best friend in the world was on his way to your cabin and that Ellie would be safe. There's no blame here. But there are some changes I believe you should consider."

Raphe looked up at him. "Like what?"

"This might be hard to hear, Raphe, but I don't think Ellie should go back to your cabin, at least not now, and—well—maybe not ever."

"But it's our home."

"I know. And up until now, it's been filled with good memories for Ellie—marrying you and making a home for Remy and finding the life she was searching for when she came here. That all changed yesterday, Raphe. Combat vets aren't the only ones who suffer flashbacks. Anybody who goes through something as frightening and life-threating as Ellie did can have them. What used to be her safe haven might now remind her of the worst day of her life."

"We don't know that will happen, do we?" Raphe asked.

"No. But there's something else. Your wife and mine—they didn't grow up here like we did. Florence and Ellie both had homes with running water and electricity. They were used to traveling in cars, not boats. The difference between them is that Ellie loves the bayou as much as we do. Florence has never been comfortable there, so she asked me to meet her halfway out here on the river. Ellie's never asked you to make that choice. But, Raphe, I think maybe you should. I know it's none o' my business, and I hope you'll take this in the spirit of friendship in which I offer it. I believe you need to think about the future—about the children you and Ellie might have. I think you need a fresh start. And I know where you can get it."

LATE IN THE NIGHT, Ellie awoke to find Raphe lying beside her in bed at Doc's. He was wide awake, staring at the ceiling. It was raining outside.

She reached over and touched his hand. "I'd offer a penny for your thoughts, but I don't think that would begin to cover everything swirling around up there."

He turned on his side and propped up on his elbow, looking down at her and tracing the line of her cheekbone with his fingertip. "You have such pretty bones."

"Merci . . . I guess?"

They laughed quietly together so they wouldn't disturb Remy next door. Raphe lay back down on his pillow, and she rested her head on his shoulder.

"How do you feel, Juliet?"

"Like a train ran over me. No matter what I do, I can't stay awake very long, and when I sleep I have the craziest dreams."

"Just rest. Everything will be different tomorrow. Everything. I promise."

ON TUESDAY MORNING, Ellie felt fully awake for the first time since coming to Doc's. Raphe's side of the bed was empty. Sunlight was streaming through her window. It must be seven o'clock at least. She heard her door open and turned to see Remy peeking in. She smiled and pulled the covers back. He grinned at her as he came inside and climbed in.

"You're about the best thing I could possibly see right now," Ellie said as he snuggled into her shoulder.

"I was afraid you wouldn't ever wake up," he said.

Ellie tightened her arms around him. "I'm sorry I scared you, sweetheart. We've had quite a few days, haven't we?"

"Oui, M'Ellie."

"Where's Nonc?"

"I can't tell you."

"Why not?"

"It's a secret," he said, smiling up at her.

"So you and Nonc have secrets from me now?"

Remy nodded.

"I guess that's what I get for having two men in my house. You'll always have your secrets."

"This is a really good one," Remy said. "And I'm supposed to take care of you till Nonc gets back."

"You are? Well, that makes me feel a lot better."

"Nonc says we'll spend tonight at Doc's and then we can go home tomorrow."

Ellie held Remy a little closer—for his protection or hers, she wasn't sure. "Home," she said.

Remy squeezed her tightly. "Don't go back to sleep again, M'Ellie, okay?"

"Okay, sweetie. I won't go back to sleep."

FORTY-EIGHT

THAT NIGHT THE MOON WAS HIGH and full as Raphe paddled through a watery tunnel of green and returned once again to the remote slough, dwelling place of the white alligator. Soon he would take Juliet and Remy home. He would devote himself to their protection and happiness. But on this night, with the two of them safe at Doc's, there was something he needed to do.

He entered the slough, its waters bathed in silver light, the surface as smooth as a river stone. The pirogue glided through it as Raphe paddled only as much as necessary, with a reverence for the beauty of this place and a respect for the alligator's sanctuary.

Aligned with the fallen tupelo gum, he laid down his paddle and waited. Around midnight, he heard the rare but familiar rustling in the swamp grass and the sound of something massive moving over damp ground. It appeared just like always, though the sight of it had grown ever more breathtaking over the years as the alligator grew in stature and might. Its hide, under this particular moon, was gleaming ever whiter.

Raphe expected it to climb onto the tupelo tree, but tonight the alligator did something it had never done before.

It went straight into the water and dove under. About thirty seconds later, the alligator surfaced, its snowy form marred by mud on its snout. Raphe held his breath as it dove again and then a third time. He saw bubbles on the surface of the water as the alligator glided back to its tupelo tree, the bayou waters cleansing the mud from its ivory skin.

As the alligator took its position on the fallen tree, drinking in the moon's muted light, a horror followed the bubbles to the surface of the water. Raphe saw it and remembered, with a familiar sickness, the many bodies he had pulled out of the water after the great storm. And here was another one, facedown in the bayou, a frayed rope tied around one leg. The alligator had freed it from its anchor down below. Now it floated in these waters, a silent accusation demanding justice for a son betrayed by a father's greed.

FORTY-NINE

ON WEDNESDAY MORNING IN BATON ROUGE, Lura Poteet put through a call to the senator. As was her custom, she listened in. The boy had been found by a Cajun fisherman who couldn't remember the way back to whatever backwoods swamp Boone had landed in but had delivered the body— and the strange knife buried in it—to the local deputies. The parish sheriff wished to express his deepest regrets.

Lura disconnected from the line before the call ended. She knew the senator would summon her soon. And he did.

"Lura," he said as she entered his office, "they found Boone."

"Was it as you expected, Senator?"

"It was. I need you to plan the funeral. And make it nice."

"Of course. Do you anticipate any . . . repercussions?"

"No. Been in the water too long for much evidence. For all anybody knows, that knife belongs to the preacher. Luetrell dead, preacher locked up for Boone—that takes care o' that. And I thank you, Lura, for all your help."

"Yes, sir." Lura quickly removed herself from the senator's office and prepared to make arrangements for the boy. She was about to dial the funeral home when she saw the senator's private line light up. Lifting her receiver, she pressed the button and listened.

"Loyal as she can be . . . Served me well . . . Just unfortunate that she knows too much . . ."

As always, Lura heard all she needed to know and hung up as soon as the call ended. She sat motionless at her desk, considering her options. Hubris was the great weakness of powerful men. Having paid you to do their bidding, they convinced themselves over time that you served them out of love and devotion, out of admiration for their wisdom and strength, when, in fact, it was their money and the power they shed that made you stay. Ego blinded them to the transactional nature of it all.

Lura wasn't blinded by anything. She had the combination to the senator's safe and the ability to duplicate his signature. With those two in hand, she didn't need the man himself any more than he now needed her. As she had done so many times before, she would make her exit and close the door behind her.

FIFTY

ELLIE CHANGED INTO THE DRESS RAPHE had brought her from home and stripped the bed where they had slept at Doc's. She looked out the window and saw Raphe and Remy readying the boat.

Both Doc and Florence, she knew, had been busy coming up with excuses to keep her with them. Raphe and Remy, who normally would be eager to get home, had been surprisingly compliant. Maybe it had something to do with Remy's secret.

Whatever their reasons, she hadn't exactly fought them on it. The truth was, Ellie dreaded returning to the cabin, and that made her sadder than anything. It was her home. Before that, it had been Raphe's and Remy's. But instead of picturing the three of them together around the table, she kept seeing Gig Luetrell. Would it be the same with the bayou? Would she see the birds and the turtles in the here and now, or would memory forever carry her back to the eerie sight of an alligator speeding toward the sound of evil thrashing in the water?

She would find out soon enough. They had been at Doc's since Saturday night, and now it was Thursday morning.

Enough. "Back your ears and get on with it," Mama Jean would say.

"How are you, dear?" Florence came into the bedroom and joined her at the window.

"I don't have enough merci's to cover all you and Doc have done for us," Ellie said.

"You don't have to thank us. We've been happy to have y'all—brought a little life into this quiet old house."

"I'll take your sheets home and wash them. I'll get the ones from Remy's room too, and I can bring them with me to the dance hall Sunday morning if that's alright. Reckon we'll be having church there for a while."

"You'll do no such thing. I'll pitch those sheets in the washing machine when I get good and ready. Nobody needs them anytime soon. Come and sit with me, honey."

Ellie sat next to Florence on the edge of the bed.

"I can't begin to imagine the trauma you've been through, Ellie, but setting that aside, I doubt anybody in Bernadette understands your situation like I do."

"My situation?"

Florence laid her hand over Ellie's. "You fell in love with a man who not only comes from a different place than you but from a whole different world. You're separated from your family. You're living in the middle of a bayou, paddling a boat instead of driving a car, doing without electricity and running water."

Ellie smiled. "I see your point. But I love my life with Raphe."

"I know you do. I love my life with Doc. But that doesn't mean it's always easy." Florence lifted Ellie's hand and turned it over. "I'd be willing to bet you use a lot more hand cream than you used to. Emmett keeps a big supply of it—his wife makes sure of that. A washboard is rough on your hands."

"Yes," Ellie said as Florence gave her hand a gentle squeeze. "It certainly is. But it's not like I had a houseful of servants in Alabama. We had to work hard there too."

"I know. But the bayou is different. You've probably built muscles you didn't even know you had, right?"

Ellie rubbed her upper arm and nodded.

"Don't be afraid to let Raphe know when it's just too much for you, Ellie. He loves you. He wants to make you as happy as you want to make him. But he can't read your mind. When you need him to make things easier for you, just say so. I believe he'll do it."

Ellie felt the tears coming. "Thank you, Florence," she whispered as they hugged each other. "Could you hold on to me for just a minute?"

"I won't let go, honey," Florence said. "I'll hold on to you as long as you need me to."

FIFTY-ONE

ELLIE TURNED HER FACE TO THE SUN and felt the warm river breeze as Raphe steered the boat toward home. A pat on her arm made her open her eyes to see Remy, a concerned frown on his face, looking up at her. "Are you going to sleep again, M'Ellie?"

She smiled and put her arms around him. "No, sweetie. I'm just enjoying the sun."

They weren't even a quarter mile from Doc's when Raphe turned the boat down a channel Ellie had never seen before, one just off the lower Atchafalaya. "Making a stop on the way?" she asked him.

"It won't take long," he said.

Remy was suddenly grinning ear to ear.

"What are y'all up to?" Ellie asked.

Raphe put a finger over his lips. "*Dis pas rien*, Remy."

"Say nothing about what?" Ellie smiled at her husband. "Watch yourself—my French is getting better."

Raphe pulled up to a dock in front of the prettiest river cabin Ellie had ever seen. It was made of cypress, with a deep porch and tall, shuttered windows across the front, a steep metal roof, and three gables. It sat on heavy pilings five or six feet tall.

"Who lives here, Raphe?" Ellie asked him.

"Go ahead, Remy, before you explode," Raphe said.

"We do!" Remy shouted. "C'mon, M'Ellie, let's go see it! I'm going upstairs!"

Ellie was too overwhelmed to speak. Remy was already scampering up the dock to the porch as Raphe helped her out of the boat.

"Raphe, what is this?" They were standing together at the foot of the steps.

He held her face in his hands and kissed her. "It's a fresh start, Juliet."

He put an arm around her and guided her up the steps to the porch lined with rocking chairs. A swing was hanging at one end, the hammock Heywood had given Raphe at the other. Ellie turned and looked out at a beautiful watery view, dotted with cypress trees yet wide and open, making it seem part bayou, part river.

Raphe opened the front door. "I think I'm supposed to carry you over the threshold," he said, picking Ellie up and carrying her inside.

The first floor was open. To the far left was a farm table and chairs, with a large kitchen filling a whole rear quarter of the house. To the right was a real living room with a sofa and two easy chairs clustered around the fireplace. A landing to the right of it led upstairs.

Raphe guided her down a short corridor that ran between the living room and kitchen and opened a door on the right. Ellie gasped and grabbed his arm. There stood a full bathroom with indoor plumbing. Before she could take it all in, he led her into the kitchen, where she could see a gas stove and hear the hum of an electric icebox. Instead of a pump at the sink, there was a modern faucet.

"Raphe, it's—it's just beautiful," she managed to say.

"Hold on," he said, leading her into a spacious bedroom with a fireplace and tall windows that overlooked a creek running along the back of the house.

Ellie raised a window and closed her eyes, listening to the swift-flowing creek water and the plop of frogs, the birdsong and crickets.

Raphe put his arms around her waist. "Don't get lost in the creek music. I have one more thing to show you."

She followed him out to a back porch, where, in all its glory, stood a washing machine.

Ellie put her arms around the basin of the heavy machine. "Raphe," she said, "I want to be the mother of your children."

FIFTY-TWO

LATE IN THE AFTERNOON, Remy was fishing off the dock while Raphe and Ellie sat in the swing on their new front porch.

"I still can't believe this is ours," Ellie said.

"You aren't angry with me for buying it without showing you first?"

"Of course not. You bought it to give me things I didn't even know I wanted. But what about you?"

"It's the same for me. When Doc showed it to me, I saw so much I didn't even know I was missing."

"What about the distance from Kitty and Footsie?"

"There's a shallow cut-through from the creek to a main channel back into the bayou. Remy could handle it fine. And then in the other direction, we're only a few minutes from Doc and Florence."

"Are you sure we can afford it?"

"We can," Raphe said, watching Remy cast his line toward a cypress stump. "I haven't been fair to you, Juliet."

"Don't say that."

"It's true. I should've done this at the beginning. I never should've had you scrubbing clothes on a washboard or living in a house with no plumbing or electricity. What was I working all those long days in Morgan City for if not to give you and Remy a good home?"

"Raphe, it's not like I lived in a castle in Alabama," she said with a smile. "We didn't get electricity till the Army built a plant near our farm, and we didn't get indoor plumbing till after the war."

"I should've given you the best I could, and I didn't," he insisted. "I didn't do it because I couldn't let go."

"Of what?"

"My family."

Ellie kissed him on the cheek. "Nobody wants to let go of their family, Raphe. I don't fault you for that. You grew up in that cabin and—"

"No, I didn't."

"I guess I just assumed . . ."

"No, the place where I grew up got washed away in the storm. So did every other cabin in my family except for the one my oldest brother built when he married. That's the cabin we've been living in. That and my grandfather's pirogue—those were the only pieces of them, of all of them, I had left. And I guess I just couldn't let it go. Can you forgive me?"

Ellie put her arms around his waist and laid her head on his shoulder. "Nothing to forgive. But what changed your mind?"

Raphe ran his fingers through her hair. "Doc. He made me see how hard it would be for you to go back to the cabin after everything that happened there. How hard it might've been all along. I guess after the storm—losing everything like that—maybe I just didn't want to have anything to lose ever again."

"You know I'd be happy anywhere with you." Ellie wanted to make him laugh. "Anywhere with you and that washing machine."

He was smiling at last. "Gold digger."

"I'm gonna clean out your pockets, mister. Oh, look—Remy got one."

They watched as Remy reeled in a big catfish, then sat quietly rocking in the swing.

"Raphe—do you think it's possible for a dream to be a vision?"

"I imagine so. Why?"

"I had a lot of strange dreams at Doc's. Some of them were just the medicine. But there was this one I can't shake."

"Did it scare you?"

"No, just the opposite. It sort of hopped around. One minute I was at the school with Gabby and Bonita, and then I was at Tante Dodo's and she was teaching me to cook, but then I turned around and all the older girls from school were there too. I saw you and Lawyer playing music in my classroom, and then I saw five boys—two white and three colored—standing in a pirogue, holding accordions and fiddles."

"What is it saying to you?"

"That children can learn in so many ways. That I'm not the only one who can teach them. Lawyer makes his own accordions. So many of you play music. Tante Dodo has the whole history of your people in her heart and in her hands when she cooks. Why not share it? Why not share every bit of it, Raphe—with *all* the children?"

"I think you're about to put the bayou to work," he said, bending down to kiss her. "And I think it's a wonderful thing, your vision."

They looked out to see Remy smack himself on the head and reel in his line.

"Guess that one got away," Ellie said. They listened to the early evening call of cicadas as the sun began to set. "I should start supper."

"I'll cook," he said. "You rest." The squeaking of chains as they rocked back and forth added to the lazy river sounds of another day slowly fading into night.

"Raphe," she said, "do you think we might do something about Remy—something official? Should we adopt him and make it clear once and for all that he's ours, that he has a home?"

"You would do this?"

"I would do this."

"*D'accord.*"

FIFTY-THREE

A LAZY SATURDAY MORNING found Ellie reading in her porch swing when she heard the familiar chug of the *Whirlygig*. Three weeks had gone by since Ellie and Raphe moved into their new cabin, and they hadn't seen hide nor hair of Heywood. Now here he was. Raphe was coming out of the house to join Ellie when Heywood climbed out of his boat, tucked what looked like a newspaper and a bright yellow envelope under his arm, and offered his hand to Gabby. They made their way to the front porch.

"It's about time y'all turned up." Ellie smiled as she and Raphe greeted them. "Pull up some rocking chairs. Can I get you anything?"

"No, thank you, Mrs. Broussard, we dare not tarry," Heywood said as he pulled up two chairs and held Gabby's for her before sitting down next to her.

She grinned and gave him a nudge with her elbow. "He means we can't stay."

"Brought you something." Heywood handed Raphe the newspaper.

Raphe sat down with Ellie in the swing as they read the paper together. The whole front page was a tribute to the late

Senator Roy Strahan, killed by an unidentified shooter using the senator's own gun at his fishing camp on the Atchafalaya. The state police had no leads. The senator's funeral and that of his late son were arranged by his longtime secretary, who was—Ellie read the last part out loud—"now on a leave of absence from the statehouse as she copes with her grief."

"That's so strange," she said. "All of them gone—the senator, Boone, Luetrell, and now this secretary."

"Read the tiny little item at the bottom of the second page," Heywood prompted.

Ellie turned the page and read the headline: "'Evangelist Freed, Charges Dropped.'"

"Brother Lester's out of jail?" Raphe said.

Heywood nodded. "Doc and Leo helped get him released. Once Ellie identified the knife that killed Boone, they had no reason to keep the preacher in jail, especially without that senator around to try and pin it on him."

"Who do you think killed the senator?" Raphe asked.

"Bet you my good pair o' shoes it was that secretary," Gabby said.

"And why is that?" Heywood smiled at her.

"Any woman that's got to put up with a man's 'do this, do that' all day long's bound to wanna kill him."

"I shall keep that in mind, *ma femme*, and sleep with one eye open," Heywood said.

"Wait—what?" Ellie said.

Gabby held up her left hand so Ellie could see the ring. "We went and got married in New Orleans last weekend."

Ellie squealed as she jumped up and hugged them both.

"Congratulations, *mon ami*." Raphe smiled and shook Heywood's hand.

"There's just one thing that worries me, Heywood." Ellie winked at Gabby. "How did Claudette take it?"

"Poor thing was crushed, utterly crushed," Heywood replied. "Said she was leaving Louisiana, never to return."

Ellie shook her head. "Well, I for one won't miss her. That girl couldn't carry on a conversation if her life depended on it. But what's got y'all in such a hurry that you can't stay? Raphe's making gumbo."

"Well, now, that is tempting. But the missus and I are headed back to New Orleans to shoot the engagement portrait of a well-to-do bride."

"Really? Oh, Heywood, that's great news! By the time you get everybody's lumber milled, you'll be a famous photographer who won't give us common folks the time of day."

Heywood put his hand over his heart. "Just be thankful for the time we had, Broussards. Be thankful for the time we had."

"Maybe now you can do what you always wanted to," Raphe said.

Heywood smiled at Gabby. "I give all the credit to the missus. She says the best way to become a successful photographer is to act like I already am one."

"Fo' sure," Gabby said. "You got the talent, so go on and say so."

"She's got a cousin in New Orleans that helped her sniff out some rich debs lookin' to wed, and the next thing I knew, she had three of 'em booked. All Gabby's doing. One hundred percent. Any brides complain about the pictures, I'll just say, 'You need to take that up with management—let me put you through to my lovely wife. And by the way, I wouldn't cross her if I were you.'"

"I imagine you two won't be in Bernadette long," Ellie said.

Heywood shrugged. "Another year at least. Gabby thinks it'll take that long to make me world famous."

"You don't know, *cher*, I might do it in six months," she said. "Then I'm gon' make him move me to New Orleans. It's where the work is, and he's always wanted to live there. We gon' travel all over the place. I can keep him fed an' outta trouble while he earns a good livin', and I can make sure he's got the free time to take his pretty bayou pictures. Somebody's gotta keep all them mamas o' the bride off him."

"I've seen her in action, Heywood," Ellie said. "Those New Orleans mamas better fall in line if they expect an audience with *the* Heywood Thornberry."

"Well," Heywood said to Gabby, "you booked it and now I've got to shoot it." They stood up to go. "I have one more thing for you." Heywood handed Ellie the yellow envelope he had been holding. "Wait till we're gone and then open it together."

"Sounds very mysterious," Ellie said.

"Oh, it is," he said. "Top secret."

Raphe and Ellie walked them to the dock, said their good-byes, and waved as the *Whirlygig* pulled away.

Ellie took Raphe's arm as they walked back to their porch. "It's funny—it used to make me so blue when Heywood left, but I don't feel that way now. I always thought I was sad for me. But now I think I was sad for him because I knew how alone he was, no matter what big front he put on. He's not alone anymore, Raphe."

"No, he's not." Raphe bent down to kiss her. "And neither am I."

315

She smiled. "And neither am I."

They sat down in the swing together, and Ellie opened the yellow envelope. It held three portraits Heywood had printed. The first was the picture Ellie had taken of him in New Orleans when he still wondered if he'd live past thirty. It was a tight profile with Heywood staring out at the Mississippi, his Panama hat shading his face but not hiding his expression. It brought a pang of sadness to Ellie's heart even now, though she knew those days were past him. She turned the picture over and laughed. "Stop crying, Ellie, I'm fine now," Heywood had written.

Raphe put his arm around her and smiled. "He saw you coming."

Next came a portrait of Raphe, taken when he was completely unaware of the camera. He was leaning against a tree, holding his fiddle, looking at something in the distance. There was the slightest trace of a wistful smile on his handsome face.

Ellie lightly ran her hand over the portrait. "Nobody else on earth has eyes like yours."

"I never saw that picture before," Raphe said. "But I remember what I was doing. I was watching you walk away."

Ellie looked up at him and laid her hand against his face for just a moment before turning back to the pictures. She flipped over the portrait of her husband. "My boy Raphe's in love," Heywood had written, which made both of them laugh.

Finally came the third picture, the portrait of Ellie that Heywood had taken by the river in New Orleans, right before she and Raphe finally found their way to each other. Raphe took the picture from her hands and stared at it. The sun

316

was on her face, which was tilted toward the sky, the river breeze in her hair, her expression part love, part longing.

Raphe couldn't seem to stop staring at the portrait. "This is the most beautiful thing I've ever seen. When did this happen?"

"Before we married, right before you got back from Morgan City and came to Doc's cabin to be with me," Ellie said. "Remember I told you Heywood took me to New Orleans for lunch?"

"Yes."

"We stopped for lemonade by the river and he liked the afternoon light, so he asked me to close my eyes, tilt my head back, and think of the most incredible moment in my life. I thought of moonlight on the white alligator and your arms around me, how you were sharing it with me and protecting me from it all at the same time. I thought of your face against mine and how there would never be any such thing as enough time with you—on the bayou or anyplace else. That's when Heywood took the picture. It's a picture of how I feel about you, Raphe. It's how I've felt from the beginning."

He silently turned the image over to read Heywood's inscription, but the back of the picture was blank. "I guess he thought such a perfect thing needs no explanation." Raphe turned the image faceup again and traced the line of Ellie's face with his fingertips.

She took the picture from him and slipped it back in the envelope with the others, then rested her head on his shoulder and closed her eyes. Raphe held her and rocked the swing as they listened to a spring breeze stir the trees on the riverbank. A boat could go by. A bird could take flight. This day could unfold however it chose. Raphe and Ellie had found their way home.

Epilogue

"COULD THERE BE a more *jolie brune* in all of Louisiana?"

"I know what Maman would say to that, Uncle Heywood—hush up and gimme a hug."

"You sound just like her—and a tad like my beloved wife, for whom your parents wisely named you." Heywood put his arms around Gabby Broussard Cheramie and hugged her tight. "How are you, baby girl?"

"Middle aged. You?"

He shook his head sadly. "Ancient. Positively ancient. Allow me." He offered Gabby his arm and escorted her into the front parlor of his Garden District home, with its thick tapestry rugs over heart-pine floors, crystal chandeliers, and elegant fireplaces. "May I get you anything?"

"I'm fine," she said as she took a seat in an armchair by the hearth.

Heywood sat across from her. He was quite the dapper ninety-year-old with his finely tailored suit, a red rose on the lapel. His shoes were of fine leather the color of cognac. He walked with a wooden cane hand-carved in New Orleans.

318

"And how are things at the best dining establishment on the entire Atchafalaya River?" he asked.

Gabby shrugged. "Same as always. Remy's in the kitchen, making Papa's recipes, and will likely never retire as long as there's one gumbo pot remaining in the state of Louisiana. Franklin just expanded the market for the third time."

"Franklin?" Heywood frowned and rubbed his brow. "Now why can't I place him?"

She smiled. "Would it help if I called him Footsie?"

He clapped his hands together. "Oh, for heaven's sake—Footsie. I guess I'll never get used to his real name after calling him that for so many years."

"Don't feel bad. Remy still slips up and calls him by his nickname. Would you believe the two of them *still* honor Papa's rule and won't sell anything to compete with Emmett's boys at Chalmette's? And Franklin's family made so much off their oil rights that he doesn't even have to work, but he's there beside Remy every single day, just like always."

"Knowing those two, I have no trouble believing that. And the Broussard sisters?"

Gabby rolled her eyes. "The sisters are the sisters. All three of 'em still try to boss me around like I'm twelve."

Heywood crossed his long legs and folded his hands in his lap. "Ah, but my guess is you'll have none of that."

Gabby laughed. "I guess I come by it honest, given who I'm named after." But then her smile faded and she grew serious. "You sure you're up to this long drive, Uncle Heywood? Because if you're not, we all understand."

"I shall repeat myself: You are just like your mother and a tad like my beloved late wife. And I adore you for the aggravation you cause me, but I'll be fine."

Gabby looked around the parlor, where the front-facing wall held soaring windows that flooded the room with sunlight. A fireplace sat opposite the cased entrance, while the rear wall held three large, framed prints of her uncle's favorite images: one of his wife, taken at the dance hall when she was young; another of Gabby's father, so handsome, leaning against a tree; and finally, the most beautiful shot of her mother, taken on the riverbank in New Orleans.

"It's worth the drive here just to see those hanging together like that again," she said.

Heywood gave her a wistful smile. "Never took a shot I liked better than 'The Trio'—included it in every show I ever did."

"Your 'shots,' as you call them, are in highfalutin galleries all over the place."

He gave a dismissive wave of his hand. "That's not so important, as it turns out. What matters are the people and places in those frames." He pointed a finger at each of the images as he spoke. "My Gabby gave me the courage to aim my camera and believe in the results. And she was a fine companion for all my adventures. Your dear mother set me straight whenever I drifted and was always there with a place at her table. She did that for everybody. Freeman Richard just got featured in the *New York Times*, but he'd be the first to tell you he never would've gotten into art school without your mother fighting for his education in Bernadette. As for your daddy—well, there's never been a better friend. Never been a better husband and father. Never been a soul on this earth I respected more."

"I have it on good authority that he felt the same way about you."

He adjusted the rose on his lapel and sighed. "Oh, baby girl. Life is short, even when you live a really long time."

"Do you miss the French Quarter, Uncle Heywood?"

"I certainly do." He stretched out one leg and slowly flexed his knee. "Alas, the ol' boy can't handle all those steps at the townhouse anymore. But I can't complain." He looked around the beautifully appointed room. "At least I got to spend some time here with my Gabby before she passed. Makes it feel more like home. I have a fine nurse and plenty of help, so I doubt I'll end up in the street."

"You know we'd kill to have you move in with us."

Heywood smiled. "I love you for saying it. But you have your own life, just like I do, and we should both be about it." He looked at his wristwatch. "Speaking of which, I guess we should get going before this old geezer turns into a sentimental puddle of mush."

Gabby stood and went to his side to help him up. "You're *my* old geezer, and I'll fight anybody who says otherwise."

That brought another smile. Heywood's eyes twinkled with their old mischief as he put his arms around her and held her tight. "You were always my favorite."

Gabby looked up at him and grinned. "I know."

THE LAST OF THE GUESTS had gone from Gabby's house on the river when she looked out a front window and saw her Uncle Heywood sitting in a rocker on the porch. Now and again he would hold up his palms, thumb to thumb, creating a square to frame an imaginary picture. She poured them both a small glass of his favorite port and joined him on the porch.

UNDER THE BAYOU MOON

He smiled up at her when she handed him the glass. "You were raised right."

They sat silently together, looking out at the Atchafalaya.

"There's not a more beautiful river in the whole world," he said.

Gabby took a sip of her wine. "If one more person had told me they wished we could be gathering under happier circumstances, I might've jumped right into that river."

Heywood threw his head back and laughed. "People say some mighty strange things when they're at a loss for words, don't they?"

"They do indeed."

He slowly turned the glass in his hand. "Your mother always had considerable patience with that sort of thing."

"And Papa?"

"Not so much."

They watched as a heron took off from its nest, flew in a wide circle, and then turned downriver.

"I suppose," Heywood said after a while, "I must face the inevitable."

"You sure you want to go back, Uncle Heywood?" Gabby reached out and laid her hand over his. "It's been a pretty long day already."

He gave her a sad smile and then turned his gaze to the river. "I don't want to, but I need to, baby girl."

After they finished their wine, Gabby brought him his hat and cane, then helped him down the steps and into the car. She followed a narrow, paved road that wound its way to a bluff overlooking the river, where the people of Bernadette buried their dead.

Heavy rains were in the forecast, but for now only a damp

mist was falling from the Louisiana sky. Gabby got out of the car and opened the passenger door, holding a large black umbrella above it as Heywood gingerly stepped out and slowly rose to his full height. These days, his aging body needed extra time to unfurl itself.

"Feel pretty steady?" Gabby asked.

"The veritable picture of balance," he answered.

She smiled. "I guess that means you want me to leave you alone?"

"It sounds so antisocial when you put it that way. Let's just say I see an opportunity for the both of us to enjoy a moment of solitude."

"I know when I'm not wanted. I'll be right here. Want the umbrella?"

"No, my hat will keep me dry. And the more I carry, the more likely I am to trip and wind up in the nursing home, eating oatmeal and dry toast instead of having breakfast at Brennan's."

"D'accord."

He bent down and kissed her on the cheek. "It does my old heart good to hear my boy Raphe's child speaking French. Bananas Foster on me when we return to New Orleans."

HEYWOOD TOOK HIS TIME, stepping carefully on the damp grass, as he made his way to a simple headstone facing the water. It marked two graves, one older and carpeted in green, the other brand-new, its freshly dug bayou earth covered with a mountain of funeral-home flowers.

Standing beside the grave on the left, he read the dates aloud: "March 3, 1920–April 20, 2005." He reached into his pocket, took out an oyster shell, and laid it on the granite. "Five years and I still miss you every day, *mon ami*."

He leaned on his cane as he carefully stepped around to the new grave and shook his head. "Those who supposedly know best tell me I can't make this trip again, but I had to say a proper goodbye." He removed the rose from his lapel and cradled it in his hand. "My Gabby never cared for roses. She used to say, 'Who'd want a flower that means to make 'em bleed?' But as I recall, you adored roses, thorns and all. I don't think the missus would mind if I gave this one to you." He carefully placed the delicate flower on the mist-covered stone, then took off his hat and laid it over his heart.

"Goodbye for now, Miss Ellie Fields—for now but not forever."

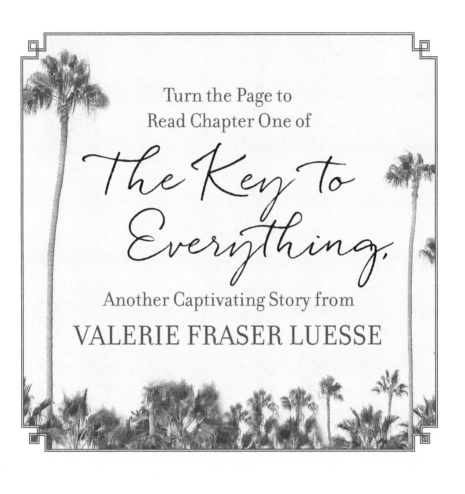

Turn the Page to
Read Chapter One of

*The Key to
Everything,*

Another Captivating Story from

VALERIE FRASER LUESSE

ONE

April 1947

THOUGH HE COULDN'T HAVE KNOWN, nor ever guessed, Peyton Cabot had just witnessed a bittersweet kiss goodbye. There they stood, a man and a woman, in the center of his grandfather's library, a mahogany-paneled sanctuary that always smelled of polished wood and old leather, parchment and pipe tobacco. It was empty now, with all the family outside for their annual picnic—empty but for these two.

As Peyton looked on, the couple shared an embrace so passionate that he knew he should turn away, for he realized in that moment that he had become the worst kind of intruder, spying on his own parents. Right now they didn't look like parents—she a blonde all-American beauty, he a larger-than-life movie idol. They looked like two strangers whose past he didn't share, whose present he couldn't comprehend. More than the embrace itself, that's what he found so arresting—the realization that his parents were more than a mother and father, that they did, in fact, have a life before him, apart from him entirely, one they would've shared even if he had never been born.

The revelation took him by surprise, and he fled to the

cover of his grandparents' front porch, sinking into their boisterous Georgia clan as he longed to sink into a pool of water that could wash away his transgression, for he knew good and well that he was guilty of theft. He had stolen a private moment that his mother and father never meant to share.

Peyton would spend this afternoon like so many others—swapping jokes with his boy cousins and listening to the uncles tell their stories (the same ones they told at every family picnic, but everybody laughed just the same). Still, the image of that kiss would be etched on his memory, not just for the rest of this sunny afternoon but for the rest of his life.

FOR YEARS, the Cabots had been gathering for a spring picnic at the family estate on the Isle of Hope. It was a show of togetherness mandated by Peyton's grandmother and held religiously, regardless of weather, on the Saturday before Easter. Attending the picnic was like performing a role in a play or a movie, the men costumed in their linen and seersucker, the ladies in tea-party dresses and wide-brimmed hats. All the children wore croquet whites, swinging their mallets in an orderly fashion until they got bored and started chasing each other all over the place, like a band of well-dressed jackrabbits.

Picnic tables were covered in starched white linens and dotted with crystal pitchers filled with fresh flowers. Even the ice cream would be served on china with sterling silver spoons. Servants ferried food out of the kitchen and dirty dishes back in. Over the course of an afternoon, the Cabots would consume platters mounded with fried chicken, country ham, and homemade biscuits slathered with fresh-churned butter; sweet potato casserole, corn on the cob, green beans, and black-eyed peas; ambrosia, Grandmother Cabot's coconut cake, Doxie's chocolate cake (she had to make three to satisfy all the family), homemade ice cream with Georgia peaches; and enough sweet tea and lemonade to float a barge—this in addition to the steady flow of cocktails mixed by the uncles.

For all appearances, the annual picnic was a grand gathering of one of the richest clans in Georgia. But the truth, Peyton knew, was that none of his aunts and uncles particularly liked each other. Moreover, they were all jealous of his father, the eldest—and reluctant favorite—son. Peyton's grandmother—instigator of the whole thing—never appeared to enjoy the picnic. In fact, it would eventually give her "a case of nerves," and she would retire well before sunset.

The center of activity was the lower front porch of his grandparents' Greek Revival house, which crowned a gently sloping, half-acre front lawn, parted down the center by a hundred-year-old live oak allée and bordered with deep pink azaleas almost as tall as Peyton. Lacy white spirea and more azaleas framed the house with its eight soaring columns. The white wicker porch furniture had been in the family for years, and while his grandmother frequently complained that it was old and needed replacing, his grandfather had it painstakingly repaired and restored every year. For whatever reason, he could not let it go.

Right now the porch was full to overflowing with relatives. Peyton leaned against one of the columns, watching a flock of his little cousins chase each other across the pristine carpet of zoysia grass that was his grandfather's pride and joy.

Though he had two gardeners, George Cabot still surveyed the zoysia daily, bending down to pull an offending weed here or dig up a wild violet there. The aunts fretted over his weeding. He was not as spry as he used to be and was starting to repeat himself more than usual. *Now, Daddy, if you fall and break a hip you're gonna be in a mess.* Still, he weeded.

With his back to the family, Peyton could listen to all of their conversations, tuning in and out as if he were turning the dial on a radio.

His father's two sisters, Aunt Camille and Aunt Charlotte, were sharing the porch swing closest to Peyton:

"Could you believe that dress Arlie Seton wore to her own daughter's wedding?"

"Ridiculous. It was cut clear to here and twice too short for a woman half her age."

Uncle Julian, the middle son, was doing what he always did—trying to sell Granddaddy Cabot on one of his big ideas: "We could parcel off a thousand acres over by Reidsville and turn it into a residential development. We'd make a fortune. Can't you see that?"

"Julian, Reidsville's not close enough to anything—not Atlanta, not Savannah. All those vets settin' up housekeepin' want to be close to a city where they can find work."

Nothing about Peyton's Uncle Julian was genuine—not his smile, not his concern, and certainly not his devotion to the family. Whenever there was any heavy lifting to be done, you could count on Uncle Julian to be needed elsewhere. Peyton's mother had once said that he was "doomed to go through life feeling cheated" because he believed any good fortune that fell on someone else rightly belonged to him.

He fancied himself a statesman but so far couldn't even win a seat on the Savannah city council.

Peyton spotted two of his cousins on a quilt underneath the Ghost Oak and decided to join them. Their grandfather had named the tree long ago, and the moniker was apt. Sit beneath it on a breezy night—better yet, a stormy one— and the rustle of leaves did indeed sound like a swirl of specters communing overhead. When they were children, Peyton and his cousins would dare each other to sit under the tree on windy evenings while the others hid in the azaleas, calling out into the darkness, "Oooooooooo, I am the ghost of Ernestine Cabot, dead from the fever of 1824 . . . Oooooooooo, I am Ol' Rawhead, swamp monster of the Okefenokee . . ."

Peyton had never been afraid of the family ghosts or the tree they supposedly haunted. There was something to be discovered way up in those branches, and he had always been more curious than fearful.

Stepping off the porch, he dipped himself some home-made ice cream from a wooden freezer that was probably older than he was and sat down on the quilt with his cousins Prentiss and Winston.

"Somebody's goin' home mighty early." Prentiss nodded toward Peyton's mother, who was walking slowly up a dirt road that led from the main house to a pretty lakeside cottage about a quarter mile away.

Peyton watched his mother's back as she moved farther and farther away from the family, now and again raising a hand to her face. Just then his father appeared, following a path that led from the back of the house, through a pecan grove, and out to the stables. In one hand was a highball glass, already filled. The other held his ever-present companion since he had come home from the Pacific, a bottle of bourbon.

Peyton's aunts said it was "the worst kind of stupid" for the Army to draft men in their thirties, but once everybody younger was already over there, they had no choice. Peyton's father was gone for just over a year before the Japanese surrendered, but by then the war had done its damage. The war was still doing its damage.

"Don't look good, does it?" Winston asked him.

"No," Peyton said, watching his father disappear into the pecan trees.

Winston swatted at a bee circling his head. "Hey, Peyton, how come you didn't bring Lisa?"

"To face the whole clan? Way too early for that. Might scare her off." Peyton finished his ice cream and stretched out on the quilt. Closing his eyes against the sun filtering through the branches overhead, he pictured the girl who was never far from his thoughts.

Lisa Wallace had transferred to his school in January, when her family moved to Savannah from Augusta. She was the prettiest girl in the whole town, the prettiest girl Peyton had ever seen. But there was more to her than that. For one thing, she didn't flirt, a rarity in a Georgia beauty. Then again, she didn't have to. Every boy in school wanted to go out with her. Her hair was deep auburn and fell in long glossy waves down her back. Her eyes were blue, with just a hint of green, and she had a complexion like ice cream.

The minute she walked into his homeroom class, he knew. He felt it in his gut or his heart or whatever you want to call it. While all the other guys were working up their nerve,

Peyton made a beeline for Lisa in the lunchroom that first day and offered to carry her tray to her table. She had smiled up at him and said, "You don't waste any time, do you?"

As beautiful as she was, Lisa wasn't interested in sitting on anybody's pedestal and looking pretty. Once, Peyton had invited her to a skeet shoot Winston put together. After watching all the guys complete their first round, Lisa had tapped him on the shoulder and said, "Don't I get a turn?" He handed her his gun and watched her take down every clay.

Peyton often found her sitting next to unpopular kids in the cafeteria so they wouldn't feel lonesome. One girl in their class was a little slow and didn't have the nerve to ask the teachers questions, so she came to Lisa, who would spend her whole study hall tutoring instead of doing her own homework. When Lisa was excited about something, she talked with her hands, and Peyton found himself staring at them as they lithely fluttered in the air, waving her timid pupil toward the correct answer.

Winston interrupted his reverie. "Lisa and Peyton sittin' in a tree, k-i-s-s-i-n-g. First comes love, then comes marriage—"

"Oh, shut up, Winston." Peyton threw an acorn at him.

The truth was, he was already thinking about marrying Lisa—daydreaming about it anyway. He had asked her out right after she moved to Savannah and just about every weekend since. Only a month ago, he had taken her to the spring formal, when his whole life seemed as close to perfect as it would ever get . . .

Again his cousins pulled him away from Lisa and back into the fray of a Cabot family picnic. "Listen—here it comes," Prentiss was saying, pointing toward the porch.

The boys listened as their Uncle Gil retold his favorite

story, the same one he told at every spring picnic. "Marshall says to me, he says, 'I believe I've seen all this ol' camp has to offer.' And I says, 'What you plan on doin' about it?' That's when he pointed at the bicycles Papa had left for us. He says, 'I'm gonna ride my bicycle to Key West and see what those islands look like.'"

The cousins finished the story with their uncle, repeating his favorite line in unison: "And *that*, ladies and gentlemen, was the last time Marshall Cabot ever let anybody tell him what to do."

Winston leaned back to rest against the oak tree. "How many times you reckon he's told that story?"

"How many spring picnics we had?" Prentiss answered. "Every time he tells it, Uncle Marshall makes the trip in less time."

Looking up at the sprawling branches above, Peyton watched one squirrel chase another, spiraling up the trunk for several feet and then racing back down again. They repeated their circular journey over and over, as if they were following a racetrack around the tree.

"Reckon they know there's a whole big world outside that oak?" he said.

"Who you talkin' about?" Winston asked.

Peyton pointed to the squirrels above. "Those little guys. Reckon they think this tree is all there is—the whole wide world up in those branches?"

"Seriously?" Winston threw a twig at him and missed. "I think a squirrel's a squirrel."

The boys were quiet for a while before Prentiss said, "How long *did* it take your daddy to get to that dang island?"

Peyton listened to the oak tree sighing in the spring breeze.

"I got his old map out and figured it up. Looks like it's somewhere in the neighborhood o' six hundred miles from that old boys' camp on the Okefenokee to Key West, so twelve hundred there and back. And he wrote dates on different spots on the map—not everywhere he stopped because the dates are too far apart. No way he pedaled two hundred miles without resting somewhere—doubt anybody could make it more than fifty in a day. And it looked like he stayed awhile in St. Augustine. But judging by the dates after he left there, I'd say that leg of it, at least, took him about a month."

"And nobody came after him?" Prentiss wanted to know.

"He said he promised Granddaddy Cabot that if they'd let him be, he'd call collect every Sunday to let 'em know he was alright, which he did."

"Ain't no way he saddled a bicycle for a month," Winston said. "He musta thumbed some rides."

"Well, hold on now," Peyton said, sitting up. "'Course you'd have to stop and rest along the way. You'd have to figure all that out before you left. And you'd prob'ly wear out your tires over and over, so that'd have to be worked out. Then there's your clothes and food . . ."

"You sure have given this a lotta thought." Now Prentiss was interested. "Why don't you just ask Uncle Marshall how he did it?"

"I have—lotsa times," Peyton answered. "He just smiles and says that's something I'll have to figure out for myself."

"Uncle Gil always tells the story like it was a spur-o'-the-minute thing," Prentiss said.

Peyton ran a finger along a seam on the quilt where they sat, absently tracing its north-south path. "I don't think so. The map has a price tag on it from the Savannah Shop 'n Go, so he bought it here. And it's dated 1921—that year Daddy woulda been 13, but he didn't make the trip till he was 15, same as us. Maybe he didn't mark all his stops ahead o' time. Can't really tell. But I believe he was thinking about it before he left for camp."

"You believe it's possible—that he rode the whole way on his bike, I mean?" Prentiss asked him.

Peyton nodded. "Yeah, I do. It wouldn'a been easy, but it's possible. I know his first stop in Florida was Aunt Rosalie's in Jacksonville. That's seventy-five miles from the camp. Aunt Lily's family lives in St. Augustine—maybe he stayed there awhile to visit with them because he didn't get to Flagler Beach till nearly two weeks later, and it's only thirty miles away. The trick would be figuring out where to stay and where to get supplies—food and water and someplace to wash your clothes. 'Specially if you went in the summertime, it'd be hot as blue blazes, so you'd be sweatin' like a pig."

"I got fifty bucks that says you'll never do it," Winston said.

"Me too," Prentiss said. "I'll put down fifty bucks."

"I never said I was gonna *do* it. I just said I think it's possible."

"Sounds like he's bailin'," Winston said.

"Yep," Prentiss agreed.

"'Course I'm bailin'," Peyton said. "Why would I want to spend my summer pedaling a bicycle and let some other guy move in on Lisa?"

"You got a point," Prentiss said.

Peyton picked a dandelion and held it up in the breeze to watch its feathers fly. "Y'all would seriously pay me a hundred bucks if I did it?"

"Yeah, but if you start the ride and quit, you gotta pay us fifty bucks apiece," Winston said. "Wanna bet?"

"Not yet," Peyton said. "But I'll think about it."

They looked up as a horse appeared from the pecan grove. Actually, they heard it before they saw it—a thunder of hooves hitting the ground as a powerful Thoroughbred named Bootlegger raced around the border of the front lawn and made his way to the rear garden before following the same dirt road Peyton's mother had taken. The rider, at once familiar and foreign, looked reckless even at this distance, holding the reins in one hand and a bottle of bourbon in the other, his boots tight against the horse's sides, his sandy hair blown by the spring breeze.

Peyton was at once sickened and mesmerized by the sight of it. He heard the familiar murmurs rippling across the porch. "I'm tellin' you, he's gonna kill hisself with that bottle . . ."

Horse and rider reached the crest of a hill that blocked the view of Peyton's house—the cottage his mother had fled to. Peyton heard the horse snort and saw it pawing at the ground, impatient to release the energy rippling through its sinewy legs. The rider kept turning to look over the hill and then back at the main house until at last he appeared resigned to his fate. Turning toward the house, he gave the horse its head and sped back down the dirt road toward the front lawn. As Bootlegger came streaking around the grand old house, Peyton saw clumps of grass fly up each time the Thoroughbred's hooves landed. It was hypnotic, the sight of his father racing into the picnic, carrying his bourbon bottle like a knight bearing a standard, ready for the joust. Without speaking, the three boys stood but remained under the tree, only halfway trusting Peyton's father not to run them through.

Years later, when Peyton was a grown man with a family, what unfolded on this spring afternoon would replay in his mind again and again, always in slow motion. Just as his father raised the bottle to his lips, leaned his head back, and took a long draw, the two squirrels in the tree suddenly raced down the trunk and scampered into the yard. Jubal, his grandfather's Irish setter, spotted them from the porch and tore down the steps after them. Barking as he laid chase, the dog startled the horse. It balked, sending Peyton's father sailing out of the saddle, over the head of his mount, and straight into the Ghost Oak, where he hit his head with such force that it sounded like a billiard ball dropped onto an oak floor. And then nothing—lifeless silence for a split second before all the women screamed and the whole family swarmed the fallen rider.

In an instant, the slow-motion scene accelerated to lightning speed, and Peyton couldn't keep up. The three boys were unceremoniously pushed aside as an ambulance was called and a cousin visiting from Birmingham—the only doctor in the family—ran to his car to get his medical bag.

Suddenly, it hit Peyton. His mother knew nothing about this. As the ambulance sped away with his father—and before anyone else thought to do it—he ran into the library and called home.

Author Note

"YOU SURE ABOUT THIS, VAL?"

I can still see the look on my husband's face as he and I stood outside a small, unassuming brick building in the blink-and-you'll-miss-it town of Mamou, Louisiana. I was on assignment for *Southern Living* magazine, and Dave was my travel companion, navigator, and courage. We had arrived at Fred's Lounge on a Saturday morning. (You read that right—Saturday morning, the only time it was open.) The parking lot was full of Harley-Davidsons. We couldn't hear a sound.

"It's *famous*" was my only justification for pressing on.

About that time, someone opened the front door to Fred's, and a blast of live accordion and fiddle music hit us like a tidal wave. The place was brightly lit, and well before lunch, couples were waltzing and two-stepping around the band. Suddenly, Dave was smiling ear to ear, and I knew we were about to have ourselves an experience.

We would have many adventures together as we journeyed through towns like Mamou, Eunice, Opelousas, Breaux

Bridge, New Iberia, and St. Martinville, all scattered around the Cajun cultural hub of Lafayette. And our odyssey began with, of all things, a misguided story idea: "Be a Cajun for a weekend."

Fortunately for all concerned, my first interview was with historian and author Carl Brasseaux. Ten minutes with him and I realized the error of our ways: The notion that we could partake of a centuries-old culture just by sampling gumbo and learning the two-step had to go. My editors agreed and replaced our original idea with a yearlong exploration of Acadian Louisiana that I'm still very proud of, as much for the people I met as for the work I did with photographer Art Meripol. (A writer couldn't ask for a better collaborator than Art, especially if you happen to be in a bass boat on the Atchafalaya River before daybreak.)

I spent time with author and musician Ann Savoy, whose husband, Marc, is a renowned accordion maker. They have traveled the world with their family, playing music and sharing Cajun culture. I interviewed Christine Balfa, whose father, Dewey, and his brothers helped revive Cajun music in the 1960s, when it was seriously endangered. So many more incredible people shared their stories—and their homes—with us, including Harold and Sarah Schoeffler, who took Art and me out on the river in the aforementioned bass boat. I don't say all this to imply that any of these kind people endorsed my book—they haven't seen it—but I do want to express my appreciation to them for giving me even a surface understanding of their rich culture and heritage.

Under the Bayou Moon was written primarily from the perspective of an outsider discovering Acadian Louisiana for the first time, just as I did. My sincere hope is that you've enjoyed discovering this singular place with Ellie Fields and that you fell in love with it just as she (and I) did.

I highly recommended the following books, which I used for research and inspiration:

Bernard, Shane K. *The Cajuns: Americanization of a People*. Jackson: University Press of Mississippi, 2003.

Brasseaux, Carl A. *Acadiana*. Baton Rouge: Louisiana State University Press, 2011.

Link, Donald, with Paula Disbrowe. *Real Cajun: Rustic Home Cooking from Donald Link's Louisiana*. New York: Clarkson Potter Publishers, 2009.

Savoy, Ann. *Cajun Music: A Reflection of a People*. Eunice, Louisiana: Bluebird Press, 1984.

Valdman, Albert, ed., et al. *Dictionary of Louisiana French*. Jackson: University Press of Mississippi, 2010.

Vetter, Cyril E. *Fonville Winans' Louisiana: Politics, People, and Places*. Baton Rouge: Louisiana State University Press, 2016.

Winans, Fonville. *Cruise of the Pintail*. Baton Rouge: Louisiana State University Press, 2011.

Winans, Melinda Risch, and Cynthia LeJeune Nobles. *The Fonville Winans Cookbook: Recipes and Photographs from a Louisiana Artist*. Baton Rouge: Louisiana State University Press, 2017.

Acknowledgments

MUCH LOVE AND GRATITUDE to my husband, Dave, for his endless patience and support, and to my parents, who read every draft of every book, reminding me again and again to stop worrying and write.

Many thanks to my extended family, church family, and dear friends for all their encouragement and support.

How to thank literary agent Leslie Stoker? Meeting Leslie at *Southern Living* was one of the great blessings of my life. Thank you, my friend, for believing in my work and guiding me every step of the way.

What were the chances that the manuscript for my first novel, *Missing Isaac*, would make its way from Birmingham, Alabama, to Leslie's desk in New York, to a brilliant Michigan-based editor with an affinity for the South? (I do not believe in accidents.) That's exactly what happened, and Kelsey Bowen has been my editor/spirit guide ever since, offering thoughtful questions and laser-sharp insights. Thank you, thank you, Kelsey, for elevating every manuscript you touch and for championing my work. My deep gratitude also goes to Jessica English, an amazing editor whose unfaltering attention to detail is rare and wonderful. Thank you, Jessica! And many thanks to yet another fine editor, Sadina Grody Brott, who shepherded the final manuscript and dealt with a million last-minute "do you think we should we change this" questions from me. Thank you for your good judgment and your patience, Sadina.

Proofreaders are the unsung heroes of the editing process, saving writers like me from many an embarrassing oversight. Sincere thanks for the time and talent of Sandra Judd, Robert Ludkey, and Julie Davis.

To Gayle Raymer and her creative team, my sincere thanks for your beautiful, evocative covers. I can't even imagine how many book buyers are stopped in their tracks by your fantastic work.

To Michele Misiak, Karen Steele, Brianne Dekker, and the marketing and publicity teams at Revell Books, my thanks (and maybe some complimentary Milo's sweet tea) for all that you do, all year long, to move those books off the shelves! I value your support and your friendship so very much.

I'd like to say a special thanks to the friends who kindly agreed to read advance copies of *Under the Bayou Moon*: *Southern Living* editor-in-chief Sid Evans and executive editor Krissy Tiglias, and four wonderful authors I truly admire—Erin Bartels, Nancy Dorman-Hickson, Lynette Eason, and Susie Finkbeiner. Many thanks also to Chris Jager of Baker Book House for all her encouragement and support.

To my dear friend, photographer Mark Sandlin, thank you (again) for the gift of your author portraits (#howdidyouputupwithme).

As always, my heartfelt thanks to Sid Evans, Krissy Tiglias, Nellah McGough, and the *Southern Living* editorial staff for your continued support, and to Kristen Payne for promoting my work to fans of the magazine. I owe Raphe's name to another *Southern Living* friend, Louisiana native Jorie MacDonald, who channeled her Cajun cousins to help me with my character.

I want to thank all the readers, booksellers, and media who have supported my writing, as well as the book clubs and writers' clubs who have invited me to join you in person or on video. It's an honor to share my stories with you.

As for my inspiration . . .

I credit Ellie's passion for teaching and her love of history to my Aunt Patsy, who spent endless hours researching the history of our hometown so that her students would know the story of their own community. Her faith and love were shining examples to me and will stay with me always. (Uncle Bud, her husband, gave me many a colorful expression for my books and an appreciation for storytelling itself.)

Doc and Florence were inspired by two wonderful friends and neighbors, Ed and Julia McKinney, who lived next door to us until he was called home and she moved away to be closer to family. Just recently, we lost her as well. For years, Mr. McKinney tried unsuccessfully to persuade Dave and me to call him "Ed," but that always felt disrespectful to us. Once he became ill, I found myself calling his wife "Miss Julia," and later just "Julia." I guess a sort of sisterhood grew between us during the long goodbye they said to each other as his health declined. She once told me that people sometimes asked her the secret to her long and happy marriage. "It's just mutual respect and unconditional love," she said matter-of-factly, as if those two things were easy to give. Dave and I watched the two of them walk through this life together in love and faith until they were united with God. The McKinneys and their family have been a great blessing to us. Any admiration you might feel for Doc and Florence Talbert is a direct reflection of my love for Ed and Julia McKinney, and my gratitude for their friendship.

Finally, I want to thank Fonville. (We're way beyond the formality of surnames now.) At the very beginning, when I was doing preliminary research for *Under the Bayou Moon*, I googled my way to the work of the late photographer Fonville Winans, whose Depression-era images of the Louisiana bayou country are breathtaking. His portraits and landscapes fired my imagination with ideas for characters and bayou settings, so much so that I decided to put a charismatic photographer in my story. Heywood Thornberry became one of my all-time favorite characters, in part because some of the most talented, interesting people I know are photographers, but also because I wanted to invoke their powers of observation. (The scene where Heywood bypasses all the sights and sounds of a busy French Quarter street and instead photographs an artist quietly working in her studio, oblivious to all distractions, was inspired by one of my own *Southern Living* trips to New Orleans with Mark Sandlin, whom I watched do exactly that.) Talented photographers like Mark see things the rest of us miss. I'm hoping Heywood caught it all with his camera. It would be a shame to miss the perfect shot.

P.S. to Aunt Boots: Thank you for always being in my corner. Love, Baby Girl.

Valerie Fraser Luesse is the bestselling author of *Missing Isaac*, *Almost Home*, and *The Key to Everything*, as well as an award-winning magazine writer best known for her feature stories and essays in *Southern Living*, where she is currently senior travel editor. Specializing in stories about unique pockets of Southern culture, Luesse received the 2009 Writer of the Year award from the Southeast Tourism Society for her editorial section on Hurricane Katrina recovery in Mississippi and Louisiana. A graduate of Auburn University and Baylor University, she lives in Birmingham, Alabama, with her husband, Dave.

"A **heartwarming** story of the power of relationships
and how the most inopportune circumstances can yield
unexpectedly **rewarding** results."

—*Publishers Weekly*

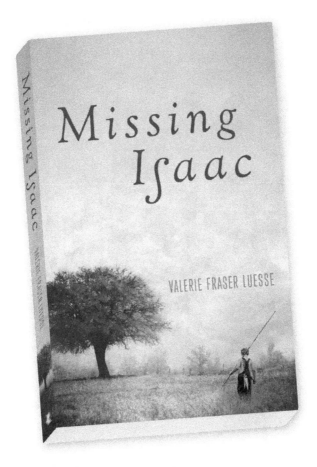

When a Black field hand disappears, a wealthy
white boy he has befriended sets out to find him.
But Pete McLean discovers more than he bargained
for—including unexpected love and difficult truths
about race and class in 1960s Alabama.

Revell
a division of Baker Publishing Group
www.RevellBooks.com

Available wherever books and ebooks are sold.

"Luesse, an award-winning writer and editor for *Southern Living*, demonstrates her **love** for Alabama in this inspirational romance. . . . Luesse's uplifting tale will **delight** fans."

—*Publishers Weekly*

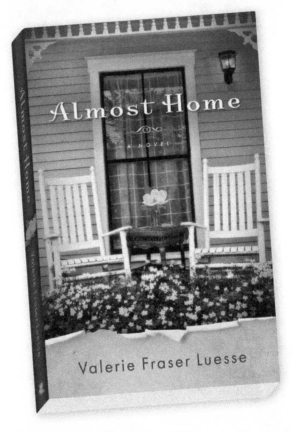

As America enters World War II, a melting pot of the displaced and disenfranchised enters Dolly Chandler's boardinghouse in Blackberry Springs, Alabama. When tragedy strikes, the only hope of salvation lies with the circle of women under Dolly's roof and their ability to discover what happened to a young bride who lived there a hundred years before.

 Revell

a division of Baker Publishing Group
www.RevellBooks.com

Available wherever books and ebooks are sold.

Meet Valerie

FOLLOW ALONG AT

ValerieFraserLuesse.com

and sign up for Valerie's newsletter to stay up to date on news, upcoming releases, and more!

 Valerie Fraser Luesse

 ValerieLuesse

GoinDownToMamas

CPSIA information can be obtained
at www.ICGtesting.com
Printed in the USA
LVHW110013270722
724513LV00002B/29

9 780800 740023